TRUMAN

ROBERT H. FERRELL

TRUMAN

A CENTENARY REMEMBRANCE

THE VIKING PRESS   **New York**

The author gratefully acknowledges the help of
JANE MOBLEY in the preparation of the text

The picture sections were compiled and written by
ROLAND GELATT

Title-page photo:
Harry S. Truman making a campaign speech at
Gilmore Stadium, Los Angeles, September 23, 1948.
Among his listeners was a future President of the
United States, Ronald Reagan (*far left*), then a film
actor and an as yet unconverted Democrat. Some other
well-known faces from the world of show business are
also seen: Humphrey Bogart, Lauren Bacall, and
George Jessel.

Copyright © 1984 Thames and Hudson, Ltd., London
Published by arrangement with Thames and Hudson
Ltd., London
All rights reserved
Published in 1984 by The Viking Press,
40 West 23rd Street, New York, N.Y. 10010
Published simultaneously in Canada by
Penguin Books Canada Limited

Library of Congress Cataloging in Publication Data

Ferrell, Robert H.
    Truman, a centenary remembrance.

    Includes index.
    1. Truman, Harry S., 1884–1972.   2. Presidents—
    United States—Biography.   I. Title.
E814.F48   1984   973.918′092′4 [B]   83–40222
ISBN 0–670–36196–8

Set and printed in Great Britain

CONTENTS

INTRODUCTION

I N. ONE of his letters to his daughter Margaret, who was barely thirteen years old at the time, Harry S. Truman wrote: "Politics is a great game. Your dad has been playing at it for some twenty-five years. It is a game of people and how they will act under certain conditions. You never can tell, but you can sometimes guess and I've been a good guesser. You must be able to tell the facts too and to believe them yourself."

In that single letter—which is dated February 23, 1937, and which he surely never expected anyone other than Margaret to read—the man who eight years later became President of the United States revealed his view of government. As a full-time man of politics, a professional politician, he made it his business to understand people, but he refused to take the easy course and give them what they wanted. He would find out "the facts," which included solutions.

Today, Truman's almost antique honesty compels increasing admiration. Here indeed was an ideal public man. The flat Missouri twang, the fighting words and slashing commentaries often appalled upholders of dignity. Highly quotable phrases, written as well as spoken, punctuated by "cuss words," brought despair to lovers of linguistic urbanity. And double-breasted suits and a penchant for garish ties and Florida sports shirts could dismay arbiters of fashion. But behind appearances stood a man who has now taken a large place in the affections of his countrymen.

He accomplished a great deal during nearly eight years in the presidency. His primary task was to turn the foreign policy of the United States in a new direction, changing it from its traditional peacetime course of non-involvement. The guiding principle of America's approach to foreign relations since the late eighteenth century had been one of isolation from the "ordinary combinations and collisions" of Europe and Asia. That principle had helped produce the international anarchy of the present century, the near chaos of two World Wars. Truman changed the direction of American policy to one of involvement and participation, with the Truman Doctrine, the Marshall Plan, the formation of NATO, and the decision to commit U.S. armed forces to fight in the Korean War. Since his time, no American President has ever considered reverting to the old ways in international affairs. In domestic affairs, his Fair Deal continued the New Deal, the effort to enlarge government so as to confront the present century's social and economic problems and realities. Although little of his program was enacted during Truman's administration, he did live to see most of the aims he espoused become the law of the land.

The late President's stock has been rising in recent years. During his second term, 1949–53, the Korean War and cries of communism and corruption in government damaged his reputation, and he retired from office in the wake of a Republican triumph that was interpreted by his enemies as a mandate for change. At the time, the Man of Independence seemed headed for obscurity. Then, in the 1960s and 1970s—a troubled era if ever there was one—people began to realize how effective a President he had been, and to look back admiringly to his honest, principled leadership. Today, Harry S. Truman has become a genuine folk-hero.

The young bank clerk, Kansas City, 1905.

BEGINNINGS

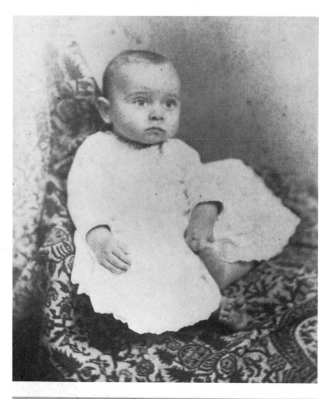

Family album

Martha Ellen and John Anderson Truman, Harry's parents, on the day of their marriage, December 28, 1881 (*right*). Truman *père* was a small man, two inches shorter than his wife, and in the few photos of them together he is always shown seated. John Anderson Truman died in 1914, but Martha Ellen lived to see her son in the White House. The future President was photographed in swaddling clothes in the year of his birth, 1884, and with his younger brother, Vivian, in 1888. The bearded gentleman is their grandfather, Anderson Shipp Truman. Harry remembered him as "a dignified, pleasant man, particularly with Vivian and me."

The years in Independence

A formal photo of young Harry, *c.* 1896, shows him with the glasses that set him somewhat apart from other boys his age. For a while he worked part-time at Clinton's Drug Store in the town center (*below*). On Sundays there was Bible school at the Presbyterian Church, where Harry first encountered his future wife, Bess Wallace.

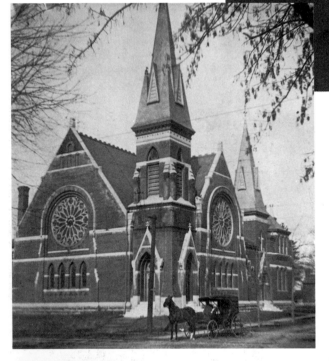

In his school years Harry read avidly, and he claimed—doubtless with some exaggeration—to have devoured every book in the Independence Public Library (*left*). The graduating class of 1901 posed for the traditional group photo in front of the school. Seventeen-year-old Harry Truman is fourth from left in the back row, Bess Wallace is on the far right of the second row, and class valedictorian Charlie Ross (Truman's lifelong friend) sits on the far left of the front row.

Kansas City

In 1902 the Trumans moved to Kansas City, where Harry found a job as "utility clerk" at the National Bank of Commerce (*right*). He is pictured at this period with his cousins Nellie and Ethel Noland and his derby-hatted friend Fielding Houchens (with whom he had pursued extracurricular studies in the vain hope of an appointment to West Point or Annapolis). Kansas City was a thriving metropolis in the early years of the century, and Harry seems to have taken full advantage of the theatrical entertainments on offer.

Life on the farm

From 1906 until America entered World War I in 1917, Harry Truman worked on the family farm near Grandview, Missouri. He is seen (*above*) standing in front of the farmhouse with his mother and maternal grandmother, Harriet Young, who died in 1909 at the age of ninety-one. A frequent guest was cousin Ethel Noland, photographed at the well which stood at the side of the house. The junior partner of J. A. Truman & Son, Farmers, is seen riding a one-row cultivator in a field of young corn; the picture dates from *c.* 1910.

Beyond the farm

Despite his long hours on the farm, Truman had energy to spare for outside activities. While still in Kansas City he had enlisted in the Missouri National Guard (the formal-uniform photo at left dates from that time) and during the farm years he still managed to attend summer camp at Cape Girardeau, Missouri, and elsewhere. He is seen (*below*) in summer fatigue uniform. In 1908 he applied for membership in the Masonic lodge at Belton, beginning an association that lasted for the rest of his life. In a detail from a group photo taken some years later, Truman (wearing glasses) is seen with fellow Masons of Consistory No. 2 of Western Missouri. Late in 1916 he invested in a company drilling for oil in Greenwood County, Kansas, and posed for the camera in front of a newly constructed oil derrick. The company stopped drilling without striking oil and sold off the lease. Later, however, another company drilled further and hit the rich Teter Pool.

Petition for Initiation

To the Worshipful Master, Wardens and Brethren
∴ of ∴

Belton _____ Lodge, No. 450

F. & A. M.

THE SUBSCRIBER, residing at _Grand View Mo_
and whose place of business is at _Grand View Mo_
and being _24_ years of age, and by occupation a _farmer_
_____ and having _____ applied for initiation
to _Belton_ Lodge _450 A F & A M_ respectfully
represents that, unbiased by friends and uninfluenced by mercenary
motives, he freely and voluntarily offers himself as a candidate for
the mysteries of Masonry, and that he is prompted to solicit this
privilege by a favorable opinion of your ancient and honorable Frater-
nity, and a desire for knowledge and sincere wish to be serviceable to
his fellow creatures, and should his petition be granted, he will
cheerfully conform to all its established laws, usages and customs.

Dated _Dec 21"_ A. L. 590 8

RECOMMENDED BY

Wm H. Meiston

SIGNED _Harry S. Truman_

The Pettibone Bros. Mfg. Co. Cincinnati O. Lodge Supplies

Bess

Harry Truman's future wife was born in Independence in 1885—the daughter of Madge Gates Wallace and David Willock Wallace (*right*). The winsome photo of Bess (*left*) shows her at about the time she and Harry first met at Sunday school. Bess's father committed suicide in 1903, and a year later Bess, her mother, and her three brothers moved in with Grandmother and Grandfather Gates at 219 North Delaware, which was to become in due course the Trumans' own home. A photo of around 1910 shows the house without the iron fence that was built to protect it after Truman became President. The young lady on the porch balustrade is Bess in her late teens or early twenties.

Courting

In 1910, Harry's and Bess's paths crossed again, and the courtship was on. He was then working at the farm in Grandview, and to facilitate his visits to Independence, Truman acquired a second-hand Stafford touring car. The proud owner is at the wheel in a contemporary snapshot. Another snapshot, taken in October 1913 at the waterworks on the Missouri River, north of Independence, shows a group of friends on a Sunday outing. Harry is kneeling in front and Bess, on the far right, is looking fondly at her by then publicly acknowledged suitor. The oval photo of Bess is one that Harry carried with him to France during World War I; later it hung in his White House office. The other photo of Bess (*below, right*) shows her in the backyard of 219 North Delaware at just about the time the courtship began. It lasted nine years. The couple were finally married on June 28, 1919, after Harry returned from war service in France, and were photographed (*opposite*) on their wedding day.

Captain Harry

Truman enlisted for army service some months after America's declaration of war in April 1917, and—in view of his extensive National Guard experience—soon became a first lieutenant. He spent the winter of 1917–18 training at Camp Doniphan, Oklahoma, before embarking for France in April 1918 as a Captain in the 129th Field Artillery. His AEF identity card shows Truman as few people ever saw him—without glasses. He looks more recognizable mounted on horseback in the French village of Coëtquidan, where his unit was stationed. In another photo taken in France during the summer of 1918, Truman is seen with a fellow officer in the 129th Field Artillery, Major Thomas McGee.

It took nearly five months from Armistice Day before Truman's unit could leave for home. In the interim he took in the sights of Paris and the Riviera, but his "greatest day . . . in France"—as a diary entry for April 9, 1919, attests (*right*)—was when he sailed for the U.S.A. aboard the S.S. *Zeppelin*.

AVRIL
9 MERCREDI — Ste Marie Eg. 99-266

Embark at 10 A. M.
after marching down
under full pack.
Greatest day I've spent
in France. Go aboard
the German (Now US); Zeppelin.

10 JEUDI — S. Fulbert.   100-265

AVRIL
11 VENDREDI — S. Léon. p. 101-264

12 SAMEDI — S. Juste.   102-263

Truman & Jacobson

In November 1919, Truman and his former canteen sergeant at Camp Doniphan, Eddie Jacobson, opened a men's haberdashery in Kansas City. The interior of the store shows ex-Captain Harry at left, with veterans of the 129th Field Artillery—his best customers—in the rear. The shop window displays an impressive assortment of the detachable collars that were then *de rigueur* for the well-dressed businessman. Dr. A. Gloom Chaser's homespun sentiment appeared on a blotter distributed by the store; it could have benefited from more careful proofreading. Despite an encouraging first year, Truman & Jacobson sailed into stormy weather during the recession of 1921–22, and the partners were forced to liquidate (*see overleaf*).

Dr. A. Gloom Chaser Says:

"I Takes 65 Muscles of the Face to Make a Frown and 13 to Make a Smile—Why Work Overtime?"

Buy Your Men's Furnishings from Us at New Prices. **YOU** Will Smile at the Great Reductions. **WE** Will Smile at the Increased Business. Then **NONE** of **US** Will Be Overworked.

Opposite
12th Street Entrance
Hotel Muehlebach

Truman-Jacobson
104 W. 12TH ST. K.C.MO.
HABERDASHERS

Phones
Home Harrison 3491
Bell Main 5393

SAVE YOUR MONEY!

We Are Quitting Business
OUR CLOSING OUT

SALE!

Lasts only a few days longer. This splendid stock of new fall Merchandise, consisting of Hats, Gloves, Caps, Men's Shirts, Union Suits, Hosiery and Neckwear, must be sold at once.

New Fall Hats

$4.00 and $5.00 values	$2.95
$6.00 and 7.00 values	3.85
10.00 values	4.85
Cloth Hats values to 5.00	1.35
Any Cap in the store, values up to 2.50	1.45

Wilson Bros. Gloves

2.00 Dress Kid Gloves	$ 89c
3.00 French Cape Gloves	1.85
4.00 Silk Lined Gloves	1.85
5.00 Imported Kid Gloves	1.85
1.00 Heavy Wool Gloves	59c
Heavy Fur Gauntlets, $7.50 values	3.95
Undressed Kid, heavy weight, sheep skin lined, a $7.50 value for	3.95
All wool cotton lined Gloves, values to $4.00	1.95

Silk and Knitted Ties

French folded Silk Ties, values up to $1.00	39c
$1.50 Grenadines, now	69c
All Knitted Ties, values to 1.00	49c
Heavy Silk Ties, values to 3.00	85c

Wilson Bros. Hose

$1.50 and 2.00 Silk Full Fashioned	95c
75c and $1.00 Silk Hose	59c
50c and 65c Fibre Silk Hose, pair 35c 3 pr.	$1.00
35c Lisle Hose, pair	19c
$1.50 Wool Hose, pair	85c

Any Belt in the store, values up to $2.00	69c
Arrow Brand Stiff Collars,	11c each
Ide Brand Stiff Collars	11c each
2 for 25c Handkerchiefs,	2 for 15c
25c Handkerchiefs 17c	3 for 50c
1.00 Silk Handkerchiefs	49c each
Wilson Bros. Night Shirts 1.75 val.	1.15
10.00 Heavy Wool Sweaters	5.95

A Nice Line of Bath Robes at Greatly Reduced Prices.

Wilson Bros. and Arrow Shirts

All $2.00 values	$1.30
All $2.50 and $3.00 values	1.95
All silk stripe and woven madras, values up to $5.00	2.65
Silk and Linen Shirts, values to $7.50	3.95
Any Silk Shirt in the store	5.45

Collar Attached Shirts Priced Accordingly

Stiff Collar to match Shirts, values up to $3.00	1.65

Wilson Bros. Union Suits—
Imperial Union Suits—
Superior Union Suits

A complete line of fall weight Union Suits at the following prices:

Heavy Cotton Ribbed	$1.29
Wilson Bros. Heavy Cotton Ribbed	1.59
Medium Weight Wool Mixed	2.15
Medium Weight	1.85
All Silk and Wool, all Silk and Silk Lisle, values up to $7.50	3.95

TRUMAN & JACOBSON

104 WEST 12th STREET.   **Opposite 12th St. Entrance to Muehlebach Hotel**

Shelving for Sale—Light Fixtures for Sale.   Show Cases for Sale—Hat Case for Sale

BORN in the era of the country's fading innocence, Harry S. Truman was at once the last of a line of yeoman farm-boy Presidents and the first of a line of global strategists. His birthplace—Lamar, Missouri—was a small farming village with a population of 700, set in the northernmost swells of the Ozark foothills, 120 miles south of Kansas City. Ironically, in the year of Truman's birth, 1884, the President of the United States was Chester A. Arthur, a man almost forgotten today except by historians, but a President whose career was paralleled by Truman's own many years later. Each man was elected Vice President and succeeded to the nation's highest office at the death of the incumbent. Arthur had begun his political career as a Republican spoilsman in New York City, and despite his contemporaries' belief that he would make a poor Chief Executive, he confounded their predictions with an honest if lackluster administration. Truman's early background was the Democratic political machine in Kansas City; his presidency, however, turned out to be one of the most distinguished in the nation's history.

In May, in Lamar, Missouri, the spring air is soft with promise. There the rocky and difficult land of the Ozark region meets the rich bottom soil from a valley that is laced with the Kansas and Missouri Rivers and many smaller streams. May is a month of peach blossoms and serious planting in Lamar, and in 1884 the sowing season meant good business for Harry's father, John Anderson Truman, dealer in horses and mules. In 1881, he had married Martha Ellen Young and the next year moved to Lamar where they bought a small frame house for $685. John Truman conducted his sometimes precarious trade in livestock across the street from the house on a lot that had cost a further $200.

When their son was born on May 8, 1884, the Trumans called him Harry S. He was named Harry for his uncle, Harrison Young, while the "S" was a compromise between the names of the child's paternal and maternal grandfathers, Anderson Shipp Truman and Solomon Young, and hence stood for no name in particular. The new father paid the doctor $15 and nailed a horseshoe over the front door to sustain the run of good fortune that had begun with the birth of a healthy son in the spring. Otherwise the nativity of a future President of the United States received little attention.

Shortly afterward, the Trumans packed up their son, and their unsold livestock, and moved to Harrisonville, north and slightly west of

Lamar. It was to be the first of a long series of moves for the family, although they stayed in western Missouri. Harry spent his early life on a succession of farms near the villages of Harrisonville, Belton, and Grandview. John Truman evidently lacked sufficient good fortune or skill in his trading because he never managed to remain successful in one place for long. Socially, the nearly nomadic life was difficult for a child. Although Harry seems never to have resented his father's profession, the life of a livestock dealer's son involved contact with many people but the opportunity of friendship with few. Later, he wrote to his sweetheart, Bess Wallace:

> You know—horsetrading is the cause of the death of truth in America. When you go to buy they'll tell you anything on earth to get your money. . . . I am not a pessimist though. There are some honest men and they are always well thought of by the crooks. They are always the last ones you get acquainted with too. We have moved around quite a bit and always the best people are hardest to know.

The Grandview farm was the home of his maternal grandparents, Solomon and Harriet Louisa Young, and the farm Harry himself worked in his early manhood. His earliest memory was of chasing a frog around a puddle behind one of those early farmhouses, Grandmother Young laughing at his toddler high spirits. He was a sturdy little boy in a family that didn't believe in coddling.

Soon he had a brother, Vivian, and a sister, Mary Jane. When Vivian was born and Uncle Harrison Young came to see the new baby, Martha Truman dropped her elder son from a second-floor window into the waiting arms of his uncle. Another time, Harry wandered away from the house and was lost. He had been poking at toads in the yard with a stick and after a while he followed a dog down a corn row in a nearby field. His mother, unworried, remarked that when the dog came back it would lead them to Harry.

The simplicity of Harry's childhood was already in contrast to the social conflicts at work in the country. In the East, robber barons luxuriated in palatial houses so lavish that even the brother-in-law of Tsar Nicholas II, visiting Newport, Rhode Island, said he had never imagined such splendor. Meanwhile, in the West, prairie farmers despaired as they mortgaged their land to buy Cyrus McCormick's agricultural machines, and saw themselves reaping mostly debt.

The town of Independence, to which John Truman moved his family in 1890, had been founded by partisans of the Tennessee general, Andrew (Old Hickory) Jackson, who became one of young Harry's heroes and a man he later considered one of the eight great Presidents. The town in Harry's day was a jumping-off place for opportunity. The great Western trails to Sante Fe, Salt Lake City, and California began

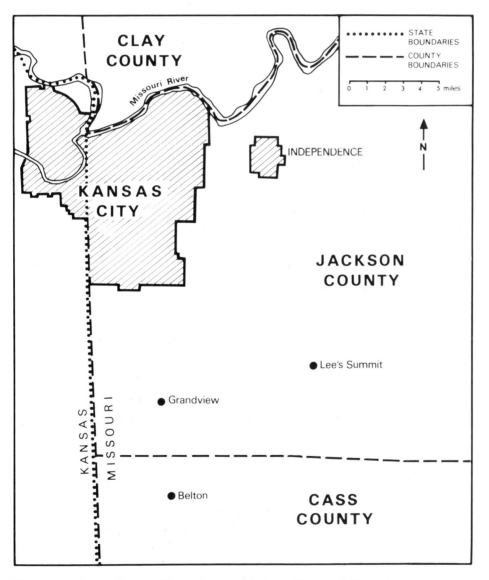

Truman territory: Kansas City and part of Jackson County, Missouri.

there. Manufactured goods came up the Missouri from St. Louis by steamboat and were loaded onto wagons, usually ox-drawn, for the long overland journeys.

Harry Truman had the dust of the trails in his own family: Grandfather Young had been one of the thousands beckoned West. From 1844 through to the late 1860s, he drove wagon trains to the Far West, leaving his wife to manage a 5,000-acre farm. During the Civil War, in 1863, he was absent when Yankee raiders came to the farm and Grandmother Young tried in vain to fend them off and save her four hundred hogs.

While Independence had been a beginning for many journeys, it had been a destination too. In the early 1830s, the Mormon prophet Joseph Smith was led to Independence by revelation. His people flourished there only for a while, however, before they were persecuted—beaten, imprisoned, impoverished by the burning of their banks—until they moved back to Illinois, where Smith was murdered by a mob in 1844.

In the 1890s, young Harry would see the descendants of Smith's followers, bearded, black-hatted men and white-capped women, standing in groups about the town square on marketing days with their horses and wagons. They were members of the Reorganized Church of Jesus Christ of Latter Day Saints (RLDS), who had returned to their frontier refuge and made it the world capital of their church; the apostate Mormons had followed Brigham Young to the Great Salt Lake.

The gentle hills and fertile farmland around Independence stopped many westward travelers at the edge of real pioneering, with the result that the town's population increased tenfold within a generation, to 6,000 citizens by 1890. It doubled to 12,000 during Truman's boyhood years there from 1890 to 1902.

Turn-of-the-century Independence had a public square paved with asphalt, a brooding granite courthouse, and a jail with a "dungeon"—a deep pit where serious offenders were held. It also had an impressive variety of homes in styles derived from the architectural pattern books of the day—mansions with cupolas and turrets, and homes of more modest size, but still ornamented with gingerbread trim and graceful porches.

On the principal residential avenue, Delaware Street, lived the town's wealthiest citizens in homes furnished with horsehair, velvet, and marble, as elaborate as any featured in the magazines "back East." One of these homes belonged to George Porterfield Gates, the manufacturer of Queen of the Pantry Flour, which was advertised as "the best biscuit and cake flour in the world." At 608 North Delaware, in a sizable home crowned by a cupola, lived the Gates' daughter, Madge, married to handsome David Willock Wallace, son of a Jackson County pioneer and himself a rising county official.

Madge was adored by her father, who even had her likeness printed on his mill's flour sacks. Her only daughter, Elizabeth, who was known as Bessie or Bess, was born in 1885, and would later become Harry Truman's wife. Bess Wallace was five years old and attending the Presbyterian Church's Sunday School when she first met the six-year-old Harry, whose mother, although a Baptist, had enrolled him with the Presbyterians because she believed her own rural Baptist church to be overrun with unbelievers.

The Independence of Harry's boyhood was divided according to church affiliations, wrote Mary Paxton, Bess's best girlhood chum, many years later. The Presbyterians were at the top of the social order, according to Mary, followed by the Campbellites (now called the Disciples of Christ or, simply, Christian Church), the Methodists, the Baptists, and the Lutherans. Independence had a large Roman Catholic church, but most of its congregation came in from the country to attend Mass and did not count in the hierarchy of the town itself. The RLDS members and the town's smattering of blacks were at the bottom of the order.

Because of these church-related social classes, Harry might as well have lived in a different community as far as Bess Wallace's family was concerned. As Bess grew older, he saw her daily at school—she sat behind him in the sixth, seventh, and high-school grades. He carried her books when she encouraged him. In high school, Harry also had a chance to see Bess outside class. His cousin, Nellie Noland, lived near Delaware Street and she excelled in Latin, then required for graduation. Two evenings a week Harry and Bess met at Nellie's house, where she would help them with declension and conjugation.

Harry simply wasn't as financially blessed as the granddaughter of the prosperous George Porterfield Gates. Years later, when they were courting, Harry wrote to Bess, "I certainly did enjoy myself Tuesday night. That stew couldn't *be beat*. You know I have always had a kind of a desire to be a chafing dish artist, but I never even had the dish."

Moreover, Harry had to work. For one thing, as he later recalled, he had tasks around the house:

> I had to milk a cow night and morning, carry the milk to the house, and put it in a cooler so I could have milk for breakfast.
>
> . . . When I was a boy, we didn't have any mechanical dishwashers. I had to wash the dishes, and wash the lamp chimneys, so that we could have clean dishes for the next meal, and for light. I had to split wood and carry it and put in the woodbox behind the stove, so I could get up in the morning and start a fire so that we could have breakfast. Now all you do is turn on a gadget . . .

When he was about thirteen, Harry went to work before and after school and on weekends at Clinton's Drug Store. It was an instructive experience, over a period of several months, for he saw the town's respected elders drop by for drinks of whiskey, dispensed furtively by the druggist. For the most part, however, his job was hard work. Many years later, he wrote his daughter Margaret:

> I can remember the first $3.00 I received for working a week — seven [*sic*] days from seven o'clock until school time and from four o'clock until ten at night, all day Saturday and Sunday. I had to wipe off bottles, mop the floor every morning, make ice cream for sodas, and wait on the customers. . . . That three silver dollars looked like three million and meant a lot more. I bought a present for Mamma and tried to give the rest of it to my dad and he wouldn't take it. It was as I say a great day all around when I got that $3.00. I've never had as much or as big a payday since.

The drugstore job may have taught him the meticulous attention to the task at hand that characterized most of his later life, but at the time it set him apart from Bess's crowd still further. Mary Paxton recalled that one day a group of girls riding around the square in a surrey had seen Harry sweeping out the drugstore and Bess had said she wished Harry didn't have to work so hard.

Later, Mary and others of the little group of friends in Independence looked back with intense longing on those days when their world seemed very small, very simple, and very lovely. Sometimes the most pressing concern of the Delaware Street girls was pestering their mothers to lengthen their skirts (not until they were eighteen were Bess and Mary allowed to wear floor-length skirts like their mothers'). Other times it was choosing party clothes. "We all had much the same kind of party dresses, mull with silk sashes, colored or striped," recalled Mary. "And Bess wore what the rest of us did; the difference was that she always looked more stylish than anyone else we knew."

The dresses had a lot of wear because most social activities were group affairs. In Harry's youth, boys and girls didn't date. The teenagers in Bess Wallace's group would gather on lawns in summer for lemonade, in parlors in autumn for cider. On winter nights they skated on frozen farm ponds; on summer evenings hay wagons drawn by farm horses rumbled down country roads carrying the boys and girls of the Delaware Street gang.

In those years, in that social setting, a girl was either "nice" or "fast." Nice ones behaved like ladies; if, however, a girl spooned—perhaps allowing a boy to put his arm around her in the hay wagon, or worse, kiss her in her papa's garden behind the lilacs—she never again received an invitation to a party. There was no "going steady" in the group to which Bess belonged. Of some twenty young people in the Presbyterian circle, only two married each other. Later, Mary Paxton asked Elmer Twyman, who had often come to her house to read Herbert Spencer, "Elmer, why do you suppose we didn't fall in love with each other?" "I think it was because we liked each other too well," he replied.

During their school years, Harry Truman was never invited to any lawn parties, hay rides, or skating parties given by Bess Wallace's group. Baptists went with Baptists, but Harry didn't consort with them either, preferring to keep to himself. It may have been the habit of a nomadic childhood that kept him from fitting easily into a group, but his reserve was more likely the result of childhood illness.

When Harry was ten, in 1894, he had contracted diphtheria. His recovery was slow, and for a year his mother had to wheel him around in a large baby carriage. Before that, at age six, he had been taken to an eye specialist who diagnosed "flat eyeballs," and to correct his faulty vision, Harry had been bought an expensive pair of glasses that immediately set him off from the other boys and prevented his playing rough games or organized sports of any kind.

As a result of the diphtheria and the glasses, he became a bookish child. His mother had already taught him to read before he was five, and he at first read only the big family Bible because of its large print. By the time he was twelve, thirteen, or fourteen (as he got older, the age varied with the telling) he had read the Bible through two, three, or four times (this number also varied with the telling). On Harry's twelfth birthday, his mother gave him an impressive, four-volume set of books, bound in brown leather and trimmed in gold, entitled *Great Men and Famous Women: A Series of Pen and Pencil Sketches of the Lives of More Than 200 of the Most Prominent Personages in History.*

Now psychologists say that the years between ten and fourteen are role-modeling years when a child is susceptible to finding heroes to emulate. At the time, all Harry knew was that the books, edited by Charles Francis Horne, fascinated him. He avidly read and reread them, poring over the sketches of illustrious figures draped in classical garments, captured in studied Victorian poses. The ancient world drew him; he went on to read Plutarch and Gibbon, found in the Independence Public Library.

The library, presided over by Miss Carrie Wallace, one of Bess's relatives, consisted of two rooms, cavernous, with high ceilings, and with books shelved neatly along each wall. The rooms housed about 2,000 volumes, although Harry later said it was 4,000. He also claimed to have read them all, even the encylopedias, but if that were so he would have had to read almost a book a day for every year he was in the town's public schools. However, it was no exaggeration on Harry's part to suggest that he read widely. Apparently most of his serious reading was done during his Independence school years, and he paid attention not only to the authors he enjoyed, but to Bess's favorites as well. In 1910, nine years after they left high school, Harry sent her a book as a gift and followed it with this note, "I am very glad you liked the book. I liked it so well myself I nearly kept it. I saw it advertised in *Life* and remembered you were fond of Scott when we went to school."

Many years later, when he was President, Truman held at bay reporters who obviously doubted the range of his reading, slyly asking him absurdly complicated historical questions. He confounded them by citing battles, dates, and kings, with little-known doings of the Founding Fathers and of Presidents of the United States.

Once high school was over, his daily schedule never again permitted the broad reading of his adolescence. By his own description, in another note to Bess, he was soon reading mostly "*Everybody's* and one or two other fifteen-cent or muckrake magazines and numerous farm publications." Certainly, after he finished school, Harry rarely went back to the classics. Instead, he developed a love for a "contemporary" author who may have contributed a great deal to the pithy wit for which Truman eventually became famous. He went on to tell Bess:

> . . . I have been reading Mark Twain. He is my patron saint in literature. I managed to save dimes enough to buy all he has written, so I am somewhat soaked in Western slang and Mark Twain idioms. My mother has been trying to persuade me to read Alexander Pope. She got a copy of his poems for her birthday. I haven't been persuaded yet, except a few of his epitaphs, which are almost as good as those we used to read of Bobby Burns.
>
> When it comes to reading though I am by it [sic] as I am by music. I would rather read Mark Twain or John Kendrick Bangs than all the Shakespeares and Miltons in Christendom.

If his spectacles and books had not been enough to set Harry apart from the forty other members of his class in Independence High School, his piano lessons would have done it. Harry was a promising piano student. He practiced two hours before school every morning and once a week he rode the streetcar to Kansas City to study with a pupil of Theodor Leschetizky, Mrs. E. C. White. Then suddenly, when he was a sophomore, he decided—to the dismay of his teacher—to quit. His love of the piano and of piano music stayed with him, however, and all his life he was particularly moved by Chopin. During his presidency, the White House piano—often with Truman playing it—got more press attention than many matters of policy.

While Harry may not have moved in the social circle he would have liked, these years in Independence were stable ones. His family only moved twice. During the first six years they lived on Crysler Street, where John Truman pursued his business, trading horses, cows, sheep, goats, and selling to the Kansas City stockyards. Then they moved to 909 West Waldo Avenue at North River Boulevard, into what was the formula house of the 1890s in the Midwest: a two-story dwelling with front and side porches and a one-story kitchen in the back. It was a respite in a way of life that once again would see moves and changes.

* * *

HARRY TRUMAN graduated from high school with ten other boys and thirty girls in 1901. In the class portrait, stylish Bess was on the right, at the end of the second row, smiling at the camera. Harry, on the back row, fourth from the left, posed seriously in a neat suit and knotted tie. The new graduate did not know what he wanted to do when he finished school, nor did he really know for years thereafter, and his life became a series of efforts to engage and focus his energies, to satisfy family responsibilities yet still find his own way. Not until he was nearly forty, in 1922, did Harry find his life's work. Meanwhile, he tried one thing after another: banking in Kansas City (1902–06), farming (1906–17), war service in the army (1917–19), a haberdashery business (1919–22). Certainly some of his decisions during these years were framed by circumstances—his parents' need for help on the farm, and the entrance of the United States into World War I—but to some degree Harry's slow start came from his own inability to take a long view. He had tremendous energy—Margaret once described it as demonic—but he did not always have an appropriate channel for it.

Truman had an enormous capacity to respond to a need, and once he established a task or a focus, he worked diligently and carefully—often brilliantly—on it. When John Truman broke his leg on the farm and Harry had to add his father's chores to his own, he wrote a letter to Bess that suggests he was aware that he wasn't moving along on what today would be called a "career path." But he also showed an awareness of the strength that stood him well throughout his political career: the ability to meet a challenge. "I don't think I'll ever make much of a mark as a farmer or anywhere else," he said, "but some times I have to come across. This is one of them."

Shortly before he graduated from high school, Harry thought he would seek an appointment to West Point or Annapolis. He and a friend, Fielding Houchens, went two evenings a week to the house of the high school history teacher, Miss Maggie Phelps, for special lessons in history and geography to get them through the entrance tests. In the event, Fielding gained admission to Annapolis in 1904, only to fail academically after a few months. In Harry's case there was no hope of admission: he could not read the fine print of the eye chart used for the physical examination.

About the same time, John Truman speculated in grain futures and lost everything the family had: a 160-acre farm Martha Ellen had inherited, and between thirty and forty thousand dollars in cash, stocks, and personal property (including the house in Independence). In 1902, the Trumans moved to Kansas City, hoping that John would find work there. Harry, too, was obliged to go to work to help keep Vivian and Mary in school, and he took a job with the Commerce Bank. He went to work in the basement "cage," where tellers cleared checks for the country banks.

The work was routine paper processing—receiving, counting, crediting—of the kind eventually automated. But Harry turned his attention to the repetitive tasks and did well. At Commerce he was a "utility clerk," doing any chore that came to hand. In 1905 he moved on to another bank, the Union National, for a better salary, $100 a month, a fairly impressive sum in those days. There he was a blotter clerk, a teller's assistant: while the teller waited on customers in the cage, the blotter clerk kept a record, writing out the give-and-take of the day in longhand.

Although careful on the job, the young bank clerk failed to take much interest in banking outside work hours. He might have attended classes at business college or studied accounting by himself, but he did neither, and showed little ambition to move past clerking. Just before he went to work with the bank, he spent a few weeks at Spalding's Commercial College, and sent a typewritten letter to Grandmother Young and Uncle Harrison to say that he was coming to the farm for the Fourth of July to set off firecrackers. If he ever typed another letter himself, it has not survived (his long correspondence with Bess was written entirely by hand).

During his time in Kansas City he lived in a boarding house with another bank clerk, a young man named Arthur Eisenhower, brother of another future President who was not yet in high school in Abilene, Kansas. Harry and Arthur were both country boys, though Harry was the more sophisticated of the two, and years later he recalled, according to his daughter Margaret, that Arthur "didn't know how to turn on a gas jet when he came to Kansas City—asked old Mrs. Trow, our boardinghouse keeper, for a coal oil lamp."

It was the one period in his growing up when Harry evidently had time for entertainment and high jinks. He went about then in the company of other young men and even took part in some practical joking. One extended joke was at the expense of Truman's roommate, Ed

Green, who went fishing on the Blue River, a nice little stream east of Kansas City; there, he and Harry's cousin, Fred Colgan, put a message in a pop bottle addressed to a nameless girl, telling her "all about what handsome young men we are, and promising young businessmen, and just fairly perishing for love, and asking her if she won't write back to us." The bottle floated lazily down the Blue River toward the Missouri, and the boys speculated that it might reach the Mississippi, maybe the Gulf of Mexico, perhaps even Brazil. About ten days later, a letter arrived postmarked Greenville, Mississippi, apparently sent by an eighteen-year-old girl who lived on a big plantation, in a house with tall, white pillars. Her mother, she told them, would just have had fits if she knew she was writing to a couple of boys she had never been introduced to, but they sounded so attractive; would they please write and tell her about Kansas City and much, much more about themselves? Answering at once, the boys told her plenty, and the correspondence went on and on. At last, she wrote and told them that she planned to come to Independence. Soon the boys received a note: the girl had arrived, unpacked her trunk, pressed her summer things, and was just ready to leave her aunt's household to meet her correspondents when a plague of scarlet fever descended and she found herself quarantined; she hoped that the paper she wrote on would not carry the dread disease, and she asked for more letters to comfort her . . . One night, a crowd of young people who had met at the Colgan house were led into the dining room by Mary Colgan. On the table was a pile of letters sent by Ed Green and Fred Colgan to the Greenville princess, and Mary began to read them aloud, to the delight of the crowd and the discomfiture of the two correspondents: Harry Truman was the "princess" and it was he who dictated the letters for Mary to write; she had then sent them to a friend in Greenville to be remailed to Fred and Ed with a convincing postmark.

Some of the fun of Kansas City at the time was less artful. For a young city, Kansas City had a rich night life and Harry spent many evenings at the theater. He ushered at the Grand on Saturday afternoons in exchange for free admission to such shows as "The Four Cohans" (including George M.). At the Auditorium he paid his way to see the Metropolitan Opera and hear recitals by some of the great romantic pianists—among them Josef Lhevinne, whose playing of Chopin he admired. He also heard Ignaz Jan Paderewski. (Some years earlier, when he was studying with Mrs. White, he had met Paderewski. Harry had been having trouble with a turn in the pianist's "Minuet in G" and, after a concert, Mrs. White had taken him backstage, where Paderewski had showed him how to make the turn.)

Generally, he felt about the afternoons at the Grand as he did about Mark Twain, and about the opera performances as he did the poems of Pope. He wrote to Bess:

> I have some cousins in KC [Kansas City] who affect intellect. They once persuaded me to go to a season of Grand Opera with them. It happened to include *Parsifal* and some others which I cannot spell. Well, I haven't recovered from that siege of Grand Opera yet. Perhaps if they had given me small doses I might have been trained because I do love music . . . But when it comes to a lot of would-be actors and actresses running around over the stage and spouting song and hugging and killing each other promiscuously, why I had rather go to the Orpheum. Perhaps if I could understand Dutch and Dago I could appreciate it better for I did hear an opera in English once that sounded real good. They say though it isn't good form to appreciate singing in English. I am sorry.

In addition to taking in the cultural delights of the city, Harry at this time also signed up in the service of his country. He joined the Missouri National Guard. Although there was an Independence artillery unit, Harry signed on with the Kansas City unit, Battery B. To pay the rental of a meeting place, he and his fellow members gave 25 cents a night, and he got a bright-blue uniform. The new uniform pleased him so much that he dressed up in it for a visit to Grandmother Young. The old lady was horrified, for its color was too close to that worn by the Yankee raiders. "Harry," she said, "this is the first time since 1863 that a blue uniform has been in this house. Don't bring it here again."

Harry gave up banking as unexpectedly as he had come to it. In 1906, another family emergency took him back to the farm, and there he stayed until the United States entered World War I in 1917. Trading still, John Truman had exchanged a Kansas City house for an 80-acre farm sixty miles to the southeast, near Clinton, and there his business had failed again when a flood washed away his corn crop. John and Martha were forced to move once more to the Young farm near Grandview, where they had lived between 1887 and 1890. Uncle Harrison wanted to retire; John Truman couldn't work the farm alone, and the Trumans asked their older son to come home. So ended Harry's banking career and his social life in the city.

The farm was a challenge to Harry after the fairly easy schedule of city life. It was still the era of horses and mules, which had to be cared for early and late, and the demands of a big farm were exhausting. Once Harry responded to Bess's invitation to a winter party, "I suppose skating is fine. I haven't the time to go see at present. I have only a few things to do such as feed hogs and cattle, build a mile of fence and a barn, and be at the house as much as possible [to do heavy chores while his mother tended his father recovering from a broken leg]."

Harry reported to Bess that farm life as an everyday thing was not very exciting, but it was clearly consuming if done with the attention he gave it. Planting, cultivating, and harvesting had a predictable—and time-consuming—rhythm; the pulling team had to be rested every twenty-five minutes. Harry had to watch the horses to see that they didn't drink too much water or eat anything while hot. When a farmer was not working in the fields he had animals, equipment, and buildings to look after. In his farming, as he had been in his bank work, Harry was meticulous. He took off the buckles before oiling his harness; a sloppy farmer would have left them on, shortening the job, but running the risk of the buckles shifting during work. Twice a year Truman would move his fence rows in order to clean them of weeds and waste.

To help feed the animals Harry put in the first local derrick and swing for stacking hay, and after feeding cattle on hay he baled the uneaten bits and pitched the bales into gulleys to stop erosion. He played midwife to birthing cattle and used his mother's homemade dip to combat lice. He kept Hampshire hogs and refused to wait, as most other farmers did, for the cholera to break out before vaccinating his animals; his veterinarian, Ed Young, recalled that Harry had sixty hogs vaccinated in 1914.

He was one of the "weed fighting-est" farmers around, contemporaries remembered. When he came into the store in town to buy extra hoes, the storekeeper knew that Harry had gotten extra help to attack cockleburs and thistles. But hired help cost 15 to 20 cents an hour plus meals and a place to sleep. The Grandview farmhouse was small, and the place to sleep usually meant Harry's own room. In the beginning he didn't always have hired help, but he needed it increasingly as his methods and planning became more thorough. In 1911, Harry broke a leg, but by then he had the farm work systematized enough that he knew he could simply supervise and still have the work go well.

It was on the farm, his mother claimed, that Harry got his common sense, and not in town. That may have been true, but farming was not all common sense—Harry studied farm management, too. He knew how to handle machinery, and a half-century afterwards remembered how he had done things. "We had riding plows, two twelve-inch mold-boards on a three-wheeled frame, pulled by four horses or mules or two of each. The big wheel on the hind side was just nine feet in circumference. I had a mark on it so I could count the revolutions. So you see I could tell exactly how much plowing was done in twelve or fourteen hours. It was usually about five or six acres. For five acres it took about ten hours at two-and-one-half miles an hour." After the field was plowed and harrowed, "along in September wheat was sowed with a twelve-disc drill which covered eight feet. I had a marker on the drill so that no skipped places would appear when the wheat came up. Those drilled wheat rows were as straight as the corn rows in the spring when corn was planted. When wheat was ripe in July it was cut with an eight-foot binder, shocked, and sometime later threshed."

Maybe what his mother meant by "common sense" was in fact dedication, for Harry approached farming with creative diligence. "J. A. Truman & Son, Farmers," as the stationery read, treated farming as a science and improved the soil at a time when most farmers were exploiting their fields year after year. Harry hauled manure from the barns and stables. He rested the soil with clover, usually "sown on the wheat, and a crop of stubble and clover would be cut in the fall, and the next year a fine crop of hay and a clover seed crop would be harvested." He handled the clover in a novel way: after stacking the first cutting, he would cover it with boards for protection against weather, and when the second cutting was ready he simply removed the covering and put the new hay on top of the old. After a year or two of clover, "fall plowing would prepare the field for corn the next year. When corn was gathered the stalk field was used as a pasture all winter and then the stalks were cut up and oats would be sown and then after fall plowing wheat and the rotation. It worked fine and more than doubled the yield for all crops."

The farm was not enough for Harry, however demanding the work, and after two or three years he began to turn his attention elsewhere. He had re-enlisted in the National Guard for a second three-year period and continued to go to Kansas City for meetings. In 1908, his cousin came into the barn lot to tell him about the fraternal organization of Masons. Shortly afterward, he applied to join the lodge in nearby Belton. Later, he organized a lodge in Grandview and became its first master. In preparation he followed a Masonic organizer from lodge to lodge, learning the complex ritual, and he liked to say that as he worked on the farm, running the cultivator, he taught the ritual to the horses. Although he was later criticized for using Masonry as a political crutch, his fascination with the order preceded his entrance into politics by many years. In 1940 he became Grand Master of the Grand Lodge of the Masons of Missouri.

Politics drew his attention in 1912, when John Truman took up the cause of a local Missourian, the Speaker of the House of Representatives, Champ Clark, who was seeking nomination as the Democratic Party's presidential candidate at the national convention in Baltimore. He lost to Governor Woodrow Wilson of New Jersey. Years afterward, when talking with John Hersey, who was preparing a profile for the *New Yorker*, Truman remembered how he had been driving a binder in a wheat field on July 2, 1912, when the convention came to a vote. The field was 160 acres, a two-mile circuit for the animals. He had to rest the horses, so after every circuit he tied them up and ran over to the telegraph station at Grandview, a quarter mile away, to see how matters were going in Baltimore. He was delighted when Wilson won. Thirty-three years later, on that darkening evening in 1945 when he took the oath as President of the United States, it was under a portrait of Woodrow Wilson in the Cabinet Room in the White House.

In 1914–15 Harry served a few months as postmaster of Grandview, but he gave the salary to a needy widow, a Republican and friend of his sister Mary. The women had met at meetings of the Order of the Eastern Star, the women's auxiliary of the Masons. At this time he also served as road overseer of his township, an appointive post for supervising work on the roads by local property owners who were required either to work themselves a day or two each year or to hire labor for the purpose. In 1914, John Truman, then road overseer, lifted a huge boulder off a road, developed a hernia, underwent surgery, and some weeks later, on November 2, died; as a direct result, Harry inherited both the minor responsibilities of the road overseer's post and the major work involved in running the farm.

Young Harry seemed briefly the heir to his father's trading spirit as well when, in 1916, he invested and lost several thousand dollars in a lead and zinc mine near Commerce, Oklahoma. Later in 1916, he went into the oil business with two partners. He put in $5,000, loaned to him by his mother. Harry and his associates managed to sink a well to a depth of 900 feet, but hired help was hard to find and drilling equipment was costly. In the spring of 1917, his little company sold its half-section lease near Eureka, Kansas, to the Empire Company. While Harry went to war, the Empire Company continued to drill and did, indeed, strike oil—the famous Teter Pool—and made millions of dollars for the partners in the enterprise. Eventually, the Empire Company became the Cities Service Oil Company.

ALL THE WHILE he farmed, Harry was courting Bess Wallace, by all accounts the only girl he ever loved. Today, their courtship seems a glimpse of a bygone age, so gentle and restrained was it, compared to "courtships" today; but the tender dignity of their courting and the loving respect of their marriage reflected Harry's character and values perhaps even more than his remarkable public life could. "I guess I am something of a freak . . .," wrote Harry to Bess, shortly after he was twenty-seven and she had turned down his first proposal of marriage. "I really never had any desire to make love to a girl just for the fun of it, and you have always been the reason. I have never met a girl in my life that you were not the first to be compared with her, to see wherein she was lacking and she always was."

Although Harry's public life featured a long series of capable responses to surprising events, his domestic life took a direction made by choice in his youth and pursued unswervingly ever after. For Harry Truman, Bess was the foundation of a life he had always hoped for and never really expected. His grateful wonder at her affection for him still shines in even the last letters he wrote her when they had been married many years. In the beginning of their serious courtship, Harry could scarcely believe that Bess would consider him as a suitor. "I have been so afraid you were not even going to let me be your good friend," he told her. "To be even in that class is something." He had no reason to expect that much would come of the acquaintanceship once their school days were over and he still had made what appeared to be very little impression on Bess. She always had several boy friends, and Harry was not even a member of her social group.

In 1903, however, Bess's carefree life changed abruptly. Mary Paxton, who lived next door, was awakened at five one morning by her father. "Go over to see Bess," he whispered urgently. "Mr. Wallace has killed himself." Mary found her friend walking back and forth behind the Wallace house. Her hands were clenched, her face set; she was not crying. Mary could think of nothing to say, so she paced silently along beside Bess as the gray light turned into morning.

No one has ever been sure why David Willock Wallace sat down in the bathtub and put a revolver to his head. If anyone in the family guessed the reason, it was not discussed. His widow took her four children—the youngest a boy aged three—to Colorado Springs for a year, then came back to move in with Grandmother and Grandfather Gates at 219 North Delaware. No one inside the Wallace household ever spoke openly of David Wallace again, though somewhat later Mrs. Wallace told Mary Paxton that she felt utterly humiliated by the suicide. After returning from Colorado, she sent Bess to Barstow, a private finishing school in Kansas City. Bess did not board there, but continued to live at home. Mrs. Wallace probably leaned heavily on Bess, who at eighteen was now mature enough to be her mother's confidante. As well as having the sole responsibility for bringing up three sons, Mrs. Wallace had been left with a deep sense of shame. Later on, "Mother Wallace" (as she came to be called) became a force to be reckoned with, not only in her own household, but later in Harry's. He learned to tread lightly with Bess where her mother was concerned, and the frame of his domestic life always had room for his mother-in-law until she died in 1952.

Perhaps her mother's sorrows and her three young brothers' needs kept Bess from making a marriage with one of her other suitors. For whatever reason, she was still single and at home on Delaware Street when Harry found his first real chance to court her seriously. One day in 1910, Harry was visiting Aunt Ella Noland and her daughters Nellie and Ethel, who by then had moved to 216 North Delaware, a little house right across the street from 219. His Aunt Ella mentioned that she had a cake plate of Mrs. Wallace's that needed returning, and (according to Margaret Truman, who heard the story from family talk) Harry seized the plate "with something approaching the speed of light" and took it across the street. When Bess answered his knock, the courtship was on.

At first he and a friend, Stanley Hall, went "sparking" together, driving Stanley's horse and buggy to Stanley's girl's house in Dodson, a small cluster of homes and shops in south Kansas City several miles north of the Grandview farm. Harry would then take a streetcar into Kansas City and another over to Independence, a ride of almost an hour. Or else he caught the train at Grandview and rode half an hour north to a junction named Sheffield, and then took a streetcar.

By 1914 these trips became too time-consuming for an increasingly successful farmer, and Harry paid $600 for a 1911 Stafford—one of 314 automobiles manufactured by Terry Stafford, first in Topeka and later in Kansas City. Thereafter he was able to travel to see Bess more easily, although the pressures of the farm kept him from getting to Independence much more often. Although she had other boy friends, Harry gradually became her acknowledged suitor. In June 1911, he sent her a letter complaining that if the drought they were having continued, "water and potatoes will soon be as much of a luxury as pineapples and diamonds." "Speaking of diamonds," he went on, "would you wear a solitaire on your left hand should I get it?" For several pages he apologized and stumbled, protesting that if he were "an Italian or a poet" he would use all the "luscious language of two continents" to persuade her. He called himself "a kind of good-for-nothing American farmer." "I've always had a sneakin' notion that some day maybe I'd amount to something. I doubt it now though like everything. It is a family failing of ours to be poor financiers. I am blest that way."

He didn't offer much promise beyond devotion and he wasn't surprised when Bess turned him down—only pleased that she didn't ridicule him. He thanked her for listening to his declaration of love. "You see I never have had any desire to say such things to anyone else. All my girl friends think I am a cheerful idiot and a confirmed old bach. They really don't know the reason nor ever will." Finally, in 1917, after seven years and dozens of letters and as many visits as the "good-for-nothing farmer" could manage, Bess accepted Harry's proposal. Naturally the happy young couple could not know that their lives and the lives of their countrymen were about to be critically affected by decisions in faraway Europe—especially the decision of the Imperial German Government in January 1917 to institute unrestricted submarine warfare against Great Britain. The Germans were trying to end the war, and hoped to starve the British into surrender by cutting off vital supplies. They had no particular quarrel with the United States but perforce had to include American vessels within the comprehensive shipping ban.

The Wilson administration refused to accept this affront to the time-honored American principle of maintaining the freedom of the seas, and on the evening of April 2, 1917, the President drove up Pennsylvania Avenue to address a joint session of Congress. He asked for a declaration of war, which he received and signed four days later. The enormous changes that emerged from the German blunder of precipitating the entry of the United States into the war in Europe were far beyond Truman's calculations at that time, or indeed those of most Americans. Most people had believed when war was declared that America would be contributing only money and munitions, but by the time the Armistice was signed, in November 1918, the American Expeditionary Force in France numbered more than two million.

Following the declaration of war, Harry Truman soon volunteered for military service. He had enjoyed his National Guard duty, and it was a period in American history when patriotism was an uncomplicated question. As a former member of Battery B in Kansas City, Harry now helped in the task of bringing in new recruits. The enlarged Batteries B and C (the latter in Independence) were formed into a regiment consisting of six batteries—the 129th Field Artillery. Harry's efforts had brought in so many men, that he told his fellow workers in the armory that he thought he should be a sergeant. Instead, they elected him—as was still the custom in the National Guard—a first lieutenant in Battery F.

Truman's army experience, like that of so many Americans, changed his life, although for some years he did not see where it would take him. His time in the army seemed only an interlude, certainly no permanent occupation, for he came out of service in 1919 with an ineradicable dislike for Regular Army officers, believing them to be, by his own phrase, silly martinets who stuck to the old army credo that "What looks right is right." And Harry never bought the line that "Rank has its privileges." This dislike would surface repeatedly later when he was

President, but in 1919 he believed that the protection of the country lay with the National Guard. Probably his dislike of the Regular Army began at Camp Doniphan, Fort Sill, Oklahoma, before he was shipped overseas. There, in a tented camp so dusty that Harry reported contests for the blackest face, he found the physical discomforts of army life nothing compared to his two great aggravations: the regular officers who disparaged reservists and National Guard officers; and his separation from Bess. Indeed he bragged in letters home about the hot showers and the good food at Camp Doniphan, and he evidently enjoyed the horseback riding that was part of army life at the time. When he had taken as much as he could from the Regular Army officers, he would gallop off across the flat countryside for hours of "equitating."

Just as he had managed the unexpected turns in his life before, Harry settled into army routine with wry wit and unflagging energy. He was a regimental canteen officer, and pay days were, by his own description, hellish. He would sometimes make $5,000 small change in a day and, as he put it in a letter to Bess, "I am generally about as tired as if I'd followed a plow all day and as hard and impolite as a paying teller in a national bank."

Harry had met Eddie Jacobson, an experienced men's furnishings buyer, and made him the canteen sergeant. They assessed the men $2 each and, with $2,200 to spend, went to Oklahoma City to buy items not issued to troops, then sold these at a modest profit, which they eventually returned to the men. Harry was proud of his canteen, proud of the effort it took to run it as a regular business in addition to his other army duties. He boasted to Bess, "They say I have the best canteen on the reservation, and every regiment has one."

His colonel was a particular bane to Harry, checking the canteen for cleanliness (occasionally, on a hunch, Harry would be up before reveille seeing to the cleaning, and the disgruntled colonel, upon making his surprise inspection, would find it spotless). The colonel also ordered audits of the books, but—in Harry's phrase—they were always "clean as a whistle."

Once the colonel stopped Harry as he was leaving camp and surveyed his uniform of "woolen O.D.," made for him by his Kansas City tailor. The colonel "made me take off my coat," wrote Harry, "and then went and ordered one like it. He said he couldn't expect all his lieutenants to dress that well until they had had a chance to run the canteen a while."

In the army, Harry had a chance for the first time to show a gift for leadership and a staunch devotion to his ideal that "One fellow is just as good as another." When Harry went to France in the spring of 1918, he was promoted to captain. In July he was given command of Battery D, the most unruly battery in the regiment. All Irish and German Catholics from Rockhurst College, a Jesuit high school in Kansas City, the two hundred boys of Battery D were a rollicking, hot-tempered band who had broken three previous commanders.

The night Harry took over the battery he announced that he was in charge, and turned the group over to the first sergeant for the order to the men to fall out. According to one of the battery's members, the trouble started at once: "And then we gave Captain Truman the Bronx cheer, that's a fact." At the time, the captain chose to ignore their disrespectful gesture, but next morning, on the bulletin board, half the noncommissioned officers and most of the first-class privates were "busted." "And then," remembered Vere C. (Pup) Leigh, a member of the battery, "we knew that we had a different 'cat' to do business with than we had up to that time. He didn't hesitate at all."

The men of Battery D came to idolize their commander because he was tough and fair—and courageous. He once got them out of a tight fix, the so-called "Battle of Who Run," when after the Americans fired five hundred rounds of gas shells at the Germans, the enemy returned fire and zeroed their guns in on Truman's battery. The first sergeant panicked and shouted, "Run, boys, they got a bracket on us!" Instantly the captain was on the scene, eyes flashing, arms flailing, holding the battery in line, shouting at them, calling them all the names he could think of. It was more epithets than most had ever heard. "It took the skin off the ears of those boys. It turned those boys right around," remembered Father L. Curtis Tiernan, regimental chaplain, who was there. Despite the clump and boom of shells, the smoke, the deadly shrapnel flying, the ground heaving, the soldiers stayed. They hitched horses to the caissons and pulled the guns away to safety.

On another occasion, Captain Truman did not hesitate to stand up for one of his men. During a march through Alsace when horses were scarce, a member of Truman's battery suffered a painful ankle injury. Truman put the man up on a horse. When a colonel saw this and demanded that the horse be unburdened, Truman retorted, "You can take these bars off my shoulders, but as long as I'm in charge of this battery the man's going to stay on that horse," The colonel rode away in a huff, and the injured soldier rode on behind his captain.

For events such as Who Run and other close calls, and for his clear loyalty to them, the men never forgot Truman. On the way home aboard a former German steamer, the *Zeppelin*, that rolled and pitched in a rough sea, Truman's men spent their time in a day-and-night crap game from which they set aside a percentage of the pot to buy a loving cup to present to the man they called Captain Harry.

After the war, the battery's men held reunions year after year on Armistice Day. In 1949, when President Truman invited the "boys" of Battery D to Washington for his inauguration, they marched in single file on each side of the presidential limousine. By then a paunchy, aging group, jauntily swinging canes, they were immensely proud of their moment in the public eye and of their former comrade in arms, their Captain Harry. When they had met that day before breakfast and someone had addressed Harry Truman as "Mr. President," his rejoinder was immediate. "We'll have none of that here," he said. "I'm Captain Harry."

In 1980, there were twenty-three of the original 210 men still alive. When the old men met at their annual reunion, M. S. (Mike) Flynn declared a few drinks to be in order, to honor the memory of Captain Harry, who had boasted that "You could turn Battery D loose in the middle of the Sahara and in an hour they'd all be drunk." At Bess Truman's funeral in 1982, six of the boys were there, four of them in wheelchairs.

While he was at Camp Doniphan, Harry wrote incessantly to Bess, sometimes twice a day, longing letters urging her to write and to come and see him. "Won't you please come down and knock off some of the rough edges," he begged when he began to be appalled at the rude tone he had adopted to handle his customers in the canteen. "Jacobson says he'd go into the guardhouse thirty days for one night on Twelfth Street [Kansas City's burlesque strip]. I'd go in for forty days if I could see you thirty minutes."

Harry was in the group of ten officers and a hundred men who left in April 1918, ahead of the main body of the 129th Field Artillery Regiment, bound for training in France after months of rumored departures and delays. He called Bess from the Armourdale, Kansas, railroad yard at five in the morning. "Call her, the phone's yours," said the switchman who let Harry use the phone, "but if she doesn't break the engagement at five o'clock in the morning she really loves you." Bess answered the call with instant warmth, despite the hour.

When the war was over and the captain had returned from active duty, he married his Bess in Independence on June 28, 1919, the day of the signing of the Treaty of Versailles. "Remember how pretty you were and how my gray checked suit showed up?" he reminded her on their anniversary nearly a quarter of a century later. At the time, the gala event was reported in the Independence *Examiner*:

> A wedding of unusual beauty and interest, was that of Miss Bess Wallace and Capt. Harry Truman, on Saturday afternoon at four o'clock, at Trinity Episcopal Church. Miss Wallace has lived in Independence all her life and has a large circle of friends. Independence also claims Capt. Truman although he has spent much time away. It was in this setting of love and devoted friendship that the marriage was solemnized. The church was beautifully decorated with garden flowers in pastel shades. The altar was a mass of daisies, pink hollyhocks and pale blue larkspur against a soft green background, lighted with tall cathedral candles.

After a short honeymoon trip to Detroit and Port Huron, the newlyweds moved into 219 North Delaware, the seventeen-room house where Bess had lived since 1904.

IN THE SUMMER OF 1919, Harry and his former canteen sergeant, Eddie Jacobson, prepared to open a haberdashery in Kansas City, which they did in November in a choice location—at 104 West Twelfth Street—opposite the grand Muehlebach Hotel. Harry could never have guessed that years later this hotel would be thought of by many Kansas Citians as "Mr. Truman's hotel."

The two men each put in everything they had. For Harry that meant $15,000 which he scraped together from various sources, mostly, it seems, from loans. In years after, Harry took a great deal of verbal abuse about the haberdashery from detractors who claimed that, because he couldn't make a go of running a business, he jumped into politics, or who derided him just for having sold men's clothing. In fact, the business of Truman & Jacobson, Men's Furnishers of Kansas City, was nothing to be ashamed of, either when it was succeeding—for they sold good-quality merchandise and kept a satisfied clientele—or when it was failing, for it was then like tens of thousands of other enterprises caught in the serious business recession of 1921–22. That recession was brought about by the sudden deflation in the wake of World War I. It was a difficult time for small business, and Truman & Jacobson fared no worse than many others.

The partners did everything right until the recession came. They had chosen a first-rate location, with good walk-in traffic from local businessmen, as well as travelers staying at the hotel across the street. They attracted steady business immediately, founded largely on friendships in the 129th Field Artillery, whose members had almost all come home to Kansas City. They ran the store in a businesslike fashion, open from eight in the morning until nine at night, six days a week. Eddie and Harry worked reverse shifts and had a clerk all the time. Eddie did the buying and Harry kept the books. All business was for cash and, in its first year, the partnership grossed $70,000—a large amount in those days. (In later years, Harry's critics would claim that he allowed too much credit business, whereas in fact there was none.)

Although both partners waited on customers, the dapper Eddie probably outshone the more reserved Harry at selling. Much later, Harry told a White House assistant the story of how Eddie made a sale to a big Swedish fellow. The Swede asked for heavy underwear, and Eddie got out the heaviest they had in stock. The Swede said it was not heavy enough. Eddie climbed on a chair and dug around on the shelves until he came out with a box containing underwear of a different color although no different in weight. The customer looked at it and said that was just what he wanted. "These will cost you a couple of dollars more," explained Eddie. "I didn't know you wanted to pay that much." Harry, unable to keep a straight face, had to walk to the back of the store out of sight.

The partners' only real problem was beyond their control. When the recession came, it caught them with a big inventory of expensive items such as $16 silk shirts. They had a chance to sell out at inventory price, but they chose to stick it out, only to find that the value of their inventory slumped from $35,000 to $10,000 because of falling prices everywhere. They settled accounts with such suppliers as J. Steinberg

Neckwear Company and Kansas City Cap Manufacturing Company by paying first a portion and then the balance in small amounts over three or four years. The five-year lease on the shop, together with the two bank loans, remained. Louis Oppenstein, owner of the building, at first refused to negotiate the $3,900 owed on the lease, but Harry eventually settled with him. The Twelfth Street Bank received settlement in full of its note for $2,500 after numerous installment payments, some as small as $25. The final payment of $200 was made in December 1924, but the haberdashery debts still were not erased.

When Eddie declared bankruptcy in 1925, Harry assumed the entire loss of their business partnership. A note of $5,600 to the Security State Bank went into default, and after several bank mergers and reorganizations, during which the successive institutions added interest, the successor bank secured a judgment in 1929 against Truman & Jacobson for $8,944.78. Shortly after the onset of the Great Depression, the bank failed, and its assets, including notes of hundreds of other debtors, were sold by court order. The notes could only be disposed of at greatly depreciated prices, that of Truman & Jacobson being bought in 1934 for $1,000 by Vivian Truman, who was thereby able to help his brother with the lingering debt problem. Eddie Jacobson eventually became prosperous again—as a haberdasher—and paid back his half of the debt, but Harry was strapped for money for twenty years after the store failed.

Taking the oath as Senator, Washington, D.C., January 3, 1935.

GENTLEMAN FROM PENDERGAST

Local politics

Following the collapse of the haberdashery business, Truman found himself at loose ends. One of his wartime buddies persuaded him to run for office as eastern judge of the Jackson County Court. His army companions helped to get out the vote for Captain Harry, and he managed to squeak through with a plurality of five hundred. Politics notwithstanding, Truman for years maintained his ties with the army reserve. A 1926 photo (*opposite*), taken on maneuvers at Fort Riley, Kansas, shows him with the insignia of a Lt. Colonel—and with a short-lived mustache grown for the occasion.

My Platform

Good Roads

A Budgeted Road Fund

Economy

A Day's Work For a Day's Pay

Fewer Automobiles and More Work for County Employees

Harry S. Truman

New Road and Precinct Map Showing

WHERE TO VOTE FOR

Harry S. Truman
Democratic Candidate For
JUDGE, EASTERN DISTRICT
Jackson County

SHAME! SHAME!

That the public shall know, and not be led astray by the falsehoods and lies that have been broadcasted in this campaign for Eastern Judge of this County's Court, we the undersigned enlisted men of the 129th Field Artillery take this means of informing the public, that HARRY S. TRUMAN, was the best liked and the most beloved Captain, officer in France or elsewhere.

We unanimously endorse him as a **man, officer** and **gentleman**, worthy of anyone's support.

A MAN

Fearless at all times, and ever willing to bear his share of the burden entailed by the hardships of actual conflict; sharing his all with those he commanded. We who know him best can freely say, "Here's a Man". Always the leader, never asking one to go where he would not go himself.

AN OFFICER

Combining executive ability with absolutely fair and impartial treatment, regardless of creed and nationalities; Capt. Truman exercised his rank, not for his own glorification, but for the glory of the country which he served. We who know him best can freely say, "Here's an officer".

Judge Truman

Following a two-year hiatus out of office, Truman ran in 1926 for presiding judge of the three-man County Court and served two four-year terms. At this period he used a multiple-pen device for signing county checks (*right*), but as President he always refused to use a mechanical aid and was sometimes obliged to sign his name several hundred times in the course of a day. The photo below shows Truman taking the oath in January 1931 for a second term as presiding judge, along with his associates on the Jackson County Court, Eugene Purcell (eastern district) and William Beeman (western district). County clerk Edward Becker (at left of photo) administers the oath. Throughout all these years, Judge Truman had to deal with burly "Boss Tom" Pendergast (*left*), the man who made Democratic politics work in western Missouri.

"New wonders, new beauty"

Truman's greatest accomplishment as presiding judge of Jackson County was the planning and completion of a modern highway system. In a letter accompanying a booklet illustrating the results of this roadbuilding program, Truman wrote: "Even to those of us who have spent our lives here, [the highway system] has opened up new wonders, new beauty." The pictures for this booklet, taken by Decatur C. Millard, are not only splendid examples of landscape photography, but are marvelously evocative of the Middle West a half century ago.

Truman's courthouse
The old county courthouse dominating the center of Independence served as Judge Truman's headquarters. For most of his years in office there, it appeared as in the 1920s photograph shown opposite—a no-nonsense structure that blended admirably with the local architecture. But the place needed a renovation, and in the process it acquired a neo-Georgian façade better suited to New England than to western Missouri. Truman was mighty proud of it, however, as he joined in the formal dedication (*left*) on September 17, 1933.

TRUMAN RALLY

Saturday, August 4, 1934
8:00 P. M.

Elmo, Mo.

V. H. SANDERS
AND
LEO D. LEWIS
The most outstanding twenty-two year old Orator of Mo.

Will Speak

Running for the Senate, 1934

A seat in the U.S. Senate came up for election in 1934, and Truman was Pendergast's candidate for it. The real contest in Missouri that year was between the three Democratic rivals in the August primary election. Truman rightly judged that his strength lay in the rural districts, and in the course of his campaign he drove to more than half of the state's 114 counties. Some recently discovered snapshots convey the small-town flavor of this 1934 primary: a crowd waiting for the candidate in Benton (*left*), the Truman campaign car in Poplar Bluff (*below*), and Judge Truman hammering home his message in Fredericktown. It was grass-roots politicking of a kind the Jackson County official understood well.

VOTE FOR

HARRY S. TRUMAN

DEMOCRATIC CANDIDATE

FOR THE

UNITED STATES SENATE

PRIMARY ELECTION
TUESDAY AUGUST 7, 1934

Running for the Senate, 1934

At the conclusion of his campaign travels, Truman had the satisfaction of voting for himself in the state primary on August 7. Thanks to the rural vote and to Pendergast's not entirely lily-white efforts in Kansas City, Truman won the Democratic nomination with a comfortable plurality. After that it was clear sailing. Missouri traditionally voted Democratic, and in November—with FDR riding high in the White House—the outcome was a foregone conclusion. Truman beat his Republican opponent by more than a quarter of a million votes.

VOTE FOR

DEMOCRATIC CANDIDATES

HARRY S. TRUMAN
United States Senator

LLOYD W. KING
State Superintendent of Schools

C. A. LEEDY, JR.
Judge Supreme Court
Division No. 2

JOHN T. FITZSIMMONS
Judge Supreme Court
Division No. 1

These Candidates Stand for Roosevelt and Recovery
GENERAL ELECTION, TUESDAY, NOVEMBER 6, 1934

The new Senator

The junior Senator from Missouri took his responsibilities seriously and began to make a name for himself during the Senate Railroad Committee hearings of 1937 (*right*). He also became a favorite of crusty John Nance Garner, the Vice President (*lower left*). Nevertheless, it was hard for Truman to shake off the widely held notion that he was merely Pendergast's stooge, and the two men's appearance together at the 1936 Democratic national convention (*below*) did little to allay such misgivings. Undeterred, the new Senator went about his business and kept in close touch with his Missouri constituents; he is shown (*left*) addressing a Masonic meeting in 1939.

Family of three

Mary Margaret joined the Truman family on February 17, 1924. By her own account, she was "a very sickly, squally baby," but that does not seem to be bothering her father in a snapshot taken during the year of her birth. The snow-suited charmer clutching a Felix the Cat doll is Margaret in the winter of 1926–27, while the backyard photo of Dad, Mom, and daughter dates from a year or so later. Shortly after Truman became the Democratic nominee for U.S. Senator in 1934, the family posed for a local newspaper photographer in the front parlor of their home at 219 North Delaware, Independence. Another newspaper photo shows the three Trumans arriving at Kansas City's Union Station from Washington, March 7, 1939.

Senator Truman boards a plane at Kansas City's municipal airport en route to Washington, April 20, 1937.

ONE AFTERNOON in 1921, a young friend from Harry Truman's army days stopped into the clothing store. He was Jim Pendergast, a lieutenant in the 129th Field Artillery and nephew of Tom Pendergast, head of the Democratic Party machine in Kansas City. With him was his father, Mike Pendergast, a leading local politician. "Run for office," they said to Truman.

The office they had in mind was that of judge (or commissioner) of the rural eastern district of Jackson County, of which Mike Pendergast was Democratic Party "Boss." Truman was interested; he had been working regularly with Mike Pendergast's Tenth Ward political club since before 1914. The members of the Tenth Ward Democratic Club were, like all Pendergast Democrats, known as Goats, while the forces of another prominent Kansas City Democrat, Joseph B. Shannon, were called Rabbits. When Truman became road overseer in 1914, his duties included attending the Goats' weekly Thursday-night meetings.

The Pendergasts' first proposal that Truman should run for office came at a time when the haberdashery was still doing well, and he refused to leave the business, but when they came back with the same proposal a year later, he eagerly accepted. His movement toward politics had been more a matter of drift than drive, through chance associations and one thing leading to another. During the war, Truman had sometimes been heard to say that he might run for Congress, and that if he were elected he could give a comeuppance to the Regular Army officers who bedeviled him and his men. Jim Pendergast had heard this talk, and he knew that his political family—firmly entrenched in the city, heavily dependent on their Roman Catholic ties—could use a good Baptist such as Harry Truman who had roots in farming areas. In 1922, the party machine needed someone for election to the three-man county court to help defeat the presiding judge, Miles J. Bulger. Bulger was known to be making a fortune from road contracts, but more outrageous to the Pendergasts were his attempts to put together a political machine to oppose Big Tom Pendergast's own. The brothers allied with Joseph Shannon and went for Bulger. Truman was their candidate.

He came from a family of dedicated Democrats. One of his friends during the presidential years, George Allen, once remarked to Truman's mother that, where he came from in Mississippi, he never saw a Republican until he was twelve. "George," replied Mrs. Truman, "you didn't miss much." There weren't many Republicans to be seen in Missouri either. In Kansas City, they were hardly recognized, so strong was the Democratic Party's hold. Tom Evans, a later friend of Truman's and owner of Crown Drugstores and radio station KCMO, used to say that in his part of the city he had never seen a Republican. The real fights for election were in the Democratic primaries; November merely confirmed the primary decisions.

Truman always believed that anyone who wished to be a politician had to learn the art, which to him meant assessing opponents, anticipating issues, then meeting the people: ringing doorbells, speaking in church basements, going to one meeting after another. It was old-fashioned stumping, the way the party of the people, the Democratic Party, had traditionally advanced itself. Truman did what was required of him during the primary campaign of 1922, but his speeches were not memorable. Indeed the first was a near disaster. "I recall it very vividly," he wrote many years later. "It wasn't a speech. It was a thoroughly rattled fellow on the platform who couldn't say a word.... They had a meeting down at Lee's Summit. They had all the candidates there and when it came my turn to talk, I couldn't talk. I was scared to death!" Then and for many years afterward, Truman was an ineffective public speaker. His flat voice—when he found it—simply put audiences to sleep.

Fortunately for Truman in 1922, his army friends laced his audiences and made up in enthusiastic support what the candidate himself lacked in oratory. They loudly applauded Captain Harry, sometimes known as Major Harry since his promotion in the reserves. Family, church, and Masonic connections also helped, but the army was crucial. Truman knew this and much later commented, "My whole political career is based upon my war service and war associates." His own Battery D and the 129th Field Artillery as a whole were the foundations of victory in the 1922 election.

Much has been made by Truman's biographers of his remarkable work during his ten years of service on the county court—he was eastern judge from 1923 to 1925 and then, after a defeat because of a falling-out of the Pendergast and Shannon factions, ran for presiding judge, won, and served two four-year terms between 1927 and 1935. Truman proved a model administrator in Jackson County, which then comprised a half million people. He foresaw the need for road building, because of increasing numbers of automobiles and trucks, and insisted on good concrete roads, not the pie crusts of the Bulger regime. He inherited a public system of nearly 1,100 miles of roads—70 unimproved, 670 graded and oiled, and 350 paved. Built by county judges who knew little about engineering, the existing roads cost $900,000 a year to maintain, and repairs consisted only of a little surface work on the worn places.

Something had to be done. Truman appointed a nonpartisan board of two engineers, one of them a Republican, who proposed to build an entirely new system, consisting of 224 miles of properly constructed highway. As presiding judge, he then arranged two large bond issues, $6.5 million in 1928 and $7.9 million in 1931, mostly for roads. He tried to distribute the new network so that no farm in the county was more than two-and-a-half miles from a concrete road. Then, in 1932, Truman arranged for the publication of a 122-page illustrated booklet—*Jackson County: Results of County Planning*—showing the progress made in road building and also the proposed remodeling of the courthouse in Independence and the new skyscraper courthouse in Kansas City erected during his administration.

No ANALYSIS of Harry Truman's political work in Jackson County can ignore his relations with the Pendergast machine. Without its backing he never could have won office on the county court. The relationship was subtle, defying easy analysis, and leaving Truman vulnerable to incessant criticism once he arrived on the national scene.

For any aspiring Democrat in Jackson County—and Truman soon was one, for he found politics exciting, exactly what he wanted to do with his life—it was necessary to deal with the Pendergasts. The head of the machine, the redoubtable Tom, had come into control of two of Kansas City's poorest wards in 1911 upon the death of his older brother Jim, founder of the machine. At that time the Pendergast brothers, Jim, Tom, and Mike, were crude, pushy men who could make their ways in a barroom brawl. Boss Tom especially looked a brawler—heavy-shouldered, thick-necked, ham-fisted.

As years passed, Tom became more sedate in his ways. In 1931 he established himself in the fashionable Ward Parkway district of Kansas City by purchasing a $115,000 French Regency-style house. He frequently visited New York, where he stayed at the Waldorf-Astoria, and he spent summers in Europe. He was head of a well-ordered household and attended Mass almost every morning. His office was at 1908 Main Street, Kansas City, on the second floor. Up a flight of stairs, a turn to the left, then a couple of steps, and visitors were in a waiting room where Pendergast's secretary, a tall, heavy-set man known as "Cap," regulated traffic into the boss's office. All visitors, high and low, sat in the waiting room and waited their democratic turns. The boss listened to their wants and gave them what he saw fit, all with the door wide open so that those in the waiting room heard what was going on.

It was there that Tom Evans sat one morning and heard the boss and Judge Truman and a group of road contractors have it out. The judge had insisted upon sealed bids for construction contracts under his first new bond issue, and the contractors had appealed to the boss. At the meeting Truman again insisted, and so did they. Finally Pendergast said, "I told you he was the hardheadedest, orneriest man in the world; there isn't anything I can do. That's it, gentlemen. You get your price right and get the best material. You heard him say it; you'll get the business." That was that, for when the boss gave his word, which was not often, it was (Truman fondly recalled, after dealing with many other politicians) as good as gold.

In this manner Judge Truman got along, and about this time, the year 1929, Mike Pendergast died, and Boss Tom installed Truman as Mike's successor as his lieutenant for the eastern part of the county. The judge never balked at giving the boss patronage, the practice of giving political appointments as favors; from his earliest days on the court he voted with the Goats on patronage, for it was the Goats who had backed him. Where he drew the line was between patronage (giving jobs to deserving Democrats) and graft (diverting money unlawfully and cheating the public interest). Boss Tom respected his position, as he needed a loyal lieutenant in the rural part of the county. He also liked a man who stood up and said what he thought, for that was the boss's own way.

Truman was not in the inner circle of the boss's lieutenants. He was an outsider compared to such men as Henry F. McElroy, who was on the county court when Truman first joined it. McElroy became city manager of Kansas City, after a good-government campaign had led to the introduction of the city-manager system, and soon was funneling money to the party machine. Truman easily sensed his outsider status, and in his second term as presiding judge he sought to help redistrict the state for elections to the House of Representatives, an effort mandated by the drop in Missouri's population in the census of 1930. He arranged a district composed of two Kansas City wards, together with the eastern part of Jackson County, a district made to order to guarantee his own election to the U.S. Congress, for he knew that two terms as presiding judge were all a man customarily could expect. Shannon, the Rabbit leader, went to the House of Representatives in 1930, and Truman hoped to do the same, but then Pendergast nominated as his candidate Kansas City Councilman C. Jasper Bell, who had cast the crucial vote in the choice of McElroy as city manager. Bell duly went to Congress in 1933, and Truman began to anticipate a return to the Grandview farm; he would be fifty years old in 1934.

Once again, however, opportunity came unexpectedly. One day in the spring of 1934, Truman was at a meeting in Sedalia when he received a telephone call asking him to see the county Democratic chairman, James P. Aylward, who was in a hotel room in Warsaw. There Truman learned he was Pendergast's candidate for the U.S. Senate. Apparently he was the boss's fourth choice, but Pendergast was in trouble, up against the machinations of Senator Bennett Champ Clark (son of the Champ Clark who had fought against Woodrow Wilson in Baltimore in 1912). Clark was from St. Louis, but was trying to dictate a Senate choice for Kansas City, which traditionally nominated the candidate for one of the state's two Senate seats. For the forthcoming Democratic primary Clark had put up a candidate, Jacob (Tuck) Milligan, from Richmond. It soon became clear, however, that the real contest was going to be between Truman and Representative John J. Cochran of St. Louis.

During the campaign Truman drove all over the state, to more than half of the 114 counties: he was on the road from morning to night, day after day. A typical day's itinerary could involve 250 miles of travel, with stops at sixteen towns and fourteen speeches. He kept an expense account of everything, for—despite the boss's endorsement—he received almost no money and virtually had to finance himself, not easy when the failure of the haberdashery had wiped out his savings. Early in the campaign, on April 17, 1934, he wrote a typical entry in his expense book which showed that he used thirty-four gallons and two quarts of gasoline that day, costing $7.33, and had taken a hotel room at $8.50 and three meals that totaled $5.10.

As well as serving as presiding judge in Jackson County, Truman had been president of the Missouri County Judge Association, and this prominence tended to help—he knew 342 county judges who frequently were influential in local Democratic party organizations. They were well acquainted with Truman's excellent record as an administrator, for he had sent to each courthouse a copy of *Jackson County: Results of County Planning.*

He campaigned thriftily and energetically, only to have Senator Clark, who was a member of Truman's own party, declare in friendly fashion that "Mr. Truman has been conducting a campaign of mendacity and imbecility unparalleled in the history of Missouri." The St. Louis Senator would live to regret his words, for eventually he failed to gain reelection to the Senate, and was forced to ask Truman, who by then was President, to appoint him to the appeals court of the District of Columbia, which he did. By that time, 1945, Truman had other things to think about, but in 1934 Bennett Clark was hard to take.

In the end, the outcome of the primary was decided not through oratory but through indiscretion, for at one point in the campaign a leading figure in the St. Louis Democratic machine boasted that Representative Cochran would carry the state's eastern metropolis by polling 125,000 votes, a remark that forced Tom Pendergast to add to the total vote he had already planned to bring in for Truman in Kansas City. In the event, the St. Louis machine produced 104,265 votes for Cochran, while 6,670 went to Milligan, and 3,742 to Truman. The Kansas City machine rolled up 137,529 votes for Truman, while 8,912 were cast for Milligan, and only 1,525 for Cochran.

Pendergast's candidate won the nomination state-wide by a margin of some 40,000—with a total of 276,850 votes, compared to 236,105 for Cochran, and 147,614 for Milligan; in November he duly went on to win the Senate seat. (If every vote from both of the big city machines had been thrown out in that primary, and only the rural counties' votes accepted, Truman still would have won—by 135,579 to Cochran's 130,315.) The St. Louis *Post-Dispatch* liked to compare the division of Missouri to the division of Gaul into three parts: Kansas City, St. Louis, and the country districts. Truman won the country districts.

It nonetheless was clear that in a contest between cheaters, St. Louis and Kansas City, the latter's machine was considerably more effective. Cochran got only 104,000 votes in St. Louis, with its population of

822,000, whereas Pendergast obtained 137,000 votes for Truman from Kansas City's much smaller population of 399,000. The Kansas City machine could produce between 50,000 and 85,000 ghost votes. Approved lists showed some persons registered as many as thirty times; fifty to a hundred persons were registered as living together in tiny apartments; voters were shown as living in empty lots and vacant buildings; thousands of persons long dead were still listed as accredited voters (inspiring the election-day quip that "Now is the time for all good cemeteries to come to the aid of the party"). Tom Evans, the drugstore magnate and dedicated Goat Democrat, in his youth was tall for his age and began voting at age sixteen. High school students could make pocket money on election day by serving as repeaters.

It was Harry Truman's good fortune in 1934 to have run for the Senate when the Kansas City Democratic machine had reached the height of its power. The redrawing of districts for election of members of the House of Representatives, caused by the census of 1930, had proved a veritable act of providence. The initial effort to redistrict had in fact produced such an absurd gerrymander that the governor threw it out, and as a result all House candidates in Missouri had to run at large in 1932—and had to seek Boss Tom's favor. That year he secured the election of a governor, who out of gratitude allowed him to name every state appointive official. Pendergast's office on Main Street in Kansas City became known as the State Capitol and the statehouse in Jefferson City became known as Uncle Tom's Cabin. In those years the Missouri artist Thomas Hart Benton painted a mural for the statehouse and included a likeness of Pendergast, who unselfconsciously posed for the portrait. There was some considerable fuss about the inclusion of Pendergast, but Benton considered him an essential part of Missouri. Many years later, after Harry S. Truman had left the White House and retired back to Independence, the artist and the former President met at a dinner party, and Benton gave Truman the original sketch of the Pendergast portrait.

In the mid-1930s, when everything seemed to be going fine for the boss, Pendergast's precinct men frequently outdid themselves. In 1934 they confronted a very real challenge from the St. Louis machine, but in other years they got out far more votes than necessary to secure the election of the machine candidates. In 1936 ghost voting in Kansas City reached absurd proportions: the city's Second Ward, with a population

of 18,478, gave a Pendergast candidate 19,202 votes, his opponent 12.

Perhaps no action would have been taken even then, for party machines everywhere in the 1920s and 1930s—Republican and Democratic alike—got out the vote this way. However, the zeal of the machine's ward heelers combined with the virtual physical and mental collapse of Boss Tom to bring this political idyll to an end. After the 1936 election 259 ward heelers were convicted of stuffing ballot boxes. Meanwhile, Boss Tom himself had suffered a series of physical blows—mastoiditis, a severe heart attack, a serious cancer operation—and in addition, he now succumbed to the horses. His penchant for horse races had turned into a mania and by the mid-1930s he was betting on races right across the United States. Pendergast's consistent losses at the racetracks compounded his other needs for money, and he began eyeing a $10 million state-impounded fire insurance fund. He arranged with his complaisant state superintendent of insurance, R. Emmett O'Malley, to pick up $750,000 in bribes if he passed 80 percent of the fund back to the companies (234 insurance firms) that wanted the fund freed. The bribes were passed. Pendergast thereby opened himself up to investigation for income tax evasion and was caught. He confessed in 1939, and, as well as having to pay a $10,000 fine and $434,000 in back taxes, he was sentenced to serve fifteen months in the federal penitentiary at Leavenworth.

All the while, Senator Truman, who had nothing to do with these shenanigans, nor with Boss Tom's unhappy end, was fighting to become a respected member of the U.S. Senate. He was known as Pendergast's man, and was called in the Senate "the Gentleman from Pendergast." Boss Tom may even have encouraged this remark by saying loosely that because some Senators represented oil and steel, utilities and railroads, he had decided to send his "office boy" to represent Pendergast. Unfortunately there were other unflattering descriptions, all easy to remember. The veteran head of the Missouri Farmers' Association, William Hirth, referred to Truman as a "bellhop," while Tuck Milligan had said during the primary campaign that Truman would get "calluses on his ears listening on the long-distance telephone to his boss." Perhaps because of such disparagements, President Roosevelt treated Truman casually, and five months passed before the new junior Senator from Missouri was given an appointment for a fifteen-minute meeting with the President—and even then he emerged after only seven.

There was another reason why Truman must not have appeared to warrant much of FDR's attention: the junior Senator did not threaten to bolt on close votes, or in any way show himself unpredictable. He was a loyal New Deal Senator because he believed in the New Deal's economic and social measures. Other Senators would occasionally make difficulties for FDR, to trade off votes for favors. Truman's Missouri colleague in the Senate, Bennett Clark, was one of those who played the political game with Roosevelt, although the alcoholic Clark was unpredictable anyway. As a result, the President gave him all the state's patronage as if he deserved it, and Clark accepted it without so much as an "if you please" to Senator Truman.

Determined not to let critical remarks and slights engage his attention unduly, especially if there was not a thing he could do about them, Truman swallowed his pride and attended to his business as Senator. In this respect he showed what a professional he had become. In fact, he was not Boss Tom's stooge, nor was he a rubber stamp for Roosevelt, but he had no real way to announce the fact. When in 1938 a fight arose in the Senate over who should become the next majority leader— Senator Alben Barkley of Kentucky, who was Roosevelt's nominee, or Senator Pat Harrison of Mississippi—Truman gave his promise to Harrison; whereupon the chairman of the Democratic national committee, James A. Farley, probably with Roosevelt's blessing, telephoned Pendergast to have him bring Truman into line. Boss Tom put in a call, but when the Senator explained that he had given his promise to Harrison, Pendergast said no more. It was the only time, Truman later remarked, when Pendergast ever tried to intervene in his activities as Senator.

IN HIS FIRST SENATE TERM, 1935–41, Truman was responsible for drafting the Civil Aeronautics Act of 1938 and was co-sponsor of the Transportation Act of 1940, major enactments and remarkable achievements for a freshman Senator. He had received assignment to a three-man subcommittee of the Interstate Commerce Committee to determine how to regulate the fast-growing civil aviation industry, and when the subcommittee chairman, the lackadaisical Senator Vic Donahey of Ohio, failed to attend his own hearings, Truman and Warren Austin, a Republican from Vermont, put together a bill that would give authority to the chairman of a Civil Aeronautics Board and make the chairman directly responsible to the President. Truman insisted that the legislation follow closely the Interstate Commerce Act, because that enactment's terms—its words and phrases—already had undergone judicial examination and the precedents were fairly clear. The new agency hence would avoid much time-consuming litigation in interpreting the meaning of the act. In an underhanded maneuver, Senator Pat McCarran, Democrat of Nevada, tried to weaken the bill, but it was passed largely as Truman had drawn it up.

Much of the rest of his time went to investigating railroad chicanery, prevalent in the 1930s because of the bankruptcies of major lines. Each night the Senator would bring home a briefcase full of papers, staying up late to study hearings and depositions and newspaper accounts, together with books on railroad finance and management and history drawn from the Library of Congress. Some of what he read was astonishing. A box among his papers in the Harry S. Truman Library of Independence contains handwritten speeches of the later 1930s, page after page of description of financial irresponsibility. In preparation for a statement issued in Washington on October 12, 1938, he wrote:

> The difficulty with the railroads is a long-standing one, and came about through banker management. Every road in the country was built by subsidies furnished either by the federal government or by the states, cities, and counties through which it ran. It has been the policy of the financial managers of the railroads to load them with all the debt that they can possibly carry in times of prosperity and then run them through expensive reorganizations out of which they usually come with debts bigger than before. No intelligent plan for debt retirement has ever been followed by the Wall Street bankers who control the railroads. They have taken it for granted that all inland transportation is a monopoly and that the railroads will forever carry it and that if the public and the people who pay the transportation bill do not like it they can "be damned."

Thus, according to Truman, it was the cupidity of bankers and lawyers that had brought the railroads to ruin during the Great Depression—27 percent of the country's railroads, 75,000 miles of track, $5 billion in assets. "Some of the country's greatest railroads have been deliberately looted by their financial agents," he told the Senate. The first train robbery was committed on the Rock Island Railroad in 1873, he said, just east of Council Bluffs, Iowa. He went on: "The man who committed that robbery used a gun and a horse and got up early in the morning. He and his gang took a chance of being killed and eventually most were. That railroad robber's name was Jesse James." The same train robber also held up the Missouri Pacific three years later and took $17,000 from the express car. "About thirty years after the Council Bluffs holdup, the Rock Island went through a looting by some gentlemen known as the 'Tin Plate Millionaires.' They used no guns but ruined the railroad and got away with $70 million or more. They did it by means of holding companies. Senators can see what 'pikers' Mr. James and his crowd were alongside of some real artists."

And after all this, of course, had come the reorganizations of the Depression years, in which insiders again pumped money out of the railroads into their own bank accounts. Truman was disgusted with the looting of the railroads' assets in the midst of the most desperate business depression the country had ever known. But it was all true— reports of bankruptcy courts displayed the bankers and lawyers incessantly at work, and especially the lawyers, "the highest of the high-hats in the legal profession," who resorted to "tricks that would make an ambulance chaser in a coroner's court blush with shame."

Things got rather warm for Truman when he was investigating the railroads, especially the Missouri Pacific, where he delved into records that cast doubt on the actions of such financial friends as William T. Kemper in Kansas City. Undaunted, the Senator went ahead; if his investigation touched his friends, that was their problem. In April 1937, when Truman's life was threatened in an anonymous letter, Senate gallery police watched carefully for several days, for the letter said he would be killed in the Senate.

Part of the reason for the appalling behavior of businessmen who looted the railroads, Truman maintained, was that they had created a kind of anonymity for themselves through the sheer size of their corporations. It was easy to forget whose money was involved. Truman wrote:

I believe that the country would be better off if we didn't have sixty percent of the assets of all the insurance companies concentrated in four companies. I believe that a thousand insurance companies, with $4 million in assets, would be just a thousand times better for the country than the Metropolitan Life, with $4 billion in assets. The average human brain is not built to deal with such astronomical figures. I also say that a thousand county-seat towns of seven thousand people each are a thousand times more important to this republic than one city of 7 million people.

Truman was against centralizing ownership, as executives of many leading railroad companies desired. Nor did he go along with proposals of some of his fellow Senators for public ownership. In Washington he met Justice Louis D. Brandeis of the Supreme Court, with whom he enjoyed long and intimate talks, and perhaps it was from Brandeis, an old Progressive who had wielded great influence with President Woodrow Wilson a generation earlier, that he came to champion regulation, rules for corporate good behavior.

In 1937, by example and in his public statements, the Missouri Senator also offered the Senate a special prescription for reform, something that would undergird any rules—for he believed rules often only defined the situations wherein skulduggery might continue. Harry S. Truman at the very bottom of his soul was no legalist, despite his admiration for law. He was an unabashed moralist. Americans, he said, worshipped money instead of honor. To such idolaters it made no difference if a billionaire rode to wealth on the sweat of little children and the blood of underpaid labor. "No one ever considered Carnegie libraries steeped in the blood of the Homestead steelworkers, but they are. We do not remember that the Rockefeller Foundation is founded on the dead miners of the Colorado Fuel and Iron Company and a dozen other similar performances." He called for a return to ancient fundamentals, to "the Giver of the Tables of the Law and His teachings."

When he first went to the Senate, Truman had listened to the advice of Senator Carl Hayden of Arizona, who told him he could either be a workhorse or a showhorse. Truman was a workhorse; he hated the Senators who failed to do their duty. As early as the summer of 1935 he had taken their measure, and wrote Bess about Senator Gerald P. Nye of North Dakota, then much heard about because of an investigation of the munitions industry constantly in the headlines. Nye, he opined,

> . . . is one of the good-looking, egotistical boys who play to the gallery all the time. He's had the limelight on the munitions investigation

for six months and he never comes to the Senate except to make a speech or introduce a bill to abolish the army and navy or to get more money for more investigation and more publicity. Several so-called people's friends in the Senate would be in a hell of a fix if there were not some good old workhorses here who really cause the Senate to function . . . . There isn't a so-called progressive who does anything but talk.

The junior Senator from Missouri was no talker, and during his first term surely proved his worth in legislative accomplishment.

DURING THESE YEARS Truman lived with Bess, their daughter Margaret, who had been born in 1924, and Mother Wallace in a succession of cramped, two-bedroom apartments in Washington. He loved having his family with him—his Bess, whom he still thought of as the light in every day, and his beloved Margie, "my beautiful baby," as he continued to call her even when he was President and she a young woman. Even the indomitable Mother Wallace helped turn the Washington flats into something more like the Independence home he missed. Of course, Bess, her mother, and her daughter missed Independence too, and they often went back. During the whole of the Trumans' time in Washington, Bess never found a laundry that suited her, and the family laundry was sent home to Kansas City to an old local firm. Other things in Washington didn't suit the Trumans very well either. Their life style and values were essentially small-town mid-American, and the family didn't mesh well with Washington high society. Moreover, they had little money for keeping up the image or the pace of Washington life, for they were still paying out campaign debts. Not until 1946 were they finally clear of that burden and able to buy back the family farm, lost to foreclosure by county officials in 1940, at which time Truman's mother and sister were forced to move into a tiny rented house in Grandview.

The Washington apartments varied, year after year, as the Trumans frequently rented one only while the Senate was in session. In between times, when office routine or special sessions made Truman's presence in Washington necessary, he lived in hotels near Capitol Hill, such as the Continental or LaFayette or Carroll Arms. Meals he managed when he was alone by taking breakfast in the apartment, lunches at the Senate office building, dinners at the Hot Shoppe or Harvey's. It was neither a glamorous life nor an adventurous one. Mostly it was busy—and when Margaret, Bess, and Mrs. Wallace went home to Independence, it was lonely. Still, the Truman family looked back on the Senate years as good years—particularly in comparison to the years of strain that came later.

At work in the Senate Office Building, 1940.

SENATOR IN HIS OWN RIGHT

The 1940 Senate race

Although an incumbent Senator, Truman faced a bitter fight for reelection in 1940. Again, the crunch came in the primary, and this time—with Pendergast in disgrace and his machine in shambles—Truman was on his own. His rivals for the nomination were Lloyd C. Stark, Missouri's governor, and Maurice Milligan, the District Attorney who had Pendergast sent to prison. Fitzpatrick's cartoon shows how the St. Louis *Post-Dispatch* rated Truman's chances. Ignoring the omens, Truman set up his campaign headquarters in Sedalia (*below*) and began putting his case to the people, including the state's large black community.

The 1940 Senate race

The heat of the 1940 primary campaign is evident in a photo of Truman addressing a meeting in Sedalia during the month of July. President Roosevelt maintained an equivocal silence over the Democratic free-for-all in Missouri, but Truman—as a loyal New Deal Senator—had every right to ride on FDR's coattails. In the end, much to most people's surprise, he won the primary. The Kansas City *Journal-Post*, which had come out for Truman early in the campaign, exultantly sent Governor Stark back to his apple orchards, and the Truman family could beam delightedly at a sheaf of congratulatory telegrams. More were to come in November, when the Senator won an easy victory over his Republican opponent.

91

CLEARING THE WAY TOWARD VICTORY

The Truman Committee

When Truman returned to the Senate in January 1941 for a second term, he was very much his own man. Soon he gained national prominence as head of a Committee to Investigate the National Defense Program, better known simply as the Truman Committee. He is pictured above with Senator Harold H. Burton, inspecting an army camp in Ohio. Back in Washington there were endless Senate hearings. A photograph taken on March 24, 1943, shows Senators Truman, Ralph Brewster, and Homer Ferguson concentrating on testimony relating to the manpower situation, while below Truman is caught in conversation with Senator Tom Connally of Texas.

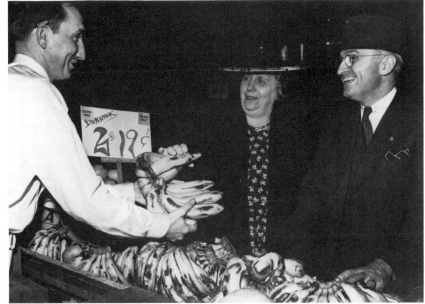

Life in Washington

During the Trumans' early years in Washington, the family lived frugally in a succession of two-bedroom apartments. A Senator's salary at that time did not go very far, even with two pounds of bananas selling for 19 cents. In the series of photos here, taken by a news photographer in the early 1940s, Bess is shown helping with the correspondence, Margaret hands Dad a record from a 78-rpm album of Victor Herbert, and the Senator does his bit with the morning toast.

Reluctant candidate

Truman's nomination for Vice President at the 1944 Democratic national convention in Chicago was engineered by Robert E. Hannegan, chairman of the party's national committee. The two are shown together during the convention (*left, above*). Truman did not seek or even desire the nomination, but he appears properly elated as the convention chairman, Senator Samuel Jackson of Indiana, holds the winning candidate's arm aloft. By long tradition, a successful nominee is later formally "notified" in his home state. Truman's notification ceremony took place on September 2, 1944, at his birthplace, Lamar (*left, below*). On election day Roosevelt won an unprecedented fourth term. Four days later, the President and Vice-President-elect met at Washington's Union Station and rode to the White House in an open limousine.

The only occasion on which Truman and FDR were photographed together during the election campaign: lunch on the White House lawn, August 18, 1944. The President's failing health was already a matter for concern among leading Democrats, and on this occasion FDR left Truman in no doubt about the extra burden he would have to bear in nationwide campaigning.

JUST when Senator Truman was beginning to build a reputation based on hard work and effective legislation, his first six-year term approached its end, and in 1940 he faced a primary fight for reelection that was to prove the most difficult, grueling contest in his political career, and certainly the experience that persuaded him to defy polls and predictions in the presidential election of 1948. In 1940 the essential problem was the recent downfall of Tom Pendergast, and the rise of one of his antagonists, Lloyd C. Stark, governor of Missouri since 1937.

Stark owned a multimillion-dollar nursery, largest in the country, known for Stark Delicious apples. Like almost all successful Democratic officeholders in the state, he had enjoyed assistance from the Kansas City machine, but when Boss Tom became vulnerable, Stark turned against him and helped the brother of Tuck Milligan, Maurice Milligan, federal attorney for the western district of Missouri, have Pendergast sent to Leavenworth. Stark believed that Truman too was vulnerable, and planned to take his Senate seat from him. One of the first signs Truman had of what was coming occurred when the governor—accustomed to breezing in and out of Washington on errands, visiting with President Roosevelt and not always paying his respects to Senator Truman—stopped by the Senator's outer office and told his secretary, Vic Messall, that he, Stark, would never think of running for the Senate. Truman knew instantly that Stark would run.

In the primary of 1940, Truman was on his own, for Tom Pendergast's machine was in shambles. The boss's nephew Jim, Truman's friend, controlled only a ward or two in central Kansas City. Nor did Senator Truman have the public support of President Roosevelt, who was the boss, so to speak, of the national scene and who, through myriad federal activities, including relief rolls that reached out to all the states, could have exerted irresistible influence on Truman's behalf. Roosevelt, to be sure, had other matters to think of. The New Deal had run into trouble because of the recession of 1937–38, and although the President had rescued it by a new series of domestic measures, the recession had shaken his confidence in getting the country on its way again. Moreover, on September 1, 1939, World War II had begun.

Roosevelt confronted his domestic critics with all the guile he could master, which even his supporters agreed was a great deal. Having lost his fight to "pack" the Supreme Court in 1937, and having failed to prevent the reelection of conservative and mainly Southern Senators in congressional races the following year, the President decided in 1940 to run for an unprecedented third term, to ensure the continuation of the New Deal and to oversee the country's preparations for war. In this situation, Senator Truman's plight in faraway Missouri hardly mattered to Roosevelt. He gave Truman a private assurance that he personally would like to see him reelected, but he refused to make a public endorsement. Roosevelt saw Truman only infrequently, much less often than he did Lloyd Stark, although in the end he drew back from publicly supporting Truman's antagonist.

FDR toyed with Stark, for he doubtless believed the governor to be the rising Democratic power in Missouri and worthy of his attention. As the summer Democratic convention approached, Roosevelt obviously was searching for a potential running mate and he probably intimated to Stark that a man with a nationwide reputation for apples could easily attract votes to the national ticket. Vice President John N. (Cactus Jack) Garner was getting old, and was an arch-conservative. In the event, Roosevelt picked his Secretary of Agriculture, Henry A. Wallace, as his running mate, but the President's build-up of Stark did not help Senator Truman's cause. All the omens were bad, and Truman made a trip to Missouri in January to see what he could do about rallying support. He wrote thirty friends, asking them to meet him at the Hotel Statler in St. Louis. Half of those invited failed to show up, and the ones who did only argued the futility of opposing Stark. Just after breakfast that morning and before this discouraging meeting took place, the telephone had rung in the Senator's suite. It was President Roosevelt's press secretary, Stephen T. Early, offering a seat on the Interstate Commerce Commission, at a salary higher than a Senator's. Roosevelt was easing the way for Stark. "Tell them to go to hell," Truman said. "I've made up my mind that I'm going to run."

Actually he had not made up his mind at that point and the meeting that followed put him in a quandary again. Truman agonized over his course of action. At last, at the Hotel President in Kansas City—with Tom Evans, Vic Messall, and a clerk, Kenneth Miller, at his side—he decided. "Go down [to Jefferson City] today, and be sure and be there and file," he told Vic and Ken, "because there's one moral cinch. If I don't get anybody's vote, I'll get the Boss's and my own." The "Boss" was Mrs. Truman. Tom said, "I can get you two more, my wife's and mine."

Truman had no money for a campaign. His close friend and former army associate, Harry H. Vaughan, said that when he took over as campaign treasurer in 1940, the campaign fund totaled "three dollars and a quarter." Years afterward, he related that the total amount raised came to $16,000 including $3,000 borrowed against Truman's life insurance. The only large contribution was $1,000; everything else was twenties and fifties. Vaughan at one point appealed for dollar bills and received about two hundred, which he used to buy stamps to send out several thousand more requests—which turned up $1,200. Stark made a radio statement that Truman was being financed by a slush fund provided by Tom Pendergast. Vaughan did not have enough money to go on the air to refute it.

Of the large daily papers in Missouri only the Kansas City *Journal-Post* came out for Truman. The *Star* was bitterly hostile, as was the St. Louis *Post-Dispatch*, which editorialized that "Truman is through in Missouri. He may as well fold up and accept a nice lucrative federal post . . ." When the Pendergast ship sank, the *P-D* said, it took Truman down with it. Of the smaller city and rural papers, only the Jefferson City *Daily Capitol News*, the weekly paper of Harrisonville, and the Dade County *Advocate* supported Truman. It is no wonder that, later in his life, he said he'd much rather spend time with politicians than newspaper publishers.

Truman ignored all the odds, and engaged his doggedly loyal friend Fred Canfil to drive him from courthouse to courthouse to talk to every rally and meeting he could raise or invite himself to. He began his campaign in Sedalia, where he went all-out to obtain the support of Missouri's 245,000 black voters, telling his audience:

> I believe in the brotherhood of man, not merely the brotherhood of white men but the brotherhood of all men before law. In the years past, lynching and mob violence, lack of schools and countless other unfair conditions hastened the progress of the Negro from the country to the city. . . . They have been forced to live in segregated slums, neglected by the authorities. Negroes have been preyed upon by all types of exploiters. The majority of our Negro people find but cold comfort in shanties and tenements.

He also sought help from the state's railroad workers, who had taken note of his fight against the roads' managers and generally against control of the nation's wealth in Wall Street. The twenty-one railroad brotherhoods came out for the Senator, 50,000 strong, and just before the election sent into the state 500,000 copies of a special Missouri edition of a weekly Washington newspaper, *Labor*. Truman considered this move important in offsetting the general hostility of the daily papers.

His position improved somewhat when District Attorney Maurice Milligan entered the primary race. Milligan was the man who had Boss Tom sent to prison, and he resented Stark's attempt to claim credit for Pendergast's conviction. His candidacy promised to divide the "good government" votes with the governor, thus giving Truman the chance of a plurality.

To outsiders it still appeared that Truman would lose, but slowly the alignment, or appearances of strength, began to change. Milligan got out on the hustings before Stark, who was overconfident, and Milligan proved an even worse public speaker than Truman; his manner turned away audiences in droves. Everywhere Governor Stark went, he was followed by a group of Missouri colonels, in uniform, who saluted him as he strode to the podium to make a speech. His state police chauffeur saluted him. And behind the flamboyance lay the fact that he had "put the lug" (to use the Missouri expression) on all office-holders making over $60 a month, whom he forced to kick in 5 percent to his campaign fund. In June 1940, the Fulton, Missouri, paper revealed that employees of the state hospital were contributing. To this Stark replied, unconvincingly, that contributions were voluntary.

Despite the errors of his opponents, Truman might have lost had it not been for a narrow victory in St. Louis, for on primary day he took only half the vote in Kansas City (as compared to 92 percent in 1934). In St. Louis a few days before the election, thirty-seven-year-old Robert E. Hannegan—son of a local detective, and ally of Mayor Bernard F. Dickmann—announced himself for Truman. The reason has never become clear; perhaps it was the urging of the mercurial Bennett Clark, or a threat by Truman's Kansas City supporters to vote against the St. Louis candidate for governor. Whatever the explanation, Hannegan instructed the heelers to go out, ring the doorbells, and bring in the vote for the Senator. Hannegan brought in just enough to give the supposedly dead Truman a local plurality of 8,411 votes, which swung the overall result in his favor.

Never, in all his thirty-year political career, did Truman savor victory more than in the 1940 primary. He went on to an easy win against his Republican opponent in November. When he took office the next January, and entered the Senate Chamber to walk down the aisle, the entire Senate arose and applauded.

Truman never forgot Governor Stark, and never forgave him. He liked to say that he had sent him back to the nursery. In May 1945, when the former Senator had become President, the question of appointing the erstwhile governor's brother Paul to a minor federal office arose. The President agreed, avowing that Paul Stark was all right, but that his brother was an S.O.B. He said he meant no reflection on the mother the two men had in common.

In his second term the still junior Senator from Missouri (Clark was not defeated until 1944) quickly became one of the Senate's half-dozen most important members. Seeking out major issues, searching incessantly for ways to resolve them, wasting no time on socializing in Washington or Missouri, Truman proved immensely effective. People naturally liked him; he described himself as affable, and he was modest and unassuming, considering himself no great man but the servant of the people of his state.

Equally important, Truman was happy in the Senate, which was as close to the camaraderie of Battery D as one could come in American politics. For the blowhards and exhibitionists he saw around him, he had little short of contempt; he felt they betrayed the people who had elected them. Long before, he had said the best people were the hardest to know, but in the Senate he met some at last, a very solid group of public servants, like himself, with whom he could work. There was Warren Austin of Vermont, a Republican who joined with him to hammer out the Civil Aeronautics Act, and Burt Wheeler, the maverick Democrat from Montana who had befriended him in 1935 when almost all Senators ignored him. And there were others such as Carl Hatch of New Mexico, and Mon Wallgren of Washington, both Democrats. The Senator from Missouri at last enjoyed being a part of a "club."

IN 1941, BESS AND MARGARET took up year-round residence in Washington since it seemed that Congress would stay in session until the war crisis was over. Margaret had been spending fall semesters at a public high school in Independence and spring terms at Gunston Hall, a Washington-area finishing school in the tradition of Southern ladies' education. Her parents decided that Margaret should spend a full year at Gunston Hall and get a diploma from there. So the family settled into temporary "permanent residence" in Washington, but ironically it was now Truman's turn to leave the capital.

Shortly after his reelection, Truman began to receive letters from constituents in his home state complaining about waste during construction of Fort Leonard Wood, going up near Rolla, in south central Missouri. He inquired at the War Department, where officers told him politely but firmly to mind his own business; he therefore decided to look firsthand at army installations in the South and Middle West, driving his own car in what he later proudly described as a 30,000-mile trip. Even if it were only 3,000 miles, it was a long journey to undertake, especially in midwinter at a time when highways were still on the primitive side. He drove in a great circle down to Florida and Mississippi, across to Texas, north through Oklahoma to Nebraska, back through Wisconsin and Michigan, and looked at the camps under construction, which inexperienced officers of the Regular Army were nominally supervising. He put together a Senate resolution providing for a Committee to Investigate the National Defense Program, and on March 1, 1941—when sixteen Senators were on the floor—he had it approved, without objection. With himself as chairman, the committee consisted of eight (later ten) Senators.

President Roosevelt, unsure of a Senate watchdog committee, may have instructed Senator James F. Byrnes of South Carolina, then head of the Appropriations Committee, to give the Truman Committee only $15,000 to investigate a defense program that in early 1941 was already approaching $15 billion. Unperturbed, Truman hired the best investigating lawyer he could find, put together a dedicated staff, and looked for the same sort of chicanery he had seen in the course of his investigation of railroad reorganizations during the 1930s.

The committee's great success is well known—for its chairman avoided either interfering with the plans of the President or making showy investigations of the obvious that would do nothing for the national defense effort. The committee's staff and chairman looked into every complaint that came their way, and when general complaints pointed to serious malfeasance they moved in. Their reports—there were thirty before Truman resigned as chairman in the autumn of

1944—were always unanimous. Publicity from the reports was pitiless, so the mere prospect of an adverse report often brought results.

The committee uncovered astonishing failures, notably in manufacture of defective aircraft engines by Curtiss-Wright, and improper steel plates made for warships by the Illinois-Carnegie plant of U.S. Steel. Truman prodded public figures without regard to their political connections: Donald Nelson, head of the War Production Board, who presided over a disorderly government office that allowed crucial mobilization issues to mill around in confusion; Secretary of the Navy Frank Knox, whose department chose to ignore losses of merchant shipping to German submarines. Friends and foes alike came to see the committee's value. General Brehon B. Somervell, head of army supply, an imperious man with a bristling mustache who at the outset encouraged subordinates to sweep the army's mistakes under the rug, admitted that Truman and his committee had saved the country $15 billion. Even Roosevelt, who had done nothing to create or, at the outset, support the committee, came around. When someone mentioned Truman and the committee to him in the spring of 1944, the President said, "Yes . . . yes . . . I put him in charge of that war investigating committee, didn't I?"

More than any other factor, the committee made Truman a likely candidate for the vice-presidential nomination in 1944. As late as 1941, when the committee was just getting started, he was so little known that the Washington *Star* ran a picture of someone else with the caption, "Senator Harry S. Truman." By 1944, however, when the time came for Roosevelt to choose a running mate, Truman suited the post in every way except, perhaps, for his own lack of desire to fill it. Margaret later wrote in *Souvenir*—her memories of growing up in Independence, in Washington, and in the White House—that "my mother was bitterly opposed to it." So, it seems, was Truman, who often related in letters and conversation that he enjoyed the Senate more than any other of the varied experiences of his life, political and otherwise. With his re-election in 1940 he had become a Senate leader, and felt secure in the performance of his duties. The Truman Committee generated massive correspondence, the largest volume of letters, calls, and telegrams in the Senate, together with hearings, meetings, and trips around the country. Because the senior Senator from Missouri, Bennett Clark, was, according to Truman, "always either tipsy or up in the clouds on some wild policy to embarrass the administration and never had time to see the ordinary customers from Missouri," it was the junior Senator who received almost all the Missouri constituent mail and visitors. He saw innumerable visitors from farms, villages, towns, and the state's two metropolises. When they weren't coming to him, Truman was going to the people because he believed it best to get out on trips to discover what people in the country really thought.

The office of Vice President, Truman thought, might be largely ceremonial. "I have no ambitions to run for any other office but United States Senator," he told his Missouri friend Harry Easley in January 1944. "A fellow is just a figurehead when he gets to be vice president of the United States. He is merely sitting around waiting for a funeral, and I don't like funerals. I have worked like a slave for nine years to try to find out what it is all about up here and I think I am getting some results. I don't see any reason for throwing that in the creek."

Still, in 1944, the Democratic Party turned to the leaders it believed would provide the best national ticket: FDR and Truman. In fact, Truman was chosen over the incumbent Vice President, Henry A. Wallace, and over James F. Byrnes, who had resigned from the Senate in 1941 to become Associate Justice of the Supreme Court, and from that post in October 1942 to become virtual "Assistant President" for the home front during the war. Wallace was no politician and Senators disliked him. Byrnes was despised by labor leaders, and he was from the South, which raised doubts about black support for the ticket. In addition, years earlier he had renounced the Catholic Church in favor of the Episcopalianism of his wife and thereby became unattractive to many Democratic Catholics in Northern cities. Truman possessed none of these liabilities; he had become a national figure because of the Truman Committee, and had the special virtue of being from a border state with a good record on black rights.

THE FIGHT for the vice-presidential nomination in 1944 was bitter, for a reason that party leaders could not voice in public: Roosevelt's health, which was obviously failing. The choice of a vice-presidential running mate at the Chicago convention in the summer of 1944 would in all probability be the choice of a President of the United States, for it seemed unlikely that Roosevelt, if reelected, could survive a fourth term in the most demanding public office in the world. After the President returned from the Teheran Conference, held in November-December 1943, his health rapidly failed; one of his assistants, Jonathan Daniels, later Truman's biographer, wrote that White House staffers had watched Roosevelt visibly decline. Wallace and Byrnes both saw the President frequently and drew their own conclusions. FDR may have sensed their thoughts, certainly observed their ambitions—in the one case to run again, in the other to take the nomination—and carefully encouraged both. Then he sent Wallace on a two-month visit to China on May 20, just before the convention, and advised Byrnes to secure the endorsement of such labor leaders as Sidney Hillman, of the Amalgamated Clothing Workers, when he had already learned privately that Hillman never would endorse Byrnes.

The President appeared blithely unconcerned about the vice presidency, and may well have been, in the way in which terminally ill people refuse to recognize their mortality. Just to be sure that he did not do something foolish, however, a group of party leaders closeted themselves with him on July 19, a few days before the Chicago convention, and obtained his endorsement of Truman, and secondarily of Justice William O. Douglas of the Supreme Court.

The maneuvers in Chicago revealed the political insiders' understanding of what was at stake—the presidency. One of Truman's supporters, Matthew J. Connelly, later his appointments secretary, remembered that "Wallace knew full well the state of Roosevelt's health. He saw him every week. He knew. Everybody else in politics knew . . ." Truman himself had heard from party leaders of their preference for him, and knew what that preference might mean. On July 9, 1944, well before the convention opened, ten days before the party chieftains met with Roosevelt, the Senator wrote his daughter Margaret about the vice-presidential nomination. "It is funny how some people would give a fortune to be as close as I am to it and I don't want it. . . . Hope I can dodge it. 1600 Pennsylvania is a nice address but I'd rather not move in through the back door—or any other door at sixty."

Back from China, Wallace threw caution to the winds and went all-out for renomination. He packed his supporters into the convention hall's galleries, and even onto the floor, by a stratagem that seems to have belied his reputation over the years for sterling honesty: someone in Wallace's entourage issued counterfeit tickets. Everywhere were the signs of "Frank and Hank," and the convention organist was playing the Iowa song: "Iowa, Iowa, *that*'s where the tall corn grows." Jimmy Byrnes meanwhile telephoned Truman in Independence, just before Truman pulled his car out of the backyard driveway en route to Chicago, and solicited his active support. "Harry," he said, "the President has given the go sign and I'm calling up to ask you to nominate me." Truman said he would be delighted, and would do what he could about lining up the Missouri delegation.

The party leaders, mostly big city bosses, who had decided on Truman, worked out their own strategy. The chairman of the national committee was Robert E. Hannegan, who in just a few years had made rapid advances from his position in the St. Louis machine; having become collector of internal revenue for that city in 1942 and commissioner of internal revenue for the entire United States in 1943, he was appointed committee chairman the following year. Just after the White House meeting on July 19, Hannegan used an excuse to go back into Roosevelt's office and get a scribbled commitment: "Bob, it's Truman. FDR."

Roosevelt did not attend the convention, but his private train passed through Chicago, en route to the West Coast (from where he had arranged to take ship for Hawaii and a meeting with his Pacific commanders). Hannegan went down to the yards, saw the President, and obtained another chit on which Roosevelt wrote the names of Truman and Douglas. Hannegan repaired to the train compartment of Roosevelt's secretary, Grace Tully, to have the endorsement typed. The secretary later recalled that FDR in fact had opted for Douglas and Truman, in that order, and Hannegan had the order reversed.

Firm tactics were needed. One of the convention leaders told the organist to change his tune to anything but "Iowa" or he would cut the organ's cable with a fire axe. The chairman ruled that the disorderly "Frank and Hank" people had packed the hall beyond capacity, thus creating a fire hazard, and adjourned the session until the leaders could get the convention under control. Even then, Truman himself wasn't convinced he should accept the nomination. He told his friend Tom Evans he didn't want to be Vice President. Evans pressed him.

"Well, I don't want to drag a lot of skeletons out of the closet," replied the Senator, defensively.

"Well," said Tom, "now wait a minute. . . . I didn't know you had skeletons. What are they?"

"The worst thing," Truman responded, "is that I've had the Boss on the payroll in my Senate office and I'm not going to have her name dragged over the front pages of the papers and over the radio."

"Well, Lord," said Tom, "that isn't anything too great." Bess was down for $4,500 a year. Truman had refused to accept payment for speeches, contrary to the behavior of many of his senatorial colleagues, but had put Bess to work in the office. Evans told the Senator he knew Bess was on the payroll because he had seen her working in the office, and that he knew a half-dozen Senators with wives on the payroll and forty or fifty Congressmen who had relatives galore on the payroll, and that Truman could not have gotten by as a Senator without Bess on the payroll, because it was expensive to live and maintain two homes.

Truman raised another point: "I just don't have any money; I can't go through an expensive national campaign. As you know, I'm still paying off on my last campaign. I never have been out of debt, and I just can't take on a campaign."

Evans assured him he should not worry over money, but when Truman reiterated that he just wanted to be a Senator, special persuasion became necessary. At a meeting in a suite in the Blackstone, Hannegan placed a call to Roosevelt, by that time in San Diego. Roosevelt's voice came on the line in its accustomed way, so loud that a listener had to hold the receiver away from his ear.

With Truman sitting on one twin bed, Hannegan on the other, politicos grouped round the room, everyone could hear what the President said. According to Truman's recollection, FDR talked only to Hannegan, who reported that Truman was acting like a Missouri mule. "Well, you tell him," said the President, "if he wants to break up the Democratic Party in the middle of a war, that's his responsibility," and hung up. According to Evans' version, Truman himself got on the phone and the President listened for a short time: "Well, I just think, Mr. President, that I've done a good job where I am and I'm happy, and I want to stay there. Yes, sir, I know you're the Commander-in-Chief, yes sir, yes sir; well, if that's what you want, that's what I'll do. I have always taken orders from the Commander-in-Chief. I'll do it."

Truman saw Roosevelt two or three times that fall during the campaign. On his return from the Pacific, the President was exhausted, and when he spoke at the Bremerton, Washington, Navy Yard on August 12 he suffered an attack of angina pectoris in the middle of the speech, and barely made it through, clutching at the podium, fortunate that most of his listeners were in the radio audience and did not sense what was happening. He met Truman for luncheon on the White House lawn on August 18, and while the two ate in their shirt sleeves, press photographers took pictures.

At that time only the highest government officials, military and civil, knew that American and British scientists were working tirelessly to develop nuclear weapons. The army was supervising the project and was fearful that word would pass to the Germans or Japanese who might speed up what was presumed, erroneously, to be their own nuclear bomb projects. It has long been thought that Truman learned about the Anglo-American atomic project only after he became President. In fact, Roosevelt told him in August 1944.

Roosevelt also advised Truman not to use an airplane, and was explicit about the reason. "Harry," he said, "I'm not a well man. We cannot be sure of my future." Afterward Truman told reporters at the gate that "He's still the leader he's always been and don't let anybody kid you about it. He's keen as a briar." Truman knew better, of course, for during lunch the President had talked with difficulty, his speech thick, and when he tried to pour cream into his coffee he spilled most of it into the saucer.

Campaigning that fall, in an arduous speaking trip that took him around the country, substituting for the ailing Commander-in-Chief, Truman had no time to contemplate the future. Altogether he gave fifty-four speeches and talks, and shook hands, he believed, with 100,000 people. Once again the newspapers were against him. He admitted to a friend that he had "to put a clamp on my tongue and tie my shootin' arm behind me," had lost two pounds, and needed to get back his "mental balance" so that he would not be tempted to shoot the publishers William Randolph Hearst and Robert R. McCormick. But such were the ways of politics—receiving the slings and arrows of the journalists.

Back in the Muehlebach penthouse suite after the election victory, his mood turned serious and he asked Harry Easley to stay overnight. Years later, Easley remembered: "And I stayed with him that night, I slept there with him. He told me just lying there in bed after things quieted down that the last time he saw him [Roosevelt] that he had the pallor of death on his face and he knew that . . . he would be President before the term was out."

Friday, April 13, 1945: an image of vigor. The new President strides to the Oval Office, having just arrived from his apartment on Connecticut Avenue.

LONESOME HARRY

The Vice President

Because of the war and Roosevelt's declining health, the inauguration on January 20, 1945, was a muted affair, held on the south portico of the White House instead of at the Capitol. The photo above shows the Trumans arriving for the ceremony. Two days later there was another ceremony to perform as the new Vice President, in his capacity as presiding officer of the Senate, raised his gavel for the first time to call the Upper House into session.

Hiatus

Truman obligingly went through the motions of appearing busy for a news photographer who came to his office shortly after the inauguration, but in truth he had less to do as Vice President than as Senator from Missouri. Often at the end of the day he could go back to 4701 Connecticut Avenue and catch up on his reading. On other evenings there were various social functions to attend. One invitation Truman regretted accepting was to a National Press Club party in February 1945. During the course of the evening he was asked to play the piano. Lauren Bacall, another guest, climbed on top of the upright, and a picture of them together made the front pages of newspapers across the country. It was better publicity for the actress than for the Vice President. Mrs. Truman was not amused and felt, according to Margaret, that it made her husband "look undignified and much too carefree for the Vice President of a nation at war."

April 12, 1945

A stunned and somber assemblage gather in the White House Cabinet Room to watch Chief Justice Harlan F. Stone administer the oath of office to Franklin D. Roosevelt's successor. Those present constituted a who's who of FDR's wartime administration. Shown here are (*from left to right*): Frances Perkins, Secretary of Labor; Henry L. Stimson, Secretary of War; Henry A. Wallace, Secretary of Commerce; Julius A. Krug, War Production Board Administrator; James V. Forrestal, Secretary of the Navy; Claude Wickard, Secretary of Agriculture; Frank L. McNamee, deputy chairman of the War Manpower Commission; Francis Biddle, Attorney General; Truman; Edward R. Stettinius, Jr., Secretary of State; Mrs. Truman; Harold R. Ickes, Secretary of the Interior; Chief Justice Stone; Sam Rayburn, Speaker of the House; Fred M. Vinson, director, Office of War Mobilization and Reconversion; Joseph W. Martin, Jr., minority leader, House of Representatives.

A time for mourning
While a flag flies at half-mast over the White House, the new President, flanked by James F. Byrnes and Henry A. Wallace, awaits the Roosevelt funeral train at Washington's Union Station, April 14, 1945. The following day, Truman, Bess, and Margaret attended the funeral at the Roosevelt family home in Hyde Park, N.Y.

In Independence the local paper declared: "City Chokes Its Sorrow to Wish Its Harry Well." Four days after Roosevelt's death, the new President addressed a joint sesssion of Congress. He pledged himself to carry on the New Deal program of

improving "the lot of the common people" and reiterated Roosevelt's insistence on Germany's acceptance of unequivocal terms for ending the war in Europe: "Our demand has been—and it remains—unconditional surrender."

Prelude to Hiroshima

Truman's decision to authorize the use of the atomic bomb—the first detonated over Hiroshima, the second over Nagasaki (*opposite*)—must be viewed in the context of Japan's fanatical resistance as the tide of war neared its shores. Japanese pilots willingly undertook suicide missions as they flew their Zero fighters into the gun emplacements of U.S. naval vessels (*above*), while in the battle for Okinawa (*left*) some 100,000 Japanese lost their lives while inflicting fearsome losses on the American invaders. Much worse was to be expected if Japan itself had to be invaded.

On to Potsdam

On July 7, 1945, two months after Germany's surrender to the Allies, Truman boarded the heavy cruiser U.S.S. *Augusta* for the first leg of his trip to meet Churchill and Stalin at Potsdam. He is seen with Secretary of State James F. Byrnes in the bow (the ship in the distance is an escorting cruiser) and sharing a meal in the enlisted men's mess with some of the crew. The ship docked in the relatively unharmed port of Antwerp eight days later, and the President was on hand to view the sights. From there Truman proceeded by plane to Potsdam, just outside Berlin. His headquarters were in a lakeside residence at No. 2 Kaiserstraße in the nearby town of Babelsberg.

The Big Three

The Potsdam Conference had been in session for eight days when the three world leaders posed for photographs outside the Cecilienhof on July 25, 1945. Later that day Churchill left for London to await the outcome of Britain's first postwar general election. Following his party's defeat, he resigned; when the Potsdam meetings resumed on July 28, the new prime minister, Clement Attlee, took his place. Meanwhile, Truman had paid a courtesy visit to Stalin at the latter's personal headquarters (*below*). Many official photos were taken during the course of the Potsdam Conference. On the back of one, showing the large table around which the Big Three and their advisers conferred, Truman scribbled the note at right. But Stalin already knew about the bomb, as the President would discover later that year, following the defection of the Russian cipher clerk Igor Gouzenko.

This is the place I told Stalin about the Atom Bomb, which was exploded July 16, 1945 in New Mexico. He did not realize what I was talking about!

HST

In the White House garden, spring 1946. The pensive mood reflects Truman's state of mind as the awesome realities of his responsibilities bore down on him.

MANY men have aspired to be President of the United States, but Harry Truman was never one of them. The position came to him as an obligation. "If ever there was a man who was forced to be President, I am that man," he said, and he accepted the prospect of succeeding Roosevelt because to have refused would have been against his code of social responsibility. When he took on the nation's highest office, it was in much the same spirit as he had taken on the Grandview farm nearly forty years before: ". . . some times I have to come across. This is one of them."

Throughout Truman's years in the Oval Office the political drama challenged him and the vision of a world seeking peace both drove the President on and sustained him. But "Harry Truman, citizen," as he sometimes called himself, never felt at home in the White House. For him, the summons to the presidency was a call to spend almost eight years as "the loneliest man in the world."

Nothing in his life had led Truman to imagine—much less anticipate—that he might some day be President of the United States. Certainly he had no family predisposition to power, nor any lifelong military career in leadership. He was not a public personality and, in fact, hated being photographed, interviewed, and quoted. To him the press was made up of "news goons," and he delighted in fending off reporters whenever he could.

Truman had not even had the kind of political career that often makes presidential material. He had served capably and honestly but with relatively little notice until he was drafted and reluctantly agreed to the vice-presidential nomination. Once he had made that agreement, however, the position he had never seen as a goal became a probability. Insiders at the Chicago convention—Byrnes, Wallace, the bosses who sent him out to campaign—had known they were in reality kingmakers when they chose the man who would run with the ailing Roosevelt. Truman had known it too, as he told his friend Easley in the long night in the Muehlebach penthouse, but then, in characteristic fashion, the new Vice President had put thoughts of the future out of his mind and applied himself to the problems of the present.

Actually, his brief time as Vice President was a respite from his exhausting terms in the Senate, when he had been almost overwhelmed by railroad hearings, seeking reelection, and the work of the Truman Committee. The nine years in the Senate were grueling. Although he complained that there was more work than anyone could manage, he also realized that worrying over not getting it done would only make matters worse. By comparison, the vice presidency was almost a cakewalk. It was an ornamental post and Truman had the use of two offices: out of courtesy, the Senate leadership allowed him to keep his old office, and he also had what he described, without much exaggeration, as the Vice President's "gold-plated" office. In a letter to his mother, he wrote that a typical vice-presidential day began when he arrived at the Senate office at eight-thirty (he preferred to be at his desk by seven, but during his vice presidency he was taking Margaret to school every morning—she was studying history at George Washington University) and met with his secretary, Reathel Odum, who

> . . . is always here at that time and we wade through a stack of mail a foot high. By that time I have to see people—one at a time just as fast as they can go through the office without seeming to hurry them. Then I go over to the Capitol gold-plated office and see Senators and curiosity seekers for an hour and then the Senate meets and it's my job to get 'em prayed for—and goodness knows they need it—and then get the business to going by staying in the chair for an hour and then see more Senators and curiosity people who want to see what a V.P. looks like and if he walks and has teeth.
>
> Then I close the Senate and sign the mail and then maybe go home or to some meeting, usually some meeting, and then home and start over.

At the outset, President Roosevelt had assigned Truman a single task, to obtain the confirmation of Henry Wallace as Secretary of Commerce. Because the Senators hated Wallace, Truman had to force the confirmation, voting himself to break a tie. Once that job was out of the way, he had little to do other than satisfy the obligations of protocol and remember the fates of Roosevelt's previous Vice Presidents, Garner and Wallace, and the remark of Wilson's Vice President, Thomas R. Marshall, that the vice presidency was only a heartbeat away from the presidency. Still, he kept the threat of presidential office sufficiently from his mind that, on April 12, 1945, when he was summoned urgently to the White House, he couldn't think what the reason might be.

The story of how Harry Truman learned that he was the President of the United States has been told many times and yet it keeps its fascination, for it is a story of both inevitability and surprise. Debate in the Upper House that afternoon was over the Mexican Water Treaty. It made dull conversation on the floor and, in his chair above the wrangling Senators, the Vice President was writing a letter to his mother. "Turn on your radio tomorrow night at nine-thirty your time," he told her, "and you'll hear Harry make a Jefferson Day address to the nation. . . . It will be followed by the President, whom I'll introduce." Bringing down the gavel at 4:56, he stepped down from his chair and went through the gray corridors of the Capitol to the House side, where Speaker Sam Rayburn had called a meeting of the "Board of Education," a group of legislators who gathered in Rayburn's private office now and then after a legislative session to swap stories and drink a little bourbon. Before Truman could sit down, Rayburn told him that Steve Early (Roosevelt's press secretary) had called. Truman returned the call at once and, after listening for a moment, he muttered "Holy General Jackson," then said to Rayburn, "I have to go to the White House immediately." He told the Congressmen present to say nothing about it, he would probably be back shortly.

Describing the day's events in his diary, Truman noted that it occurred to him that the funeral of Bishop Julius W. Atwood (an old friend of Roosevelt's) had taken place that day, and that "maybe the President was in town . . . and wanted to go over some matters with me before returning to Warm Springs." Nonetheless, Steve Early had said he should come straightaway to the front door of the White House and directly up to Mrs. Roosevelt's suite, and Truman took off at a run—not stopping to look for his Secret Service escort, although he did go back to his office to pick up his hat—through the lower tunnel leading out of the Capitol at the Senate end on the north side, where he found his driver and car. He threw himself into the back seat and the black limousine moved out into the traffic, down to the White House. When he arrived at 1600 Pennsylvania Avenue, he was escorted to a second-floor sitting room where the First Lady was waiting with her daughter Anna, Anna's husband (Colonel John Boettiger), and Early. Mrs. Roosevelt rose to meet Harry Truman, put her arm around his shoulder and said gently, "The President is dead."

It was "the first inkling I had of the seriousness of the situation," Truman wrote in his diary, with typical Midwestern understatement. When he asked Mrs. Roosevelt if there was anything he could do for her, she replied by asking the new President if there was anything they could do for him.

When Truman heard the news from Mrs. Roosevelt, it was about five-thirty and already he had been President for over an hour without knowing it. He went to the office of the President in the west wing and called home to inform Bess. Margaret answered and began to tease her father about not being home for dinner when she herself was also going out on the town. In a tight voice he said, "Let me speak to your mother," and Margaret passed over the phone in a huff. Moments later, Bess, appeared in the doorway to her daughter's room, tears streaming down her face. Margaret got out of the party dress she planned to wear on a date and dressed instead for her father's swearing-in. In the course of the next hour or so, Bess and Margaret were driven to the White House and visited briefly with Mrs. Roosevelt; Attorney General Francis Biddle called other members of the Cabinet; Chief Justice Harlan F. Stone was located and came to the President's office; and members of the White House staff searched frantically for a Bible. By seven o'clock the group, shaken but in control of their emotions, had assembled in the Cabinet Room, ready to witness the swearing-in ceremony.

The Chief Justice stood at the end of the long Cabinet table and Truman stood under the portrait of Woodrow Wilson. In his hand was the small red-edged Bible that had been finally located in a White House bookcase. The Chief Justice began, "I, Harry Shipp Truman . . ." and Truman raised his right hand and responded "I, Harry S. Truman, do solemnly swear . . ." When the oath was done, the Chief Justice added, "So help you God," a phrase not in the official oath of office. "So help me God," said the new President, as he raised the borrowed Bible to his lips. The time on the clock beneath the portrait of one of Harry Truman's heroes was 7:09.

Bess and Margaret went home to 4701 Connecticut Avenue, while the President stayed for a first meeting with his Cabinet. Then he too went home, to find that Bess, Margaret, and Mother Wallace were next door at a neighbor's apartment. "They [the neighbors] had had a turkey dinner and they gave us something to eat," wrote the President in his diary. "I had not had anything to eat since noon. Went to bed, went to sleep, and did not worry any more."

Next morning in the Oval Office in the west wing, he sat down behind the huge desk, now cleared of Roosevelt's personal belongings. An aide looked in sometime in the morning and saw Truman swiveling back and forth, gazing out uncertainly through his glasses. Most likely, he was peering ahead at his inheritance. In his diary entry for April 12 he had noted:

> I did not know what reaction the country would have to the death of a man whom they all practically worshipped. I was worried about the reaction of the Armed Forces. I did not know what effect the situation would have on the war effort, price control, war production and everything that entered into the emergency that then existed. I knew the President had a great many meetings with Churchill and Stalin. I was not familiar with any of these things and it was really something to think about . . .

TRUMAN'S TASK, beginning that morning, was to master the presidency—the office he always liked to say was the greatest in the world, and which he knew to be compounded of decision-making and public appearances in roughly equal parts. He very quickly discovered that ceremony got in the way of business, but that there was little he could do about it. Americans are brought up to respect the presidency, both the office and the person who holds it, but the President, unlike royalty, is one of the people and therefore accessible to the rest of the people through visits, handshaking, photographs, autographs, speeches, and letters. To conduct the business of his office, any President has to work diligently to keep his responsibilities in balance, and to be sure that his decisions are made in calm reflection, not in the fatigue of too much ceremony.

For Truman the pomp was a particular distraction. A genuinely modest man without the need or desire for pageantry, he always took a homespun view of pomp and most of the circumstances surrounding it. "I was the driver of the open car," he reported to Bess about a visit to the governor of Washington early in 1945, "the first time I've been at the wheel, but a time or two, since I became V.P. . . . But we had a carload of state police in front of us, a carload of Secret Service men behind us, and a carload of newsmen behind the Secret Service. At that I had a big kick out of driving once more."

Fanfare never impressed Truman, and neither did titles, but both belonged to the proper rites of his new office. "I've got to lunch with the Limey King . . .," he wrote home once about his first meeting with Britain's King George VI. The only royal treatment Truman received that pleased him enough to merit a mention in a letter to Bess was a ride in the Governor-General of Bermuda's landau drawn by two white horses. No doubt it was the simple pleasure of being behind a team of horses once again that so delighted the new President, rather than the regal conveyance and the cheering spectators.

Could the farmer from Independence handle the job and all the public scrutiny as well? Whether the farm, the army, the county court, the Senate, and a short time as Vice President were preparation enough was a question Truman certainly must have asked himself in April 1945, as he turned first this way then that in his presidential chair on the morning of Friday the thirteenth. He knew that the average American believed in the economic and social measures of the New Deal and would look to him as Roosevelt's successor to maintain them. The United States was still embroiled in a World War, and he knew that he would be charged with its successful outcome. Probably that first morning in office he reread once again the verse he had carried around in his wallet and had recopied a dozen times since high school, lines from his favorite poet, Tennyson, "For I dipt into the future, far as the eye could see, Saw the vision of the world, and all the wonder it would be . . ."

Americans who were thinking about presidential responsibilities as Truman took on his new role might well have wondered what would happen to the Republic as a result of the change. It was uncertain at the outset, for no one—especially not the new President himself—knew how he would do. And for years afterward, many Americans didn't realize how well he had done. For a generation and more after 1945, Americans underestimated Truman and his presidency. Only in recent years, after several more Presidents, have they come to recognize the extraordinary virtues of the man who replaced Roosevelt. It has taken that long for the strengths of a small-town Baptist upbringing, a lifelong commitment to the humanitarian principles of Masonry, and an inbred insistence of paying one's own way to be recognized as traits important to a great presidency. Occasionally, during his presidency, Americans warmed to Truman, as in 1948 when he fought for his political life and won (although less than half the eligible voters bothered to vote either for him or for his opponent, Governor Dewey). Mostly, during his time in office and for years afterward, they looked at him in boredom, sometimes askance, taking him at his word when he said he was an ordinary man who happened to be President.

Truman's very ordinariness has today made him something of a folk hero: a plain-speaking, straight-talking, ordinary fellow who did what he saw as his duty without turning his obligation into an opportunity for personal gain. Today, it seems that his plain ways were a throwback to the Puritan fathers' meaning of the word "plain": the unadorned life that is stripped of excesses in appearance so that it exists as a testament to the principles beneath. In 1945, however, the American public found those principles dull, and they missed the appearance of Roosevelt, who looked every inch the President, even in his wheelchair. Truman spoke with a flat twang compared to the elegant voice of his predecessor, who sounded better over the air than any of his successors save the actor-President of the 1980s. They missed the patrician head-shaking of FDR, for Truman, if he used gestures at all, only moved his hands up and down, palms turned inward. Although by nature a dignified man, Truman sometimes let his guard down in the highly quotable phrases that seem so refreshing today in contrast to the coached presentations of recent Presidents. Compared then to the demeanor of Roosevelt, who had been raised in a mansion overlooking the Hudson and educated at Groton and Harvard, Truman—with his pithy language and directness of approach—seemed to many to betray a lack of cultivation and finish.

Ironically, it may have been Truman's humble ways that suited him so well to his task. He had no illusions about the true significance of ceremonial requirements such as twenty-one gun salutes, which he knew to be for the institution of the presidency and not for himself. Truman realized that for his own good he must keep himself separate from the presidency, and he was in fact successful in keeping his sense of self from becoming the role he assumed. In some ways, this separation caused him the greatest trial of his personal life, for in the White House years the joy he took in his marriage and his fatherhood was interrupted and, as his professional life soared, his domestic life became divided from it to a degree that grieved him terribly. It was only after the White House years, when he was back in Independence—at home with the roses, Mrs. Truman's cooking, and other home-town things he had missed so badly—that Truman felt a whole man once again.

His capacity to keep himself somewhat separate from his role as President was perhaps the central difference between Truman and Roosevelt in office, but their presidencies differed in a variety of other important respects, too. To begin with, Truman was physically vigorous when he came to be President. Roosevelt was born in 1882, only two years before Truman, but the cares of the presidency had worn him down far beyond his years. When Truman hurried up the walk toward his office on the morning after his swearing-in, he was the picture of health as a crowd of photographers ran along in front of him. A scene impossible during the Roosevelt administration, it was symbolic of far more than the contrast with the late President's well-known infirmity. Truman undertook a schedule that tripled Roosevelt's, moving visitors in and out of his office with dispatch, signing letters in shifts, meeting groups for short talks, posing in the rose garden for photographers, making excursions to deliver major speeches, and often spending evenings at formal events. As he had done since the farm years, he got up at five-thirty every morning; he was at his office within minutes, long before secretaries arrived and the working day formally began.

Truman was attentive to his health; during his Senate years he had put himself in the hospital for a complete going-over because of a persistent stomach problem. The difficulty was traced to fatigue, stress, and some foods. From that time on, he said he was fine as long as he got enough sleep, exercise, and buttermilk. He walked, swam, and sunbathed every day that weather and his schedule permitted, even during the most hectic times. Evidently his brief sessions in the late morning sun served to renew him for many more hours of work each day.

For mental relaxation he played poker with friends whenever he could. Rarely more than a 25-cent better, Truman loved what he called his little "games of probability." Bess sent him pocket money for these. "Thanks for the ten," he would write to Bess. "If you need it, I'll send it back." Without money from home, he didn't play; and his letters make frequent references to his winnings—when there were any, they were seldom more than $10. Once Bess passed along $40 paid by Mother Wallace toward grocery expenses. He gravely responded that he wished her mother would just sit back and let him assume her financial worries; then he added, "Don't tell her, but I'll invest her payment . . . in a game of chance . . ."

As well as indulging in his games of chance, Truman kept himself free in other small ways from being totally consumed by the pressures of the presidency. On one occasion he slipped away to the rose garden to cut a small bouquet for the hospitalized niece of his private secretary, Rose Conway. He continued to concern himself with household matters, sometimes spending hours rummaging about through White House closets for articles as small as a black satin purse to post off to Margaret in time for a date. These personal attentions to detail appear in his own accounts not to be pressures in themselves, but rather a relief from the strains of being President.

In addition to his physical fitness, Truman's constitution set him apart from Roosevelt in another way. Truman had a tenacious ability to focus on a problem and make a decision. FDR in his last year was observably weary, putting things off in hope that problems would disappear. Perhaps he had held power for so long that he lacked a sense of urgency about the machinery of government; when people around him insisted that a particular matter was of the utmost importance, he would sometimes listen with half an ear. He had heard it all before. Whatever the reasons, FDR's ability to make decisions lessened noticeably during the war years, and as a result there had been mixed signals coming from the White House. Truman, on the other hand, had never been one to tolerate confusion. Early in 1941, when the war effort creaked and threatened to stall while businessmen and labor unions took all they could of the easy money that had suddenly become available, Roosevelt watched the confusion with benign indifference, and it was the Missouri Senator who created a committee to begin to solve the problems.

Despite his admiration for Roosevelt (he always included FDR in his pantheon of great Presidents), Truman had not failed to observe his tendency to procrastinate all through the war. From the day he stepped into his new office, Truman moved quickly and steadily through critical issues. "I have always believed right will prevail in the end. It has been a policy with me to get the facts and then make a decision. . . . If the facts available justify a decision at the time it will also be correct in future time."

Harvard political scientist Richard Neustadt, a White House staff member in the early 1950s, has written that Truman invariably made decisions on almost all subjects that came to his attention, but the new

President also knew when the time was ripe for inaction in a given situation. The Berlin Blockade of 1948–49 is a good example. Some advisers, including top-ranking generals, told him that Berlin was indefensible and he should withdraw U.S. forces; other advisers, also including top-ranking generals, said he had only one option—to push through an armed convoy from Helmstedt, the nearest American-held point, to the beleaguered city. Truman, however, took neither course. Shortly after, an altogether unexpected alternative—the airlift—solved the problem.

One of the qualities people came to admire in Truman was his straightforward dependability. General George C. Marshall, who became Secretary of State in 1947, had found Roosevelt difficult and was never sure of him; Truman, he believed, was a man to count on. Dean Acheson said, "I acquired the greatest respect and admiration for the President's capacity to understand complex problems and to decide. This is one of the rarest qualities possessed by man. Too frequently the mind vacillates between unpleasant choices and escapes through procrastination." He remembered Truman as "the captain with the mighty heart," to whom he dedicated his memoirs, published in 1969.

At the front of Truman's White House desk was the sign, now legendary, "The Buck Stops Here." His Missouri political handyman and friend, Fred Canfil, had seen such a sign while visiting the federal reformatory at El Reno, Oklahoma, and had asked the warden for a duplicate; Truman received it in October 1945. The saying originated in the old frontier days, when players at the poker tables used a marker or counter (often a knife with a buckhorn handle) to indicate the person whose turn it was to deal. If the player did not want to deal, he could pass the responsibility by passing the "buck," as the counter came to be called, to the next player. Truman's refusal to pass the buck was a hallmark of his political career from the county level up.

Part of this refusal came from his essential directness, another trait that set the new President apart from his predecessor. Roosevelt could be left-handed, devious, Machiavellian. Behind the bonhomie and exuberance he showed to White House visitors was a willingness to play both sides. As early in his career as 1913, when he was Assistant Secretary of the Navy, he had casually intrigued—with anyone who would listen—against his chief, Secretary Josephus Daniels; years later, in the

White House, Roosevelt was still open to intrigue. Truman, it is safe to say, was never in all his life sly or disloyal, and he stood by his friends even when he risked taking a public scourging for it. When the ex-convict Tom Pendergast died during Truman's vice presidency, Truman did not hesitate "for even five seconds" (to use Margaret's description) to use a government plane to get to Kansas City for the funeral. He saw no impropriety. "He was always my friend," Truman said of Pendergast, "and I have always been his." Time was too valuable, life too short, to waste in dissembling. Moreover, to have acted unfaithfully would have gone against his Baptist and Masonic principles.

ANOTHER CRITICAL difference between Truman and Roosevelt lay in their home lives. Although Roosevelt had a family, he was not a family man in the sense that Harry Truman was. It is a telling fact that his first letter to Bess from the White House began, "This is a lonesome place." Whereas Roosevelt's marriage to Eleanor had continued only in a formal way after her discovery of the now well-known liaison between FDR and her own social secretary, Lucy Mercer, Truman's marriage was the core of his life. On their wedding anniversary in 1957, he sent Bess a year-by-year outline of events in his life keyed to their anniversaries on June 28. Entries range along a line that includes "Broke and in a bad way." (1922); "Depression. Still going." (1930); "Senate Special Committee. Margie wants to sing." (1941); and "V.P. & President. War End." (1945). The one constant running through the list is the June date.

The happiness of his family life was clouded with money problems even into the White House years—certainly another way in which his life differed from Roosevelt's. It seems unthinkable to Americans now, after a succession of wealthy First Families, that the Trumans mailed $10 bills back and forth to each other to share pocket money for an upcoming week. As late as 1946, there was still not enough excess in the family accounts to afford a new car for Bess. She wrote asking her husband what to do about her old one and he replied:

> It seems to me that if you can get a good price for it you may as well sell it and buy a bond, and then when we leave the great white jail a new car can be bought. The new cars won't have the bugs out of them for two or three years anyway. Be sure that no

regulations or price ceilings are in any way infringed, no matter how good you may think the friendship of the person you sell to may be. The temptation to take a crack at the first family for pay is almost irresistible and so far we've escaped any factual misdemeanor and I'd like to finish with that reputation.

Now that presidential ladies have their own dress designers, it is harder to understand Bess and Margaret's apologetic approach to having to buy clothes for appearances' sake. At the time, Truman always encouraged their purchases, saying that he didn't want them to have inadequate wardrobes, but it is indicative of the family approach to finances that on one occasion he personally spent hours searching closets for a velvet coat Bess believed she had left in Washington. Neither of them apparently suggested that the cost of buying a new one might be less than the expense of his time.

Throughout the period of his administration, Truman refused to accept any gifts that were not a matter of protocol. Gifts to the office were in acceptable form as far as he was concerned, and some of those are housed in the Truman Library today, but he insisted that, for example, trips for the family be paid for by the Trumans themselves, not by the taxpayers. His lengthy correspondence to Bess arose partly from his unwillingness to run up large telephone bills, and when he did call her in Independence, either from Washington or from posts along his official journeys, he would often call collect.

He was something of an anomaly in the most powerful job in the world: a modest, honest, and thrifty man who, when teased by Press Secretary Charlie Ross that he would rather be right than President, replied "I'd rather be anything than President." It was perhaps inevitable that the same combination of personal modesty and public decisiveness that made Truman capable of being President would also cause doubts to be raised in the public mind about his capability and would eventually lead him into a storm of controversy; but it was also characteristic of Truman to stand firm. "If you will study the history of our country you'll find that our greatest Presidents and congressional leaders have been the ones who have been vilified worst by the current press. But history justifies the honorable politician when he works for the welfare of the country," he wrote late in his life.

* * *

WORKING FOR THE WELFARE of the United States was a confusing and difficult job when Truman took it on as President. Within months of taking office, he was forced to the most fateful decision made by any President in the country's history—the decision to use nuclear weapons against Japan. More than any other choice, this one dogged Truman for the rest of his life in questions and criticism from the press and public. Momentous and world-changing as it was, however, the decision to bomb Hiroshima and Nagasaki was not so isolated as the focus on its aftermath has made it appear. Like other matters that required Truman's decision after Roosevelt's death, the use of nuclear weapons was one aspect of the unresolved World War.

When Truman reached the presidency in April 1945, the European war was coming to an end. Early in May, following Hitler's suicide in his Berlin bunker, the German high command agreed to the unconditional surrender of their forces to the Americans, British, and Russians. Now, an immense swell of relief buoyed up the Western world, for the war in Europe had lasted nearly six years and had been smoldering for six years before that. War and the threat of war had overshadowed the lives of hundreds of millions of people for more than a decade. Now the hostilities were over, but in the White House Truman was confronted with all the problems of postwar negotiations, the matter of reparations, the peace settlements with Italy, Rumania, Bulgaria, Hungary, Finland, and Austria, the question of Palestine, and other pressing matters of international resonance.

Meanwhile, in the Far East a bitter struggle was still raging. In early 1945 a Japanese garrison on the insignificant island of Iwo Jima had fought a battle to the death of almost every man among the defenders, with losses to the invading U.S. Marines of over 4,000 dead, 15,000 wounded, and several hundred missing. It was the worst battle in Marine history, save Belleau Wood in June 1918. Within months came the battle of Okinawa, worse yet than Iwo Jima because it was larger. This time the U.S. Army fought the Japanese defenders and encountered equally fanatical resistance. To the incredulity of American soldiers, even the civilians of Okinawa chose suicide rather than survival in defeat. The battle ended June 21, 1945, with some 12,500 U.S. soldiers, sailors, and airmen killed, 36,000 wounded, as well as 36 ships sunk, 368 damaged, and 763 planes lost. By midsummer the American joint chiefs of staff, contemplating these island ordeals, were having to face up to what would probably be the bloodiest assault ever undertaken by any large military force: invasion of the Japanese home islands. The joint chiefs planned an invasion of the southernmost island, Kyushu, for November 1 with the main invasion of Honshu to follow in March 1946. Two million Japanese troops were stationed in the home islands, with another 2 million in China, Korea, and Southeast Asia; if the Japanese Navy, however weak, could succeed in ferrying at least part of the troops stationed overseas back to the home islands, they would outnumber the American invaders by four to one. On Iwo Jima and Okinawa the ratio had been the other way, and still the U.S. casualties were shockingly high.

All the argument that has swirled around the employment of nuclear weapons against the Japanese is retrospective, set in the context of American relations with Japan after the war. If one looks at the situation of the time, Truman's decision is understandable. Of the major nations, America had come into the war last, but people had tired of it by 1945, and no Americans were more tired than the troops in Europe who found themselves scheduled for rerouting to the Pacific theater. To men in the divisions in Europe, who had seen plenty of death and devastation already, the fact that the numbers of dead became suddenly greater in Japan because the atomic bomb was used there could not be more horrifying than the horror they already knew at first hand, and did not present a moral dilemma.

In 1981, when debate over nuclear weapons revived the controversy over Truman's atomic bomb decision, Paul Fussell, himself a young infantryman in 1945, stirred a fury of accusation with his commentary in the *New Republic*: "The dramatic postwar Japanese success at hustling and merchandising and tourism has (happily, in many ways) effaced for most people important elements of the assault context in which Hiroshima should be viewed. It is easy to forget what Japan was like before it was first destroyed and then humiliated, tamed and constitutionalized by the West."

Another reason why Truman could make the decision he did about the bomb was the degree of public ignorance of science at that time. Under today's avalanche of information about scientific projects and discoveries all over the world, it is easy to overlook the fact that the atomic bomb project was developed secretly, that even such knowledge as was shared with laymen by physicists was virtually incomprehensible to anyone outside the scientific community. Had the public known of the project, they could not have been expected to grasp its meaning, for they were scarcely able to judge the meaning of the rapid growth of science in this century and its practical consequences. Truman himself suffered from this shared ignorance—and suddenly he was confronted with a need to understand what a generation of physicists had wrought, and what the next generation could produce. His predecessor had been equally ignorant; to make a judgment on the bomb, he would have had to make the same quantum leap.

Once the theoretical foundations of nuclear fission were laid, science moved inevitably and rapidly toward the construction of an atomic bomb. Einstein's theory of relativity, announced in 1905, had first raised the possibility, and was followed by experiments on the structure of atoms by two Britons, Rutherford and Chadwick, around the time of World War I. In 1938, two German physicists at the Kaiser Wilhelm Institute in Berlin, Hahn and Strassmann, split a uranium atom in an experiment that caused a stir among physicists throughout the world but made no real impression on the governments it would affect. However, word soon traveled to America by an odd route.

The Kaiser Wilhelm Institute physicists were aided by a partner, Lise Meitner, who, because of her Jewish background, was forced to flee Germany before the Berlin experiment was finished. She shared with her nephew, Otto Frisch, a physicist in Sweden, her fear that the experiment might lead to a bomb Hitler could use. Frisch confided these fears to Nobel Laureate Nils Bohr of Denmark. Later, Bohr talked to Albert Einstein, who drew up a letter to President Roosevelt; this was delivered to Washington by Alexander Sachs, a scholarly New York economist who enjoyed easy access to the White House. Visited twice by Sachs, who pressed the matter, Roosevelt arranged for a government program of support that did little other than finance small-scale uranium experiments at Columbia University.

In 1940 a research team at Berkeley, California, discovered the artificial element plutonium, extractable from raw uranium. Uranium and plutonium, both fissionable, were the two keys to the bomb. On December 6, 1941, the president of Harvard University, chemist James B. Conant, announced to a select group in Washington the inauguration of a full-scale secret government program, code-named the Manhattan Project, to obtain enough fissionable material to build a bomb.

Roosevelt must have felt pressed by the possibility of a German bomb, given the Berlin experiments, but three years had passed with little action toward developing a bomb in the United States. Once begun, the all-out project moved swiftly, however. Because it was secret, the American people could not debate the issues it raised. And the scientists did not. Perhaps, given their customary insulation from politics, they would not have seen the political ramifications of their experiments. After 1945, in expiation and in recognition of the apolitical behavior of scientists whose research had for generations helped to add to the destructiveness of war, the nuclear scientists of 1941–45 organized themselves politically and established the *Bulletin of the Atomic Scientists*, as well as set up private conferences and discussions with Soviet and other nuclear scientists.

The wartime bomb program took three-and-one-half years to reach the stage at which a practical nuclear weapon was available, already too late for use in Europe. The argument arose afterward that the Anglo-American allies (the program was in part British, though conducted in the United States, at a safe distance from the war in Europe) would never have dropped such a bomb on white men and chose instead to use the bomb in Asia.

In addition to scientific secrecy, the eventual decision to use the atomic bomb was influenced by the frightful precedents of bombing civilian populations with conventional weapons earlier in the war. The escalation of violence in less than two decades of modern warfare had been dramatic, from the bombing of the Chinese sector of Shanghai, Chapei, by the Japanese in 1932 to population bombings by Italians in Ethiopia in 1935–36 and by Germans in Spain during the Spanish Civil War. The Germans bombed Poland in 1939 and destroyed Rotterdam in 1940, then turned their weaponry on the British who retaliated for the blitz of London, Coventry, and other cities by raiding civilian targets in Germany. When America entered the war it sent to England the Eighth Air Force, which bombed by day while the Royal Air Force raided by night. In Dresden, a treasure house of German art and architecture before the city was largely destroyed on February 13, 1945, the numbers of dead may have reached 135,000. Meanwhile, in the Far East, five weeks before Truman took office, American bombers dropped 2,000 tons of napalm on Tokyo, whipping up a firestorm of hurricane force. Flight crews could smell burning flesh below as 16 square miles of Tokyo burned to the ground, leaving an estimated 125,000 dead—many from asphyxiation. After similar attacks on Nagoya, Osaka, and Kobe, the American bombers went back over Tokyo and in the resulting holocaust another estimated 83,000 persons died. So, when the scientists tested a plutonium bomb at Alamogordo, New Mexico, on July 16, 1945, they were not looking for a weapon of previously unimagined power; but they found it. Although they had expected the explosive force of the bomb to equal that of 500 to 1,500 tons of TNT, it came in at 20,000.

Later, people said that the supernatural force of such a weapon and the prospect of a whole series of such bombs should have forced reconsideration of the program; but then the world was at war, and while hostilities in Europe were over, the Japanese still seemed an overwhelming threat. Moreover, by July 16, 1945, it was almost too late to reconsider, since Truman and his closest advisers were in Potsdam, a suburb of Berlin, where the victorious allies—the United States, Britain, and Russia—were meeting to settle outstanding problems left at the European war's end, and to anticipate a resolution to the war in the Far East. Already a cabinet committee and a special scientific panel had reported that there was no alternative but to drop the new bombs on Japan as soon as they were ready.

At Potsdam, Truman set down, in his diary entry for July 25, his own vision of the apocalypse: "We have discovered the most terrible bomb in the history of the world. It may be the fire destruction prophesied in the Euphrates Valley Era, after Noah and his fabulous Ark." Fearful as his vision was, the entry continued, "This weapon is to be used against Japan between now and August 10th. . . . It seems to be the most terrible thing ever discovered, but it can be made the most useful."

His diary makes it clear that he had intended the bomb to be used against "military objectives . . . and not women and children," and that he would issue a warning asking the Japanese to "surrender and save lives." On July 26 he gave the Twentieth Air Force permission to use the weapons when available, so long as it was after he had left Europe. The Potsdam Conference ended August 2 and the first bomb went down on Hiroshima four days later.

In retrospect it is clear that there should have been an explicit advance warning to the Japanese, followed by a demonstration of the awesome power of the new weapon. An Anglo-American-Chinese warning issued from Potsdam was simply a general statement that said nothing about a new weapon. If in the name of humanity, the Americans should have waited, uncertainty drove them on. With the Manhattan Project underway, it was unlikely that one man, even a President, could have stopped it. Research and development had cost $2 billion, an unprecedented sum for a single military or civilian purpose, and scientists and military leaders were eager to use the product. Had Truman refused to go ahead, he might well have been impeached. Admiral William D. Leahy, his chief of staff and Roosevelt's before him, said later that "I know F.D.R. would have used it in a minute to prove that he had not wasted $2 billion."

In after years Truman doughtily told all inquirers that the bomb saved half a million lives, 250,000 Americans and 250,000 Japanese. Sometimes he said it saved more. Privately he may have wondered, but as the years passed he continued to defend the decision steadfastly. In 1959, in a class at Columbia University, someone asked the inevitable question and he snapped back, "All this uproar about what we did and what could have been stopped—should we take these wonderful Monday morning quarterbacks, the experts who are supposed to be right? They don't know what they are talking about. I was there. I did it. I would do it again." As if he had not said enough, he explained that "It was merely another powerful weapon in the arsenal of right-eousness. . . . saved millions of lives. . . . It was a purely military decision to end the war."

The foresight in his diary entry of July 25 proved to be an accurate prophecy of what nuclear weaponry would mean, and it shows the great choices between which the new President found himself trapped in the early months of what he called in his memoirs the "Year of Decisions." "I hope for some sort of peace," he mused. "But I fear that machines are ahead of morals, and when morals catch up perhaps there'll be no reason for any of it." By midsummer, the realities of being President were unavoidable. The work itself would take him eighteen hours a day to accomplish, the problems—both national and international—seemed sown like dragon's teeth: as soon as one was weeded out, another—equally ferocious—would appear. And already people were talking to him about 1948, about the prospect of taking on a longer tour of lonesome duty.

Early in June he had written cheerfully to Bess,

My office force will soon be shaken down and so will my Cabinet
. . . It won't be long until I can sit back and study the whole picture
and tell 'em what is to be done in each department. When things
come to that stage there'll be no more to this job than there was
to running Jackson County and not any more worry. Foreign relations, national finances, reconversion, and a postwar military policy
will be the big headaches—and they can all be solved if the Congress
decides to help me do a bang-up job, and I believe they will do that.
. . . I'm facing another tall day as usual. But I like 'em that way.
I'm never half so worn out when I have too much to do as I am
when there is too little. Trouble is I'm working the help to death.

This optimism was premature and by autumn the truth was evident;
there would not be any sitting back and studying the whole picture
until his presidency was over. Already the challenges of the next seven
years were taking form: relations with Russia, the status of Palestine,
the changes in China, the social and civil accomplishments Truman
hoped to share with Congress, the character of the Congress itself; even
the White House was already showing the signs of disrepair that would
force the First Family out while the interior was gutted and rebuilt.

As Truman was discovering the awesome job he had taken on, his
wife and daughter were finding out some hard truths themselves. The
White House in 1945 was a dump. Redecorated in public spaces only,
it had private quarters that Margaret described as looking like a third-
rate boardinghouse with peeling paint and ragged furniture. And there
were rats. Mrs. Roosevelt told Bess that she had once been having a
luncheon on the south portico when a rat ran across the porch railing.
Undaunted, Bess set about having the place painted and brightened up
a bit, and she encouraged the resignation of the housekeeper, who had
been with the former tenants and took Bess's instructions with a sniff
and the grand pronouncement that "Mrs. Roosevelt never did things
that way." The housekeeper retired shortly after serving brussels
sprouts three nights in a row to the new President when she had been
told repeatedly that he loathed them.

Once the White House was cleaned up and the staff organized, Bess
and Margaret used as their home base the comfy old house in Independence, where friends did not have to run what Margaret described as

a "gauntlet of guards" to see her. But when his family was gone, the pressures of office worked harder on Truman. "I'm always so lonesome when the family leaves," he wrote. "I have no one to raise a fuss over my neckties and my haircuts, my shoes and my clothes generally. I usually put on a terrible tie . . . just to get a loud protest from Bess and Margie. When they are gone I have to put on the right ones and it's no fun."

Early in the summer of 1945 he wrote home to describe the White House ghosts in a whimsical, light-hearted way as the fancies of a history-lover might see them.

> I sit here in this old house and work on foreign affairs, read reports, and work on speeches—all the while listening to the ghosts walk up and down the hallway and even right in here in the study. The floors pop and the drapes move back and forth—I can just imagine old Andy and Teddy having an argument over Franklin. Or James Buchanan and Franklin Pierce deciding which was the more useless to the country. And when Millard Fillmore and Chester Arthur join in for place and show the din is almost unbearable. But I still get some work done.

In the fall of 1946, the ghosts were still there, but not as welcome apparitions. Now they were enough to waken a man who had slept soundly before and after every major crisis he had faced. Harry Truman was beginning to feel just how "lonesome a hole this old barn is." He confided to Bess that

> . . . I went to bed at nine o'clock after shutting all my doors. At four o'clock I was awakened by three distinct knocks on my bedroom door. I jumped up and put on my bathrobe, opened the door, and no one there. Went out and looked up and down the hall, looked into your room and Margie's. Still no one. Went back to bed after locking the doors and there were footsteps in your room whose door I'd left open. Jumped and looked and no one there! The damned place is haunted sure as shootin'.

April 11, 1947—two years in office and beset by problems, with the Truman Doctrine just announced and the Marshall Plan soon to be unveiled, the President beams from behind the desk where the buck invariably stopped.

MAKING HISTORY

The Cold War

On March 5, 1946, Winston Churchill received an honorary degree from Westminster College in Fulton, Missouri. He used the occasion to deliver a landmark address about the widening chasm between East and West. "From Stettin in the Baltic to Trieste in the Adriatic," he growled, "an iron curtain has descended across the Continent." In the photo below, Churchill is escorted by the President and the head of Westminster College, Franc L. McCluer.

Two years later the cold war broke out in earnest with the Russian blockade of Berlin. Truman responded on June 26, 1948, by ordering military planes to fly food and supplies into the beleaguered city. Finally, after eleven months, the blockade was lifted, but meanwhile Berliners grew so accustomed to the almost ceaseless transit of aircraft overhead that they did not even bother to look up. They became concerned only when, due to bad weather, the drone of aircraft ceased, giving way to a silence that could have been ominous.

The Marshall Plan

The European Recovery Program is more familiarly known as the Marshall Plan, named after Secretary of State George C. Marshall, who first broached the idea during commencement exercises at Harvard University, June 5, 1947 (*left*). Soon after, the Marshall Plan was translated into reality. Four of its prime movers are seen (*below*) in the Oval Office: the President, Marshall, Paul G. Hoffman (who administered the program), and Averell Harriman (the Plan's special representative in Europe). Over the next four years some $13 billion worth of economic aid was distributed throughout Western Europe. Among the many forms it took were (*opposite*) boiler tubes to Oslo, paving blocks to Palermo, the reconstruction of a destroyed Belgian metal works, and even a Missouri mule working in harness with a Greek gray mare.

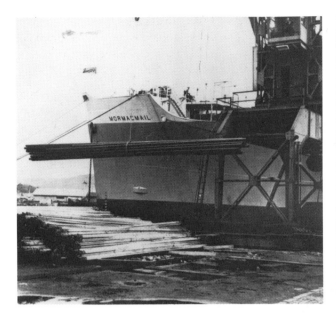

The Great White Jail

Life in the White House did not enrapture the Truman family, who keenly disliked its inconveniences and lack of privacy. Their name for the place was the Great White Jail. Some recently discovered snapshots show Harry and Bess in the family quarters (*above*) and at a pre-Christmas lunch for members of the Truman and Wallace families, held in the President's private dining room (*below*). Around the table (clockwise from the end nearest the camera) are: Fred Wallace (Bess's brother); Marian Wallace (daughter of Fred and Christine) and Bess Truman (both partly obscured); David Wallace (son of Fred and Christine); Christine Wallace (wife of Fred); Frank Wallace (Bess's brother); George Wallace (Bess's brother); Mary Jane Truman (the President's sister); and Harry S. Truman.

Official business was also briefly put aside when the President went to meet his ninety-four-year-old mother, Martha Ellen Truman, who visited Washington in 1945 (*above left*), and when a blizzard turned the White House grounds into an unlimited reservoir of snowballs.

Truman's balcony

The President raised a rumpus early in 1948 when he announced his intention of building a balcony outside his second-floor study in the White House. Traditionalist critics cried out that a national monument was being desecrated, but every President since then has treasured the privacy which "Truman's balcony" affords the First Family. The photos at left show the south portico before and after renovation, and on the opposite page the balcony under construction. "A man with my kind of work doesn't have time for sitting on verandas and porches," the President assured John Hersey in 1951—an exaggeration belied by Margaret's snapshot of her father and mother taking it easy on their new balcony in the summer of 1948.

Margaret

Margaret Truman received her degree from George Washington University on May 29, 1946, and on that occasion her proud father consented to accept an honorary degree. His daughter's burgeoning popularity as she emerged into the limelight provided the theme for a Shoemaker cartoon that is said to have been the President's all-time favorite. Determined to cut loose from the White House and to pursue a singing career, Margaret made her debut with the Detroit Symphony under conductor Karl Krueger in a nationwide radio broadcast on March 16, 1947 (*above*). This was a studio performance, without an audience. Later that year she made her public debut with an orchestra at the Hollywood Bowl. In between concert engagements, Margaret occasionally returned to Washington for brief visits with the family. One such occurred in January 1952, when she attended a dinner given by Secretary of State Dean Acheson for Winston Churchill, once again Britain's prime minister. A photographer caught him flanked by his daughter Sarah and the President's daughter.

MARGARET TRUMAN

Soprano Soloist

PUBLIC DEBUT WITH ORCHESTRA

HOLLYWOOD BOWL

★ ★ ★

Eugene Ormandy, Conducting
HOLLYWOOD BOWL SYMPHONY

★ ★ ★

SAT. EVE. 8:30 AUG. 23

The Little White House

Next to Independence, the Trumans' favorite hideaway
was Key West, Florida, where the commandant's house
at the submarine base became in effect the winter White
House. The President is shown here arriving in Key
West with Margaret, catching up on his reading, and
out fishing on the presidential yacht. Down on the dock
after a few hours at sea there was clearly a good story
to share with correspondence secretary Bill Hassett
(*opposite, below*). Truman's penchant for colorful
sports shirts was a weakness even his severest critics
could condone.

Black rights

Truman was genuinely concerned about the mistreatment accorded the country's black citizens. He set up a Committee on Civil Rights, and on June 29, 1947—in front of the Lincoln Memorial—he told the annual convention of the National Association for the Advancement of Colored People (*opposite*) that "we can no longer afford the luxury of a leisurely attack upon prejudice and discrimination." During Truman's presidency some progress was made in replacing old shanties with decent public housing for blacks (*center*), but his other stated goals were mostly realized only under later administrations. At the height of the 1948 campaign, Truman received an award (*above*) in Harlem from Dr. C. Asapansa Johnson, while an election banner (*below*) proclaimed a clear message.

Whistle-stop campaign

President Truman and vice-presidential nominee Senator Alben W. Barkley share the rostrum at the Democratic national convention in Philadelphia, July 16, 1948. A few days before, a photographer had snapped the President in the Oval Office. By turning the picture upside down, he could see that Truman was making notes for his acceptance speech in Philadelphia. There ensued the famous whistle-stop campaign, a 32,000-mile odyssey by train up and down the country. Wherever the President went, crowds gathered to hear his blistering off-the-cuff speeches. By recalling the "do-nothing" Republican-dominated Eightieth Congress for what proved to be an equally do-nothing special session in July 1948, Truman had a made-to-order target for his attacks.

Slugging it out

Truman and his Republican opponent, Governor Thomas E. Dewey of New York, were all smiles at the dedication of New York's International (later John F. Kennedy) Airport on July 31, 1948 (*right*), but on the campaign trail the President heaped scorn on the opposition party and their complacent standard bearer. Along the way Truman stopped at Uvalde, Texas, for a chat with former Vice President John Nance Garner, and in the course of their meeting the President got Dewey's goat. By the time he reached the Chicago Stadium on October 25, 1948 (*opposite*, *below*), it was clear that —whatever the pollsters might say—a lot of voters were just wild about Harry.

A delicious denouement. Truman (with Mayor Bernard Dickmann of St. Louis) holds up an early edition of the *Chicago Tribune* with its much-too-premature headline.

WHEN he was a Senator, Harry Truman called himself "just a country jake who works at the job," but as President his job was taking on entirely new dimensions, and many Americans began to wonder whether a country jake was up to the task. While he had shown he could ably tend the fields of the Republic, he was increasingly forced to oversee unfamiliar foreign fields. Now that communications satellites allow the nations of the world to share each other's daily trials as they happen, the provincialism of an Independence, Missouri, farmer is a bygone thing. Few high school students of today know as little of foreign affairs as Harry Truman did when he went to Washington, yet by the time he left the presidency he had marked a place for the United States in international affairs in ways that would shape the destiny of mankind for decades to come. Truman's presidency marked the era of the atomic bomb and the cold war. Reflecting on Truman's two terms in office, Cabell Phillips, of the *New York Times*, observed that they were "overshadowed by a danger no other President has ever had to face: the grinding rebalancing of world power between two hostile and incompatible forces, each capable of destroying the other." An era of unparalleled danger in foreign relations demanded unprecedented decisions. Truman saw the flaring problems in Russia, Iran, China, Greece, Italy, France, Germany, India, Israel, and Korea as sparks that could start a Third World War. Each of these required a decision which was in its own way momentous, and had to be made with one idea in mind—eventual world peace.

Truman had a favorite prayer and it doubtless was put to considerable use during these difficult years. A diary entry records it:

Oh! Almighty and Everlasting God, creator of Heaven, Earth and the Universe:

Help me to be, to think, to act what is right, because it is right; make me truthful, honest and honorable in all things; make me intellectually honest for the sake of right and honor and without thought of reward to me. Give me the ability to be charitable, forgiving and patient with my fellowmen—help me to understand their motives and their shortcomings—even as Thou understandest mine!

Amen, amen, amen.

During the period after Hiroshima and Nagasaki, it must have been troublesome to Truman to be sure that he had acted rightly about the bomb. After using what General Eisenhower described as an inhuman weapon, Truman appears quickly to have grasped the lesson for policy. He drew back, fearful of again using the bomb. He indignantly rejected any suggestion that control of this weapon should pass out of his hands. When Secretary of Defense James V. Forrestal proposed early in 1948 that the military services assume "tactical control" of the nuclear bombs in American arsenals, the President refused, considering the proposition not merely dangerous but unconstitutional. From the extraordinarily careful way in which he thereafter approached any possibility of employing nuclear weapons again, one senses that he felt deep regret for the apparent necessity of August 1945.

The President's second great policy decision, to take the United States into the cold war, was more characteristic of Truman than the bomb decision had been. It shows him coming to a situation without much foreknowledge, trying to take an honorable course, and eventually choosing on behalf of the needs of the Republic. This sort of decision was much more to his taste, and he did better with it. Contrary to the widespread impression that his "decision-making process" was hasty, Truman was actually a very slow decider when he had time to be.

In retirement, recalling his years of public office, he said he went into problems thoroughly and then made his decisions. "I was always thinking about what was pending and hoping that the final decision would be correct. I thought about them on my walks. I thought about them in the morning and the afternoon and thought about them after I went to bed and then did a lot of reading to see if I could find some background of history which would affect what had to be done." He admitted to making instant appraisals, which usually produced an instinctive solution. He preferred to deliberate on these instincts and choose more slowly, but it was these initial reactions that gained for him a reputation of being quick on the trigger. "I call it a jump decision. It's a decision immediately when the proposition is put up to you as it comes to your mind. Of course, you don't have to make it public but if you've had the history and background of the thing that's likely to come up, then after you study all the information you can possibly get, you'll find nine times in ten the decision off the cuff . . . is the correct one."

Decisions about Russia required more than deliberation, they demanded education first. Truman seems to have known almost nothing about the Soviet Union when he entered the presidency. In domestic politics his conclusions came from years of experience, and his policies could easily be made to fit them: he believed in the common man and thought politics should treat the economic and social needs of this great mass of Americans. In foreign affairs, however, he had few fixed points of reference. Indeed, he had not been abroad since World War I. In the year he spent in France, from April 1918 to April 1919, he was too busy soldiering to think about international relations. He had joined the army out of patriotism, but his letters home showed little of the nationalism of the era, only a few random comments about American purposes or pronouncements about the treachery of the Kaiser. When he touched on international matters, his letters were impatient with Continental politics, in particular the issues before the Paris Peace Conference, perhaps because Captain Truman wanted to go home. He decided that the Peace Conference had little to do with the interests of the people of the United States. To Cousin Ethel Noland he wrote that "Woodie" (President Wilson) should "cease his gallivantin' around" and give Europe back to the Europeans. He hoped that the people of each European nation would choose, if they wanted, their own King of the Lollipops. Such matters were none of America's business.

In the 1920s and the 1930s the future President of the United States rarely remarked on the politics of Europe or the world—his mind was on county, state, and national roads, and after he reached the Senate, on regulation of civil aviation and the financial reorganization of railroads. Beginning in early 1941, he worked on national defense, but that did not mean international affairs. His official—and informal—stand was to repeat the views of liberal members of the Democratic Party, that the American failure to join the League of Nations had encouraged the rise of Hitler and Mussolini and the aggression of Japan in the Far East; if the United States avoided any surrenders such as the Munich agreements of 1938, all would be well. The litany of half-truths that passed for thought about foreign affairs among otherwise well-informed Americans was as far as he thought—and sometimes not even that far. In the summer of 1941, when Germany attacked Russia, he said that Americans should watch the contest and that if one side were winning then the United States should help the other, to even out the fighting.

After Pearl Harbor, Truman does not seem to have paid very much attention to international developments, confining his attention to military events, which interested him because of his World War I and army reserve experience. He could have consulted journals of opinion and books on larger issues of foreign affairs, but there is no evidence that he did so.

It is remotely possible that Truman had occasional private conferences with President Roosevelt and there learned about the increasing problems with the Grand Alliance, not merely the troubles with the British but with the Russians as well. In taped interviews of 1959–60, he ventured that he had met with Roosevelt far more often than appeared on White House appointment lists. He said that he customarily came in by special arrangement, without formal appointment, and that the President talked at length about historical and other matters: "I used to get in the back door once or twice a week. Nobody knew that." It was a curious admission; there is no mention of it elsewhere. Such interviews might have taken place and helped transform the Missouri politician into a statesman. As Vice President, he was entitled to attend Cabinet meetings, but probably learned little there, because FDR held only a few early in 1945, and discussed few things of importance in them.

Upon assuming the presidency, Truman found himself surrounded by advisers with different opinions about the USSR. Some, such as Fleet Admiral Leahy, were conservative on any subject. Leahy told Truman during his first full day in the presidency, April 13, that the atomic bomb would "never go off." He said he spoke "as an expert in explosives," meaning conventional TNT, with which he had grown up (in his day the old admiral had sailed around the Horn in 1898 on board the battleship *Oregon* when it raced to get to Cuba to fight the Spanish at Santiago). About Russia the admiral also held strong opinions. Ambassador Averell Harriman flew back to Washington from Moscow for the express purpose of reinforcing Leahy's hard-line advice. Truman listened to them and seems to have given in to them when in mid-April he conferred with Foreign Minister Vyacheslav Molotov, who was en route to the United Nations Conference in San Francisco. The foreign minister, unsuspecting, "began to tell me how I could cooperate with Russia by doing what Russia wanted. I explained to him in words of one syllable and in language he could understand that cooperation is not a one-way street. He remarked that he had not been so bluntly addressed since he'd been foreign minister."

After this conversation Truman cooled off, evidently having listened to such moderate officials as Charles E. Bohlen, who had translated for Roosevelt at the Yalta Conference. The new President sent emissaries to Moscow and London. His choice for London of the former ambassador to the Soviet Union, Joseph E. Davies, rested in the belief that he was an "economic royalist" with a liking for the Soviets, and thus would have the right proportion of opposites to talk to Churchill, whose anti-Russian cables had disturbed Truman. He sent Harry Hopkins, former Roosevelt troubleshooter, to Moscow with no restrictions. "I told Harry he could use diplomatic language, or he could use a baseball bat if he thought that was the proper approach to Mr. Stalin. I also told Harry to tell Stalin I would be grateful to see him—facts in the case are I thought it his turn to come to the U.S. as our President had been to Russia . . ."

Shortly afterward, and over the objection of Churchill, Truman withdrew American troops from the Soviet zone of Germany. Churchill wanted them to remain as a guarantee of Russian good behavior. But Truman refused, and there was nothing more that Churchill could do. As he wrote sadly in his memoirs, "The American army was three millions to our one. All I could do was plead . . ." It was an action that belied the charge of Truman's contemporary and later critics that he unthinkingly brought on the cold war. Truman felt that he had to keep his predecessor's agreements. Eisenhower also had advised him to pull out because the Soviets might not otherwise have welcomed American troops into the Yalta-designated joint Allied occupation of Berlin; the German capital lay deep within the Soviet zone. It was a period when, Truman reflected, "I had the kindliest feeling for Russia and the Russian people and I liked Stalin. But I found after a very patient year that Russian agreements are made to be broken."

At the beginning of the cold war the President did not try to argue with the Russians; avoiding argument had been his procedure throughout his twenty-year career in politics. He considered what he had learned under Pendergast in Jackson County—that personalities are unchanging, purposes the same everywhere. At one point he remarked aloud that Stalin was just like Tom Pendergast, and the comment revealed an intuitive understanding of American-Russian relations. In the 1920s and early 1930s, from his vantage point of Independence, Truman could gaze down Van Horn Road toward the long slope that showed the skyscrapers of Kansas City, ten miles to the west; but from his rural courthouse what could he do about the city, against Pendergast who understood the compulsions of the trail drivers' brawling West Bottoms as well as the strategies of businessmen who prized a complaisant municipal government? Truman ran the eastern part of the county and cooperated with the boss if only because he could not control him. Stalin's Russia dominated Eastern Europe and extended far into Asia, and what was the President of the United States to do about it, short of another war? Some local citizens had trouble seeing the reality of Jackson County in the 1920s, and some Americans failed to see a similar reality about their country two decades later.

At the beginning of his presidency, Harry Truman was not especially worried about the Russians. A few of his countrymen, he thought, were worked up about them. In his diary entry for June 7, 1945, he wrote that "I'm not afraid of Russia. They've always been our friends and I can't see any reason why they shouldn't always be." But he did dislike many aspects of the Soviet system. "There's no socialism in Russia. It's the hotbed of special privilege." Russian communism was "just police government pure and simple. A few top hands just take clubs, pistols, and concentration camps and rule the people on the lower levels." He saw no difference between Moscow communists and the noblemen who had supported the Tsar. On June 13 he theorized: "Propaganda seems to be our greatest foreign relations enemy. Russians distribute lies about us. Our papers lie about and misrepresent the motives of the Russians . . ."

Gradually the President and most of his countrymen changed their minds, from tolerance to irritation over ingratitude, uncooperative participation in diplomatic conferences, and hostilities that stopped just short of downright war. Truman was indignant. He wrote:

> In all the history of the world we are the first great nation to create independent republics from conquered territory, Cuba and the Philippines. Our neighbors are not afraid of us. Their borders have no forts, no soldiers, no tanks, no big guns lined up.
>
> We are a peaceful nation. But we must be prepared for trouble if it comes.

By early 1946, Truman had come to believe that the Russians indeed were trying to push the Americans around and that his Secretary of State, James F. Byrnes, a domestic politician who had made his way in the Senate and the Roosevelt White House by compromise, was being too easy with them. In the White House in early January 1946, the President read Byrnes a memo-letter in which he said: ". . . Unless Russia is faced with an iron fist and strong language another war is in the making. Only one language do they understand—'How many divisions have you?' I'm tired [of] babying the Soviets."

Shortly, a confrontation with the Soviets arose over Russian unwillingness to evacuate the territory of Iran, contrary to an agreement of 1943 with the United States and Britain. During the war, with consent of the weak regime in Teheran, the Allies had occupied Iran in order to permit supplies to go by ship to the Persian Gulf and thence by rail to the Soviet Union. All three powers promised to leave at the end of the war, but Soviet troops remained and supported a dissident government in the northern Iranian province of Azerbaijan. Truman encouraged the Iranians to go to the United Nations and plead their case. Privately he may have done more, although no clear evidence has appeared. He always insisted that in 1946 he sent Stalin an ultimatum, telling him that if the Russians did not get out of Iran, U.S. troops would move in. Whatever the true reason for their action, the Russians indeed did leave.

The drift of East-West relations were again made apparent when, early in March 1946, Winston Churchill gave his famous "Iron Curtain" speech at Westminster College in Fulton, Missouri. During the Potsdam Conference, in July 1945, Churchill's party had been defeated in Britain's first postwar election, and he was out of office. In October, Franc L. McCluer the president of the Missouri college, visited the White House with a letter proposing the British statesman for an honorary degree. Without a great deal of thought, Truman endorsed it: "Dear Winnie. This is a fine old college out in my state. If you'll come out and make them a speech, I'll take you out and introduce you." Next month, Churchill accepted, and in the course of his trip to the United States (where he had already planned a winter vacation in Florida), he and the President traveled together to Fulton by train.

On the train the two leaders spent much time at poker; Churchill won. Upon arrival, he discovered to his dismay that Fulton, a dry

college town, was without facilities to remedy his considerable thirst. Truman ordered his military aide, Major General Harry Vaughan, to spare no effort to find Churchill a drink, and shortly before the ceremony he appeared with liquor and ice water. "Well, General," said Churchill, "I am glad to see you. I didn't know whether I was in Fulton, Missouri, or Fulton, Sahara." In the stirring address that followed, with Truman on the platform, Churchill turned his full oratorical force on the Soviet Union, and he gave a name to the separation that had occurred between the Eastern and Western spheres of influence in Europe: ". . . an iron curtain has descended across the Continent."

But the sequel to the Churchill visit showed Truman still unsure of Soviet intentions, for reporters asked if he had read the speech before it was delivered and he said he had not, when in fact he had done so and had told Churchill it was excellent. He wrote to his family, however, "I am not ready to endorse Mr. Churchill's speech." The President carefully sent a cable to Stalin, telling him that he would be happy to give the Soviet leader the same opportunity to come and talk to the American people.

The remaining months of 1946 did not bode well for peaceful negotiating. The winter of 1946–47 was one of the coldest on record in Western Europe. Wheat froze in the ground, and a food shortage appeared certain the following spring. Coal production dropped alarmingly; figures for industrial production in all the countries of Western Europe plummeted.

In February 1947, the plight of Greece and Turkey suddenly came to American attention, and became the occasion for a profound change in American foreign policy. Greece was poverty-stricken after a long wartime occupation by the Germans. Turkey had only 19 million people and was maintaining a 600,000-man army it could not afford along its border with the Soviet Union. The British Government had been supporting both countries, but the British were nearly bankrupt—in 1946 they had negotiated a $3.75 billion, fifty-year loan from the United States—and early in 1947 decided they could no longer back Greece and Turkey. Either the United States would come to the rescue, or these two eastern Mediterranean states would probably succumb to communism. On March 12, Truman announced to Congress a broad world program to assist nations in danger of communist subversion. Known as the Truman Doctrine, the program prepared the American people for the European Recovery Program which came soon after. The general nature of the Truman Doctrine had unspecific limits, but to begin with the President asked for $400 million: $250 million for Greece, the rest for Turkey.

A broad plan was needed, however, to stop economic disintegration in Europe. Great sums from the United States had been distributed through the United Nations under its Relief and Rehabilitation Administration (UNRRA) as "poor relief," but Americans were concerned that European nations did not know the source of the money. Moreover, in Eastern Europe, communist regimes used this relief money to back their own rule. Economic crisis would surely force European countries to allow Communists into coalition governments. Early in 1947, American taxpayers balked at sending more money to Europe without more control, and the UNRRA funds stopped. Congress passed appropriations for interim aid while a general plan was organized.

The Marshall Plan was unveiled at the Harvard commencement exercises on June 5, 1947, by George C. Marshall, who had replaced Byrnes earlier that year as Secretary of State. Built on the Truman Doctrine, the program provided the economic foundation for the recovery of Europe's war-shattered nations. Marshall's speech offered aid to all the countries of Europe, East as well as West, but the Russians would have no part of it, and thus the Marshall Plan became in effect a self-help program for Western Europe alone. By September 1947, the sixteen nations involved had put together proposals for a four-year recovery plan to be financed by the United States and, after some pruning and much politicking, the initial appropriation for the European Recovery Program passed Congress on April 3, 1948. In the course of the next four years, Marshall Plan grants and credits totaled some $13 billion, and the effect was to put Western Europe on the way to an unprecedented prosperity.

In 1949, Marshall's successor as Secretary of State, Dean Acheson, together with the foreign ministers of eleven other nations, signed the North Atlantic Treaty, the third great turning point in American foreign policy. The North Atlantic Treaty Organization (NATO) alliance created a military buffer around the people of Western Europe. There was no point in supporting Europe economically and then having it fall to a military attack from the East European satellite nations or the Soviet Union. Although NATO troops never reached the goals imagined, the organization did present a point of resistance to an Eastern enemy, and eased the fears of West Europeans so they could get on with planning their economic futures.

To set out the three measures—the Truman Doctrine, the Marshall Plan, and NATO—by which the government changed its policy toward Europe and the world to rearrange the postwar power balance is to make everything seem absurdly easy. In reality, the difficulties were legion. Although the structure was there, working out details created enormous pressure and the pace became hectic because of the intervention of other problems, domestic and foreign.

In the midst of this profound reorientation came not only the presidential election campaign, which preoccupied Truman for months in 1948, but two important developments in foreign affairs: Israel and Berlin. One brought belated cooperation, the other an innovative and successful opposition. Since the end of the war, the quarrels of Arabs and Jews over Palestine had been an increasing international problem, mediated in 1947 by the U.N. Early in 1948, Eddie Jacobson visited Truman, trading on their long friendship to beg his old friend to issue a statement supporting the creation of a Jewish state. Truman refused. But he agreed to see the Jewish spokesman, Dr. Chaim Weizmann. Although critics made a great fuss over Jacobson's influence on Truman, the meeting was apparently of little import to a decision dictated by international necessity. The "Palestine Question" came to an end with the independence of the State of Israel, proclaimed at 6:00 p.m., Washington time, on May 14, 1948. The United States formally recognized Israel at 6:11 that same evening. Truman, it appears, had done little to assist the new state until it announced its own existence. Afterward, he could never persuade the Arab states to join Israel in a program to develop the entire Middle East with U.S. aid. But he did manage to keep the friendship of Britain and, during his administration, most of the Arab states. In subsequent months and years Israel's military triumphs over surrounding Arab states were far more a result of the state's own military prowess and Arab incapacity than of any American help.

Meanwhile, in response to the European Recovery Program, Truman had to deal with the Russian blockade of West Berlin. Had the Berlin Blockade succeeded, Western Europe might well have succumbed to communism. When the blockade of Western sectors of Berlin became total on June 24, 1948, few of the officials of the American military government in Germany, least of all the military governor, General Lucius D. Clay, believed an airlift of essential supplies could be anything more than a show of interest in the Germans living in the U.S., British, and French sectors. When a German newspaperman asked Clay about the airlift's chances of success, the general snapped his fingers and said he "wouldn't give you that" for them. Althogh it took until April 1949 before the Soviets consented to lift the blockade, the Western Allies' airlift was successful, and continued until September to assure Berlin of supplies.

In these years President Truman twice almost lost his belief that the United States could arrange its differences with the Soviet Union without risking World War III. In the autumn of 1948, the Soviet blockade of West Berlin was working, the airlift not yet large enough to count, and the combination of signs and proposals was dismal. "Have a terrific day," Truman wrote sardonically in his diary for September 13, 1948. Military advisers had bricfed him on "bases, bombs, Moscow, Leningrad, etc. I have a terrible feeling afterward that we are very close to war." A year later, on August 31, 1949, a White House aide noted in a diary how the defection of Yugoslavia from the Soviet bloc was threatening a Russian invasion and American involvement: "During our staff meeting this morning the President commented that we are now nearer to war than we have been at any time."

In what Churchill called "this most critical and baffling period in world affairs," at a time when the cold war was beginning and its outcome was uncertain, the United States had only a fragment of the great military forces it had mustiered at the end of World War II. Then the U.S. Army, Navy, and Air Force had together totaled 12 million men (and some women); by early 1947 the defense establishment was down to 1.3 million, and Truman was worried. He feared budget deficits might bring uncontrollable inflation, so he kept expenditures down, reducing the military budget in 1949 to $13 billion. General Marshall said that year that when he was Secretary of State he had been called upon constantly to give the Russians hell, a difficult task when his "facilities for giving hell" consisted of a reserve, within the United States, of $1\frac{1}{3}$ divisions, while the Soviets had 240. Marshall and Truman had hoped for a defense system bolstered by Universal Military Training, a plan for keeping a trained force available. But UMT couldn't get past

Congress, and the United States relied uncertainly on possessing the atomic bomb. There were not many: the President privately told one of his World War I comrades, visiting the White House in 1947, that he had fourteen atomic bombs. After the presidency, when two assistants were helping him write a book, they questioned the President: "Could you have used the persuasive power of the atomic bomb to make Russia roll back its frontiers?" "I think so," was the uneasy answer, "if we had had the neccessary soldiers and sailors to back it up. But a great many of them had been discharged, so there you are. We didn't have them." Lack of conventional military power also constituted much of the reason for the poor American showing at the beginning of the Korean War in the summer of 1950.

Truman had trouble raising support for other strategies in addition to UMT. "There are liars, trimmers and pussyfooters on both sides of the aisle in the Senate and the House . . . I wish I had straight-out opposition and loyal support," he wrote. Sometimes when a nation's leader does not have sufficient support, he is tempted to interpret the future in ways that let him believe such backing to be unnecessary, and Truman seems to have done this during the year or so before the Korean War. When, in 1949, America's first peacetime alliance, the North Atlantic Treaty Organization pact, was signed, the alliance was difficult for Congress to accept, but with careful shepherding from Truman, Marshall, and Dean Acheson, NATO got through both Houses. Signing the treaty had marked a turn in defense strategy, and the President thereafter encouraged the military departments to raise their budget requirements. The three services fell to fighting over how much each should get. The first Secretary of Defense, James V. Forrestal, who resigned in 1949, proved unable to control them, especially the air force, which was courting Congress and claiming that it could defend the country alone if it had enough money for bombers and fighters. The navy rebelled at such pretensions, in what became known as "the revolt of the admirals," and Truman in disgust held back from reinforcing the military until its separate departments decided how to cut the budget pie. Truman wrote:

> We are faced with a defense problem. I have wanted a universal training program, a balanced regular setup, ground, air and water, and a reserve to back up the regular skeleton training force.

The Congress can't bring itself to do the right thing—because of votes. The air boys are for glamor and the navy as always is the greatest of propaganda machines.

I want a balanced sensible defense for which the country can pay. If the glamor boys win we'll have another 1920 or another 1941. God keep us from that! And it is so sensible and easy to keep from it—but— . . .

The National Defense Act of 1949 created a chairman of the joint chiefs, and the President hoped that the first holder of that position, General Omar N. Bradley, would bring order out of the rivalry. Meanwhile he held down the budget.

During this pause of 1949–50 before rebuilding the defense establishment, Truman turned his attention to America's economic future. He foresaw an economic phase of the cold war, in which the Americans would best the Soviets because of the productivity of the American economic system. A few weeks before Korea he went out to dedicate, in a St. Louis park, the Jefferson Memorial, a tribute to the prescience of the nation's third President who had bought Louisiana from the French, opened up the trans-Mississippi West, and ensured settlement of such states as Missouri. The Memorial's theme emboldened the nation's thirty-third President to speak of America bringing peace to the world—so that young people everywhere might behold a world of economic opportunity in which they could play their parts. Truman spoke in detail of a point he had made in his inaugural address of 1949 almost in passing—technical assistance to developing nations (the other major points of his inaugural speech had been "unfaltering support of the United Nations," continued Marshall Plan aid for the economic recovery of Europe, and a strengthened military basis for noncommunist countries to withstand aggression).

Shortly afterward, the President went to Baltimore to dedicate Friendship Airport, then flew on to Independence for a rest. He wrote a friend, "I'm going home from Baltimore to see Bess, Margie and my brother and sister—oversee some fence building, not political, order a new roof on the farmhouse and tell some politicians to go to hell. A grand visit—I hope?"

* * *

THE REMARK of the busy President about putting a new roof on the farmhouse near Grandview reflects the daily life of Harry Truman in the late 1940s, at a time when he was rearranging Soviet-American relations and dealing with such matters as the independence of Israel and the Berlin Blockade. Life in the White House was indeed life in a goldfish bowl, and neither the President nor his family enjoyed it— Bess undoubtedly least of all. It was a tense, taut existence, in which every move the Trumans made outside of their private apartments in the executive mansion was watched and interpreted, often wrongly, by the press. The Trumans found themselves to be public property.

Perhaps the worst aspect of life in the White House for the President of the United States was the First Lady's desire not to live in their official residence, but to return to Independence, to a house she knew, where she felt comfortable. In the Senate years Truman had been able to prevail upon Bess to be present while the Upper House was in session. She held the required open houses and teas and went to the social functions his office required. Bess, Margaret, and Mrs. Wallace brought life to the succession of cramped apartments the Trumans occupied, in the decade from 1935 to 1945. The White House was something else. With its public rooms uncomfortably close to the private quarters, the house was maddeningly inconvenient. Although the grounds outside were large enough, it was impossible for the First Family to walk even there without being accompanied by obtrusive Secret Service men, and their presence called the group to the attention of tourists who pressed their faces against the surrounding iron railings and often called and shouted to the Trumans, frequently cheery hellos, but also constant requests for photographs, sometimes even for autographs. At that point any private enjoyment of the grounds disappeared and the Trumans believed themselves inmates of a zoo.

The "Great White Jail" was the family's name for the White House, and while the Roosevelts had apparently enjoyed every minute of their occupancy, the Missouri President distinctly did not. Each time he said goodbye to his wife and daughter it was an excruciatingly painful experience, for he knew that he would not see them for weeks, possibly even for months. Bess and Mrs. Wallace always went by train—Bess detested airplanes. The President would take them to Union Station and usually rode with them as far as Silver Spring, Maryland, saying his goodbyes in the privacy of their Pullman quarters, but then he got off at the small suburban station, and waved to them as the train disappeared down the track. The panoply of the presidency stood about him—watchful Secret Service men, two or three White House cars with motors running, the onlookers who congregated within seconds of his appearance anywhere. After that the only way he could see his beloved Bess was to find some public task close at hand, such as dedicating the Jefferson Memorial in St. Louis, then fly into the Kansas City airport and drive hastily out to Independence, knowing that at best he could stay only a short time in the house where he had spent the happiest days of his married life. Once he waved them down the track in Maryland, there was nothing too do but get into his limousine and go back to the White House. After one such departure he wrote in his diary:

Bess and Margaret went to Mo. at 7:30 E.D.T. 6:30, God's time. I sure hated to see them go. Came back to the great white jail and read the papers, some history, and then wrote this. It is hot and humid and lonely. Why in hell does anybody want to be a head of state? Damned if I know.

The separation was trying for Bess and Margaret too. Little of Bess's aggravation is known beyond what Margaret reported in her remembrances of her family, but Bess's temper and tongue evidently gained a serious respect inside the family. On some occasions those must have been turned on a husband too long away from her. When the President dashed out to Independence for Christmas 1945, staying only one night, he found his wife extremely unhappy. Once back in Washington, he wrote to her:

Well I'm here in the White House, the great white sepulcher of ambitions and reputations. . . .

When you told me I might as well have stayed in Washington so far as you were concerned I gave up . . .

You can never appreciate what it means to come home as I did the other evening after doing at least one hundred things I didn't want to do and have the only person in the world whose approval and good opinion I value look at me like I'm something the cat dragged in and tell me I've come in at last because I couldn't find any reason to stay away. I wonder why we are made so that what we really think and feel we cover up?

This head of mine should have been bigger and better proportioned. There ought to have been more brain and a larger bump of ego or something to give me an idea that there can be a No. 1 man in the world. I didn't want to be. But, in spite of opinions to the contrary, *Life* and *Time* say I am.

If that is the case you, Margie, and everyone else who may have any influence on my actions must give me help and assistance; because no one ever needed help and assistance as I do now. If I can get the use of the best brains in the country and a little bit of help from those I have on a pedestal at home, the job will be done. . . .

Despite the lonely separations, Bess largely avoided the draining requirements of two or three teas each afternoon, interminable social functions in the evenings, and business that demanded that she keep an office complete with social secretary who handled most of the First Lady's mail. Even with a secretary, Bess had to answer problem requests with letters of a short but careful nature, soothing the disappointments of acquaintances who wanted visits or favors. Moreover, Bess kept the White House accounts; that took time, and it was tempting to let someone else do them, even if Bess retained general oversight.

The servants were an altogether mixed blessing. On one occasion, when the extensive rebuilding of the White House had forced the First Family to move into the nearby Blair-Lee House, the President commented wryly on the cosseting he received:

Had dinner by myself tonight. Worked in the Lee House office until dinnertime. A butler came in very formally and said, "Mr. President, dinner is served." I walk into the dining room in the Blair House. Barnett in tails and white tie pulls out my chair, pushes me up to the table. John in tails and white tie brings me a fruit cup. Barnett takes away the empty cup. John brings me a plate. Barnett brings me a tenderloin, John brings me asparagus, Barnett brings me carrots and beets. I have to eat alone and in silence in candlelit room. I ring—Barnett takes the plate and butter plates. John comes in with a napkin and silver crumb tray—there are no crumbs but John has to brush them off the table anyway. Barnett brings me a plate with a finger bowl and doily on it—I remove finger bowl and doily and John puts a glass saucer and a little bowl on the plate. Barnett brings me some chocolate custard. John brings me a demitasse (at home a little cup of coffee—about two good gulps) and my dinner is over. I take a hand bath in the finger bowl and go back to work.

What a life!

Years later, when Margaret asked her mother if there was anything at all she liked about the White House, Bess—who always loathed domestic chores—recalled the luxury of having so much service.

Still, the service brought even more responsibility. Apart from having to get rid of Mrs. Roosevelt's housekeeper, who tried to decide for the Trumans what they could eat at meals, Bess discovered that under the Roosevelts the virtual army of White House employees had accustomed themselves to eating breakfast in the mansion, as if it were part of their pay; Bess put her foot down and there were no more free breakfasts. Enough is enough, she must have said to herself, as her train disappeared out of Silver Spring in the direction of Independence.

Mamma Truman's health slowly declined during the first two years after her son became President. For a while she kept going on the nerve and toughness that made her the family figurehead. She had broken her hip twice in the past years—first in 1940, when the farm foreclosure forced her to move into an unfamiliar bungalow in Grandview, and again in 1944. She hobbled along when, in 1945, at the age of ninety-four she visited Washington and the White House. Her son met her at the airport, and as the little old lady looked around at the mass of people who were waiting to see her step out the plane's door, she said to her Harry, "Oh, fiddlesticks." If she had known that there would be such a crowd, she told him, she would have stayed at home. During that summer visit, a trick was played on her when she was told that she would have to sleep in the Lincoln Room, in the Great Emancipator's bed. Unreconstructed Southerner that Mamma was—the implacable daughter of Grandmother Harriet Louisa Young who had celebrated Lincoln's assassination—she told her son the President that she would sleep on the floor before she slept in Lincoln's bed. Truman knew that the joke had been carried far enough, and his mother was given another room.

Mamma Truman seems to have enjoyed the visit, save for a fall in one of the White House corridors, which she characteristically did not report to anyone until weeks after it happened. But after she returned to Grandview she again lost her spark, and when once more, early in 1947, she fell and cracked her hip, it was the end. She did not really want to recover, and spent her last days in a swinging bed, receiving visits from the President who hastily came from Washington to be with her, but dreaming more of the life in the old days when her famous son had been a farmer or in the army at Camp Doniphan. She seemed to recover a little, and then failed. The President was in a plane over Cincinnati, flying out to see Mamma Truman, when, dozing off, he dreamed that she looked at him and said, as was her custom, "Harry, be a good boy." He nodded awake and checked the time. At that precise moment, he later learned, she had died.

Family life went on, mostly in separation. Margaret finished college at George Washington University in the spring of 1946, with a major in American history, and that spring her father received an honorary degree there—which pleased him not because he tried to collect such honors but because he was momentarily in Margaret's company. Thereafter she too went away—first to New York City to study voice, and then off on a career of her own.

Margaret's singing was to become a source of much criticism of Truman, and as everyone of his time knows, a matter over which his choler would rise instantly. In December 1950, he wrote a longhand letter to the music critic of the Washington *Post*, Paul Hume, who had not liked Margaret's singing and cruelly said so. "I've just read your lousy review of Margaret's concert," Truman wrote. "I've come to the conclusion that you are an 'eight-ulcer man on four-ulcer pay.'" Her parents had taken great pride in Margaret's singing when she was a youngster, and watched her progress carefully as she studied with Mrs. Thomas J. Strickler of Kansas City. They arranged for her to study in New York with one of the Metropolitan Opera's great sopranos, Helen Traubel, herself born and brought up in St. Louis. They hoped that the two Missourians would get along, which they did until Miss Traubel balked at Margaret's going on tour. Margaret thereupon changed her teacher, to Sidney Dietch, a distinguished New York coach, and Dietch consented to the tours. The tours continued even after the fiasco over the Hume letter, but eventually Margaret changed direction, preferring to sing on radio and television and to appear in summer stock, where she was quite a success.

*   *   *

IT WAS IN 1948, of course a highly political year, that the President ruffled his many Washington critics by announcing, at the year's outset, that he was going to build a balcony leading off his second-floor White House study. The Fine Arts Commission opposed the idea, contending that the balcony would alter the mansion's historic architecture. In irritation Truman told the commission that the original design was hardly inviolate, as the colonnade at the front had been added during the Jackson era—and the colonnade itself, so much photographed and cherished by patriots and art critics, was lopsided, with pillars that did not fit the building. In addition, he said, the awful awnings that bedecked the lower back porches of the White House were rained upon and rotted out every other year, and cost thousands of dollars to replace. Moreover, the balcony he wanted was part of the mansion's original design. The critics raged, and several newspapers called attention to the fact that Mussolini and Hitler also had admired balconies.

The hullabaloo about the balcony was hardly past—the President had it built, to the horror of the critics—when the whole enterprise paled into relative insignificance because of the virtual collapse of the old building. One of the first signs of serious trouble had come when Margaret's spinet had threatened to fall through the floor—one of its legs suddenly went down through the boards of her sitting room. Trouble arose with chandeliers, which seemed to be hanging by threads. Then it became clear that the house itself had been gravely jeopardized ever since President Calvin Coolidge had added to it by building additional rooms under the roof. It was the only time, Truman waggishly commented, that Coolidge had raised the roof. The Vermont President had allowed a great deal of cement to go into the upper story he constructed, and the extra weight fatally weakened the house's beams, so that in the autumn of 1948 the entire building threatened to collapse into the cellar. Immediately after the election that year the Trumans had to move out, across the street to Blair House, which was combined internally with the adjacent Lee House. They spent (that is, the President spent, for Margaret was now gone almost all the time, and Bess not often present) the next years, into 1952, in the Blair-Lee House, while the White House was almost entirely rebuilt, the old building gutted to the walls and put back together again in a substantial way.

Some of the privacy that the President lacked in Washington, whether in the White House or the Blair-Lee House, he regained by his chance discovery, late in 1946, of the commandant's house at the submarine base at Key West, Florida. This modest mansion built in 1890, vacant because the base had no commandant in 1946, became in effect the winter White House, although the President went there at every opportunity year round. Sometimes he persuaded Bess and Margaret to go too, but most of the time he went there with his aides and combined swimming, boating, and modest lawn cook-outs with conferring and, when he allowed himself the luxury, resting.

In the first months of his presidency Truman had done his best to bring his administration into order. He had moved at once to straighten out his Cabinet by getting rid of the Roosevelt appointees with whom he knew he could not easily work. Some critics pointed out that the result was a Cabinet of cronies, but such hardly was the case. To the crucial portfolios, State and Defense, Truman made extraordinarily able appointments—Byrnes, Marshall, and Acheson to the former, Forrestal, Marshall, and Robert M. Lovett to the latter. A single appointment, Louis Johnson to Defense, proved a poor choice, and Truman in 1950 fired Johnson.

The domestic issues after the end of World War II bothered everyone at the time, for they directly affected the livelihoods of the mass of the country's citizens. The issues were really one, except that they sometimes seemed separate—prices and strikes. The same people, unfortunately, were usually involved, and one aspect led easily to the other. At the end of the war a massive purchasing power had built up, and only rationing could have controlled it. When Truman had been in charge of his Senate investigating committee in 1944, he had run headlong against the Roosevelt administration, for he favored using the country's excess industrial capacity to convert to peacetime production. The military departments, and the President himself, refused, apparently fearing that any conversion might reduce the war fever at home. Truman lost the fight, and then the problem returned to haunt him after the war—for shortages of consumer goods turned instantly into inflation. Businessmen were happy with higher prices and were unsympathetic to price controls, which would not really work without rationing. The result was half-hearted price control, and no rationing; any attempt to introduce rationing would not have worked anyway because the wartime army of rationing officials was dismantled at war's end and the government hence possessed no machinery of enforcement.

Combined with this confusion was the reaction of labor unions to higher prices, which was to urge higher wages, receive refusals from employers, and go on strike. The year 1946 was bedeviled by a railroad strike in May and a long argument by the United Mine Workers against the operators that ran from April to December. The result of these strikes was higher wages and higher prices, and 1947 was marked by the passage of the Taft-Hartley Act. This outlawed industry-wide strikes, closed shops, and mass picketing, and among other things allowed the President to obtain injunctions in strikes involving interstate commerce, public utilities, and communications. At the time, it was called a piece of antilabor legislation, and was passed over Truman's veto, but it turned out to be an enactment with which labor could manage fairly well. That same year, the employees of General Motors signed an agreement with management hitching wages to living costs—a portent of the future.

Labor troubles were vastly embarrassing to the President, who had previously been friendly to labor, although he was coming increasingly to believe that big labor was almost as dangerous as big capital. In 1940 labor had come to his assistance against Governor Stark, and he could not forget such help. Yet in 1946 during the railroad strike he did not hesitate to threaten to draft striking railroad workers into the army, and no other President has talked more roughly to union leaders.

Equally embarrassing in the first postwar years was the assertion of the President's political enemies that his administration gave in easily to grafters, so-called five-percenters, because of the "cut" that men of influence who knew their way around official Washington sometimes took in contracts they obtained. General Harry Vaughan, the President's old friend and army aide, liked to help anyone he could, and had a penchant for helping pushy individuals, especially if they were from Missouri; so that whenever any evidence appeared that someone had used Vaughan to make a telephone call, the press saw it as malign influence. At one point Vaughan secured a few deep-freezers from a friend, and one of these pantry behemoths went to 219 North Delaware in Independence—for Bess Truman frequently received massive donations of food from friends and well-wishers and had no place to store it. Word got out, to Vaughan's and the Trumans' regret.

The whole argument over the five-percenters was so overdrawn that it hardly deserves mention today, when the annals of American government must have recorded much more flagrant chicanery. Although Truman's administration faced other charges of corruption, these too seem relatively slight in restropect. The Bureau of Internal Revenue got into trouble, and a few of the troubled members happened to be from Missouri. Chiselers turned up in army uniform, including two generals. One lost his post, the other was reprimanded.

What lay at the very root of any such problems in the Truman administration was undoubtedly human nature, and also the President's nature. If Harry Truman had one weakness, Tom Evans once said, it was his willingness to stand by his friends. Tom was unsure it was a weakness, but still this quality obviously bothered him. For example, the President should have retired General Vaughan, whom he had known since 1917. When, after the war, Vaughan became a major general, Truman could not bring himself to send his old friend into retirement.

CRITICIZED FOR THE PRICES and strikes he found impossible to control, and for the friendships he did not have the heart to control, Truman also became a focus of intense hostility in some quarters because he supported the rights of black Americans when no previous President had done so. Civil rights became more than an empty slogan during the Truman administration.

In 1946 the President set out to protect the interest of America's black citizens (who represented one tenth of the population) by appointing a commission to look into the treatment accorded them. Despite the consternation of Southerners, who formed a strong part of the Democratic Party and had control of most of the congressional committees because of their sheer longevity in office, he moved to adopt the recommendations of his commission, one of the most ambitious civil rights programs in American history. The proposals protected blacks in industries with federal contracts, and forced reform of treatment of blacks in the military services. The President supported these proposals despite the increasingly poor omens for his election in 1948. This time his critics even included his mother. He wrote in a letter to his sister, "I've got to make a speech to the Society for the Advancement of Colored People tomorrow and I wish I didn't have to make it. Mrs. R. and Walter White, Wayne Morse, Senator from Oregon, and your brother are the speakers. . . . Mamma won't like what I have to say because I wind up by quoting Old Abe. But I believe what I say and I am hopeful we may implement it."

Before the 1948 election a group of compromisers pledged support to Truman if he would soften his stand on civil rights, and he told them:

> My forebears were Confederates . . . Every factor and influence in my background—and in my wife's for that matter—would foster the personal belief that you are right.
>
> But my very stomach turned over when I learned that Negro soldiers, just back from overseas, were being dumped out of army trucks in Mississippi and beaten.
>
> Whatever my inclinations as a native of Missouri might have been, as President I know this is bad. I shall fight to end evils like this.

An old friend, Ernest W. (Ernie) Roberts, a one-time corporal in Battery C, 129th Field Artillery Regiment, advised the President to go easy on the civil rights issue, appealing to him as a Southerner. Truman answered his letter privately, on August 18, 1948, in the midst of the campaign:

> I am going to send you a copy of the report of my Commission on Civil Rights and then if you still have that antebellum proslavery outlook, I'll be thoroughly disappointed in you.
>
> The main difficulty with the South is that they are living eighty years behind the times and the sooner they come out of it the better it will be for the country and themselves. I am not asking for social equality, because no such thing exists, but I am asking for equality of opportunity for all human beings and, as long as I stay here, I am going to continue that fight. When the mob gangs can take four people out and shoot them in the back, and everybody in the country is acquainted with who did the shooting and nothing is done about it, that country is in a pretty bad fix from a law enforcement standpoint.
>
> When a mayor and a city marshal can take a Negro sergeant off a bus in South Carolina, beat him up and put out one of his eyes, and nothing is done about it by the state authorities, something is radically wrong with the system.
>
> On the Louisiana and Arkansas Railway when coal-burning locomotives were used, the Negro firemen were the thing because it was

a backbreaking job and a dirty one. As soon as they turned to oil as a fuel it became customary for people to take shots at the Negro firemen and a number were murdered because it was thought that this was now a white-collar job and should go to a white man. I can't approve of such goings-on and I shall never approve it, as long as I am here, as I told you before. I am going to try to remedy it and if that ends up in my failure to be reelected, that failure will be in a good cause.

Years later, he explained himself. "When I was President," he said in a speech in Chicago in 1955, "many people advised me not to raise the whole question of civil rights. They said it would make things worse. But you can't cure a moral problem by ignoring it. It is no service to the country to turn away from the hard problems—to ignore injustice and human suffering. It is simply not the American way of doing things." The black leader Roy Wilkins, upon Truman's death in 1972, praised the President's record, naming him one of three Presidents who did the most for black Americans; the other two were Lincoln and Lyndon B. Johnson; all three, he noted, were born in Southern states.

Such was the setting for the presidential election of 1948. Truman always said, "If you can't stand the heat, get out of the kitchen" (a remark he first heard from a Jackson County politician, Judge E. I. [Buck] Purcell, in 1930). But the President decided to stay. He could have gone back to Independence, with a presidential record that might not have appeared a triumph, but at least he could have retired with honor. And, as he ruefully had reason to think about often, he would have been able to rest, at peace in Independence, in the cool, comfortable house. The year, however, was 1948, and without his participation in the campaign Truman foresaw a Republican victory that would have turned the economic clock back, producing more Taft-Hartley Acts and more unfriendly, conservative Congresses such as the Eightieth, the Republican-dominated House and Senate with which he had to deal in 1947 and 1948. Moreover, the Marshall Plan was just getting started in Europe. And the North Atlantic Treaty had not yet been signed, even though State Department officials were busily conferring with ambassadors of the West European nations resident in Washington, and were drafting the treaty itself. Europe was hardly organized, and gave evidence of collapse if the Soviets' Berlin Blockade proved successful.

This, then, was the climate in which all the pollsters believed Truman had no chance. The Democratic Party was divided into factions on the right (the Dixiecrats, or Southern states'-rights supporters) and left (followers of Henry Wallace), with the middle so weakened and itself divided that some of its members were more in favor of General Eisenhower for their party nominee than for Truman.

IF A SINGLE FACTOR contributed to making Truman President in his own right, it was his radical new approach to public speaking. The change in Truman's campaigning style came when he learned by chance in the course of a speech to a group of Washington newspapermen that he could throw away his potted text, stop reading as fast as he could (which he did when delivering speeches that he himself found boring), and stop chopping wood (moving his arms stiffly up and down, with his outstretched fingers firmly together). He found that when he abandoned these old habits and spoke what was in his heart, directly to his audience, he could make a far stronger impact. Speaking to the American Society of Newspaper Editors, he gave a dull, prepared radio address, but once off the air, he did not sit down, launching instead into an extempore talk, off the record, on national problems from his own point of view. The language was his own, the points his own, and—according to Press Secretary Charlie Ross—the audience "went wild." The President realized the difference and abandoned formal oratory for spontaneous talks, and this tactic helped win the campaign.

One GOP Senator, Robert A. Taft of Ohio, described the President's campaign speechmaking as talking to "whistle stations," places where passenger trains stopped only if someone wanted on or off, and trains announced the stop by blowing their whistles. From that metaphor came a new campaign word, "whistle-stopping," and on a 32,000-mile tour that took the President up and down the country, with so many speeches that people lost count (probably 300 to 350) he was enormously effective. He started out at the Philadelphia convention itself, at 1:45 a.m., with the words, "Senator Barkley [Alben Barkley, his vice-presidential running mate] and I will win this election and make those Republicans like it—don't you forget that!" To the accompaniment of whistles and shouts, the campaign was on.

During the initial speech Truman announced a special session of Congress opening on July 26—Turnip Day in Missouri ("Sow turnips on the twenty-sixth of July, wet or dry."). He said he would ask them to stop rising prices and meet the housing crisis. From that point on he made fun of the Republicans, when the "do-nothing, good-for-nothing" Republican-dominated Eightieth Congress met to pass the legislation it claimed it wanted to pass (and didn't, of course, as it failed to muster sufficient votes). Irrepressible, Truman, announced that the initials GOP stood for Grand Old Platitudes. At a Dexter, Iowa, plowing contest, he said with satisfaction, "we plowed under a lot of Republicans out there." And always he made fun of the last Republican regime, under the leadership of Herbert Hoover:

> You remember the Hoover cart . . . the remains of the old tin lizzie being pulled by a mule, because you couldn't afford to buy a new car, you couldn't afford to buy gas for the old one. You remember. First you had the Hoovercrats, and then you had the Hoover carts. One always follows the other. Bear that in mind now, carefully. By the way, I asked the Department of Agriculture at Washington about this Hoover cart. They said it is the only automobile in the world that eats oats.

The Republican nominee, Governor Thomas E. Dewey, a quiet, sedate man, made the fatal error of believing that the less he said the better, but perhaps he was right—for in 1948 he could never have matched Truman on the stump. That year, Truman was for the first time in his life a dynamic campaigner. In Seattle, Washington, the candidate accidentally hit on a line that reinforced his hard-hitting speeches, when a big-voiced man hollered from the galleries, "Give 'em hell, Harry!" Quick on his feet, the President shouted back, telling him that he never gave anybody hell, but "I just told the truth on the Republicans and they thought it was hell."

In Senator Taft's home territory, Ohio, the President took the voters by storm. Elmo Roper, the pollster who had quit taking samples of voter preference as early as September 9, with the comment that only a "political convulsion" could prevent Dewey from winning, didn't count on what Truman could manage in a traditionally Republican state (which went Democratic by over 7,000 votes). In Dayton, an estimated 50,000 persons gathered along the President's route to the auditorium, in a carnival-like atmosphere, and when he left there were cheering crowds at the station to wave his train on its way. It passed

through Ohio towns that the patrician Taft may never have seen—
Lima, Ottawa, Deshler, Fostoria, Willard, Rittman. Stops were short,
but at each one Truman spoke with his own practical bit of advice:
"Vote in your own interest or you will be voting for special privilege."
Each little speech concluded with, "Do you want to meet my family?"
Amid a chorus of cheers Mrs. Truman and Margaret would come to
the front of the platform, and then the train would pull out, with the
nation's First Family smiling and waving goodbye.

At Akron, nearly 300,000 people waited. In the Rubber City, Truman
had promised to "take the hide off the Republicans," and he did indeed
make a strong speech that was based on a sweeping assumption—that
all Republicans were antilabor. He then retraced his trail across northern Ohio and went into Indiana, pausing at the whistle stops to see
the schoolchildren, spending precious time in small towns that scientific
vote-getters would have ignored. But the psychological effect of the
President meeting the people was extraordinary.

As his campaign gathered momentum, his own enthusiasm began
to roll like his whistle-stop train toward what he steadfastly believed
was a kind of destiny. By autumn 1948, when the election was only
weeks away, he could write, "It looks now like another four years of
slavery. I'd be much better off personally if we lose . . . but I fear that
the country would go to hell and I have to try to prevent that." Once
elected and inaugurated, he announced a program of the Fair Deal,
reviving a group of suggestions to extend the New Deal that he first
had offered in the autumn of 1945. Without a sympathetic Congress
to push them through, however, most of those suggestions had to await
implementation by the Democratic administrations of the 1960s.

The apogee of Truman's years in the White House was reached in
1949 and early 1950—a time when he could consider himself truly Roosevelt's successor rather than merely his stand-in. A far more active
Chief Executive than Roosevelt had been in his last years, the President
from Missouri was a man of the people in a way that his predecessor
could never have been. He also differed from Roosevelt on certain key
issues, notably in the domain of fiscal policy, where his instincts were
basically conservative in contrast to FDR's rather wayward monetary
convictions, which tended to veer in response to the exigencies of the
moment. In other respects too, such as moving rapidly and forthrightly
into the cold war once Soviet hostility had become clear to him, Truman

was far more direct than his predecessor, whose foreign policies often had seemed somewhat hesitant—two steps forward, one step back.

On a personal level, the Truman family probably endeared themselves to the American people even more than the Roosevelts. Bess was a retiring person; she certainly had her own ideas, but did not believe that the country had elected her and so chose to avoid any involvement in public issues. And although Margaret undertook a career, it was resolutely her own. The Truman presidency in so many ways amounted to a change, a turning away from the past. That was the way Harry Truman wanted it, and that was the way it went.

Sunday afternoon, June 25, 1950, at Kansas City airport, en route back to Washington. South Korea had just been invaded, and the grim news is etched in the President's face.

DARK DAYS

The Korean War

June 27, 1950: a tight-lipped President, followed by Secret Service men, leaves the Oval Office for lunch at Blair House after announcing to the nation that he had ordered U.S. air and sea forces to support South Korea's troops as part of a U.N. "police action." Four ill-equipped American divisions were rushed into battle, but the North Korean advance to the south rolled on. Pfc. Elias Dissinger and Pfc. Dominic Pecchi watch enemy forces advance to the northern bank of the Kum River (*opposite page, above left*), while other American soldiers cling to the relative safety of a Sherman tank. Much of the matériel needed to supply the U.S. troops was flown in from Japan in Flying Boxcars (*opposite, above right*). Later, General MacArthur's daring amphibious landing at Inchon (September 15, 1950) cut off the invaders from their lines of supply and temporarily turned the tide of war in Korea.

MacArthur

On October 15, 1950, Truman flew to Wake Island for a meeting with his supreme commander in the Pacific. "General MacArthur was at the airport," he later complained, "wearing a greasy ham and eggs hat that evidently had been in use for twenty years" (*above*). The Wake Island Conference was nonetheless a fairly cordial affair. At that point MacArthur's successful counteroffensive in Korea made him a hard man to fault. In the photo at left he is seen chatting with U.S. Marines of the 1st Division following the Inchon landing. Six weeks later, the picture had changed dramatically. Chinese troops had gone to the aid of North Korea, and MacArthur had vastly underestimated the effect of their intervention. His forces reeled back in retreat, once again abandoning Inchon and the capital city of Seoul to the invaders. In unauthorized statements to the press, the General began complaining about the constraints preventing him from carrying the war to Chinese soil. He refused to be muzzled, and on April 11, 1951, the President

relieved MacArthur of his commands on the grounds that the General was "unable to give his wholehearted support to the policies of the United States Government and of the United Nations." There was a great public outcry for a time and much wiping of tears when MacArthur addressed a joint session of Congress on April 19 (*above*) to proclaim that "Old soldiers never die; they just fade away."

"Who does Truman think he is —— the PRESIDENT?"

MAC ARTHUR DISMISSAL

IMPEACH! TR

To President Harry S. Truman
with heartfelt good wishes
from

"Reds in government"

Public concern over alleged communist infiltration of the government crystallized in the much-publicized case of Alger Hiss, a former State Department official, accused of onetime membership in a communist espionage ring, and later convicted of perjury. Hiss had been secretary-general of the United Nations Conference held in San Francisco in 1945, and Truman had met him briefly on June 17, when he addressed the closing session (*opposite*: Hiss is shown shaking hands with the President, who is accompanied by Secretary of State Edward R. Stettinius, Jr.). However slight the connection, it was to plague the Truman administration when Hiss had to face his accusers later on (*left*). Senator Joseph R. McCarthy (*below*) seized on the affair to bolster his contention that "the State Department harbors a nest of communists and communist sympathizers." The ensuing congressional investigation gave cartoonists a field day.

You Wouldn't Hide Anything From Us, Would You?

Time for a change

On March 29, 1952, at the annual Jefferson-Jackson Day dinner in Washington (*right*), the President announced that he would not run for office again: "I do not feel that it is my duty to spend another four years in the White House." Bess, who appears notably unexcited by the revelation, could not have agreed more. Truman's choice for his successor as Democratic standard bearer was Governor Adlai Stevenson of Illinois, who eventually won an easy victory as the party's Presidential nominee—despite his initial reluctance to run. Truman escorted Stevenson to the platform at the close of the convention in Chicago on July 28, 1952 (*below*), declaring: "You have nominated a winner, and I am going to take off my coat and do everything I can to help him win." However, after twenty long years of Democratic administrations, the voters decided it was time for a change, and in Dwight D. Eisenhower the Republicans had an unbeatable candidate. To ease the transition, the President invited Ike to the White House for a thorough briefing on November 18, 1952. The wariness of the two men is evident in a photo taken on that occasion. Truman had little faith in Eisenhower's ability to lead the country, and the President-elect must have shared the cartoonist's misgivings about the legacy he was about to inherit.

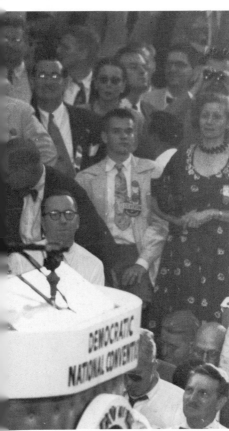

WHAT A HOPE CHEST!

STEEL CRISIS

BLUEPRINT AIR FORCE

STATE DEPT

BUNGLING

RED HERRING

SCANDAL

ARMS LAG

THE TRUMAN LEGACY

January 20, 1953: the Trumans wave goodbye to Washington.

UNLIKE previous foreign wars, the Korean War polarized American political attitudes. It ended the bipartisanship that had made possible the new policies for European economic recovery in the early postwar years. After the war's opening weeks, when Congress stood together behind President Truman and the United Nations, the question of military strategy became a party issue. For the American people, however, there were even greater problems than party politics, and the conflict in Korea proved to be extremely dispiriting and divisive. The Chinese intervention, in November 1950, made impossible the type of clear-cut victory that Americans had become accustomed to expect in war situations. The manpower of China was limitless; the United States could not set its armed forces against such a nation; and behind the Chinese stood the Soviet Union.

The Korean War also raised the frightening issue of nuclear weapons. The United States had the weapons—but could it use them? Whose territory (North Korea, China, the Soviet Union) would be bombed, and for what purpose? How could the consent of the U.N. allies be gained for such a frightful escalation of the war? Partly because of these issues, the war sparked an unprecedented public falling-out between a much-admired American general, Douglas MacArthur, and the President. Also, the war produced investigations of loyalty, rumors of traitors in high places. All these questions shocked many Americans, for they arose soon after the victory achieved in World War II.

Despite the troubled times, Harry Truman refused to give up his lifelong belief in the country's essential health and its strength to solve problems, both domestic and foreign. Even though his leadership in 1950–53 did not attract the average American (his popularity rating in Gallup polls dropped to 23 percent, similar to the rating of President Richard M. Nixon in 1974), it did not matter to him. He was buoyed by the vast material progress of the nation in his own lifetime, a progress obvious in the changes in his own Jackson County, Missouri, where Kansas City had reached out to the borders of Independence and all but engulfed the farm of his youth at Grandview. Everywhere across the country there were busy factories, growing businesses, street after street of houses. On the nation's farms the horses and mules of Truman's youth had disappeared, replaced by tractors that pulled ingenious machinery for plowing, cultivating, and reaping. In nonmaterial ways as well—societal changes, intellectual growth—the country by midcentury was flourishing. Its history from 1884 had been a great success story. If during the Korean War his countrymen underwent a crisis of confidence, Harry S. Truman wanted no part in it.

One special reason for America's success, he believed, had been the country's moral approach to issues. If the nation could maintain its moral strength, nothing could prevail against it. By 1952, Truman was more than ever sure that the world had to recognize the need "to organize the moral forces against the immoral forces." He mused in his diary: ". . . if I could succeed in getting the world of morals associated against the world of no morals, we'd have world peace for ages to come. Confucius, Buddha, Moses, our own Jesus Christ, Mahomet, all preached 'Do as you'd be done by.' So did all the other great teachers and philosophers. But along comes [sic] Marx, Lenin, Trotsky, Stalin to upset morals and intellectual honesty and a lot of 'crackpots' who want to follow them."

When, in late June 1950, Truman went out to Independence from Washington, such weighty moral and martial issues were not on his mind. He had no idea that he would have to do anything beyond fixing up the Grandview farm with a fence and farmhouse roof. He looked forward to relaxing at 219 North Delaware Street, where he could sit in the little library room behind the north parlor in a wing-backed chair and read books about American history and politics. The high-ceilinged rooms were cool in summer. He could not hear much of the traffic outside on Truman Road (so named, to his annoyance, by local enthusiasts), thanks to the house's curving porch and heavy windows. It was meant to be a peaceful interlude, back in the house he had known since he had begun to court Bess in 1910, but every one of the visits he made to Independence during his presidency had been cut short by a forced return to Washington, and he half expected some kind of interruption. When it came, however, he had not the slightest prior warning of a crisis in the Far East. Secretary of State Dean Acheson telephoned him on the evening of Saturday, June 24: the North Koreans had attacked over the 38th parallel into South Korea, but the extent of the invasion was not yet clear. When the President rejoined Bess and Margaret, he was glum. It seemed likely that the invasion might herald the beginning of World War III.

Still, war between North and South Korea did not necessarily involve the United States, and when Truman decided to fly back to Washington early the next afternoon, he was not yet certain what to do—how deeply the United States should become involved. By the the time he arrrived in Washington that evening, however, he was outraged. "By God," he told Acheson and Secretary of Defense Louis A. Johnson, "I'm going to let them have it!" This reaction over, he settled in to a more prudent course, holding conferences in Blair House; night after night, the limousines pulled up in the alley behind Pennsylvania Avenue so that, in front, everything looked normal and no panic might spread. Within days, the American Government enlisted the support of the U.N. Security Council (in the absence of the Russian delegate), and it then sent in the U.S. Air Force and Navy on June 27, and three days later the U.S. Army.

A frantic effort followed that lasted for weeks, as North Korean forces continued their advance, almost without opposition, toward the tip of the peninsula. By August, U.N. forces, mostly Americans, began to turn the tide with a bold plan to defend the vital southern port of Pusan and to recapture Inchon, only fifty miles south of the 38th parallel, then cut the North Korean supply lines; and in September, U.N. troops recaptured the South Korean capital, Seoul. For a short time it seemed that the Soviet protectorate of North Korea might also be taken and a unified Korea restored, until—in late November 1950—over 300,000 Chinese troops entered the war, moving at night, surrounding American units, suddenly attacking to the accompaniment of blasts of bugles. Within hours, the U.N. troops' advantage was lost.

In the second Korean crisis, over the Chinese intervention, U.N. forces led by the Americans eventually held the attacking Chinese, and early in 1951 (under a new commander, General Matthew B. Ridgway), began a new offensive that moved the front lines back up approximately to the parallel, where they held until the end of the war in the summer of 1953, and have held in uneasy armistice to the present day. In the sense that the outcome of the war managed to preserve the independence of South Korea, it was a victory; but in a larger sense, in its failure to unify the Korean people, the result was no more than a stalemate. In the three years the war lasted, more than 33,000 Americans were killed. Estimates of Korean and Chinese dead, military and civil, ran to half a million. This says nothing of the wounded—American, Korean, Chinese—who probably numbered a million or more.

Truman always believed that he handled the Korean War about as well as he could have in the circumstances. In that judgment he was probably correct. He did the best that any American leader reasonably could have done, considering the suddenness with which the war began, and in view of the extraordinary subtlety of many of its issues. At the time, the United States's military establishment was unprepared for another war so soon after the defeat of Japan. In the late 1940s Truman had cut funds to the army, navy, and air force, virtually starving the services, holding them down to an absurdly low budget. That this had been a mistake was obvious in June 1950, and was made evident in the scrambling that went on—the need to fly troops from the continental United States, the hastily called-up reserves, and the declaration of a national emergency.

The President had been provided with a good excuse for withholding money from the military—their public arguments during the late 1940s, over weapons, missions, and money, had persuaded him to wait out the resolution of their interservice disputes. Other factors probably had reinforced his judgment. No one really had thought that a war was likely in the Far East, or in Europe for that matter, and Truman had taken a chance.

Another error of the Korean War period was the President's failure, immediately after the North Korean attack, to ask Congress for a declaration of war. At the beginning he could have obtained it, for Congress was quite willing to pass such a resolution; but Truman chose to regard the military response as a "police action," and that description failed to give Americans enough feeling that the country was in danger and really at war. Still another error and, in retrospect, a most grievous one was to have allowed U.N. forces to enter North Korea in the autumn of 1950 after the recapture of Inchon. The Chinese in Peking had responded with threats of intervention, but everyone including the President refused to believe them.

That intervention in turn led to a series of events which precipitated one of Truman's most controversial actions: his dismissal of General Douglas MacArthur in the spring of 1951. If he could have turned the clock back, Truman surely would have managed MacArthur a bit differently—retiring him in 1945. The President never had liked MacArthur. In 1942, when he was a Senator, Truman lapsed from his usually respectful references when mentioning national figures in his letters to his daughter Margaret, and called MacArthur "Dugout Doug," the name the troops on Bataan gave to their commander on

Corregidor who only once came to visit them. Nor could he abide the general's egotism: in a diary entry of 1945 he wrote of "Mr. Prima Donna, Brass Hat, Five Star MacArthur. He's worse than the Cabots and the Lodges—they at least talked with one another before they told God what to do. Mac tells God right off. . . ."

In many ways, MacArthur appeared completely out of touch with the United States of the mid-twentieth century. He had not visited his own country since 1937, and—apart from that trip—had not been out of the Far East since 1935. Viewed with hindsight, the general's dismissal from his Far Eastern commands in 1951 now seems to have been inevitable, for two reasons. Constitutionally MacArthur was out of line. He raised policy issues with the press as if he were an elected official and, when asked by the President to confine his comments to military channels, he refused. Moreover, the general's strategic judgment was woefully lacking. "There is no substitute for victory," he insisted. He could not grasp the meaning of nuclear weapons.

Taking his lesson from history, that changing commanders in the middle of a war was bad policy, Truman at first tried to work with MacArthur despite the general's sometimes poor judgment in matters of strategy; but when MacArthur sent his own message to the Chinese without first notifying the President, thus making future negotiations between Washington and China impossible, Truman knew that the general had to be fired. The public outcry was enormous, encouraged by the interviews and speeches the general gave when he returned. Ignoring MacArthur's emotional address to a joint session of Congress, when he promised just "to fade away, an old soldier who tried to do his duty," as well as the flood of mail and telegrams from the public, Truman kept silent. He knew that public opinion is fickle and that the furor would abate. Indeed, perhaps nothing so became Truman in his White House years as his refusal to give in to popular confusions. During the difficult years from 1950 to 1953, he courageously defied the pressures of the hour. His steadiness was perhaps nowhere more sharply outlined than in November and December 1950, when—with the intervention of the Chinese—the war took a deadlier turn, and at home Truman's own life was threatened.

In November, the Trumans were living in Blair House, virtually on the sidewalk along Pennsylvania Avenue; the President's living quarters were within a stone's throw of the street. Two Puerto Rican nationalists approached Blair House from different directions, and one distracted the Secret Service guards by gunfire while the other tried to bound up the short flight of steps to the foyer of the house. The Trumans were dressing to go out and Bess, hearing the commotion, stepped to the window, then gasped, "Harry, someone's shooting our policemen!" In the space of three minutes, twenty-seven shots were fired, one of the assassins and a guard were killed, the other assassin and another guard wounded. Washington traded panicky rumors, but Truman was unruffled. "A President has to expect these things," he said, and left on schedule to dedicate a statue in Arlington Cemetery. He described the occasion in a letter to his cousin, Nellie Noland:

> The grand guards who were hurt in the attempt on me didn't have a fair chance. The one who was killed was just cold-bloodedly murdered before he could do anything. But his assassin did not live but a couple of minutes—one of the S[ecret] S[ervice] men put a bullet in one ear and it came out the other. I stuck my head out the upstairs window to see what was going on. One of the guards yelled "Get back." I did, then dressed and went downstairs. I was the only calm one in the house. You see, I've been shot at by experts and unless your name's on the bullet you needn't be afraid—and that of course you can't find out, so why worry.

THE KOREAN WAR AFFECTED almost everything Truman did during his second term in office, causing almost as much confusion in American domestic politics as in foreign relations, and preventing the President from realizing more than a token of the domestic legislation he had hoped to see passed. Almost at the outset of his presidency, in September 1945, he had sent to Congress a twenty-one-point program calling for full employment and fair employment practices bills, federal control of the unemployment compensation program, a large housing program, and development of natural resources. Then in 1949, after election in his own right, he proposed a twenty-four-point program, much of it similar to the earlier one, and began his message: "Every segment of our population and every individual has the right to expect from our government a fair deal."

In that program he asked for control of prices, credit, commodities, exports, wages, and rents; repeal of the Taft-Hartley Act; compulsory health insurance; increased coverage for social security; federal aid to education. The Fair Deal failed to get through Congress. Although some portions of it passed, such as powers to control inflation, extension of the Social Security Act to ten million more people, and a 75-cent minimum hourly wage, the opening of the war pushed domestic issues into the background. The President's State of the Union message of 1950 was preoccupied with foreign policy and defense mobilization, with the Fair Deal mentioned only as an afterthought. Dismissal of General MacArthur the next year, and the increasing stridency of the Republicans, placed a premium on Democratic unity, and threw the Democrats' congressional leadership into the hands of Southern conservatives opposed to progressive economic and social legislation.

It is safe to say that the Fair Deal failed because of the Korean War, and yet its failure was not altogether explained by the trouble in Southeast Asia. The President was pushing his luck with the Fair Deal. Domestic needs were always his first interest, and after hostilities ended in 1945 it was his intention to set forth a wide-ranging program, whether the country was ready for it or not—at least he could tell the American people what he believed was the right thing to do. In 1949, after the election, another moment of truth was at hand, and he offered a blueprint of everything that he thought would ensure the country's social and economic growth. In both instances he was asking for an ideal program. In both instances he then ran straight into a political reality, the second of which was only in part created by the Korean War.

It is far easier for a President to lead the country in foreign affairs than in domestic matters. The Founding Fathers envisioned the President as directing foreign policy but not domestic. Their domestic design was for a diffusion of power and responsibility, giving important interests a virtual veto over legislation that might affect them adversely. For limited periods, great national leaders have been able to overcome those hurdles. Woodrow Wilson in 1913–16 managed to put through a series of basic legislative acts, and so did President Franklin D. Roosevelt, beginning in 1933, until his influence began to ebb in 1937–38 with his attempt to pack the Supreme Court and "purge" errant Senators who opposed his programs. More recently, in 1964–66, President Lyndon B. Johnson pushed major bills through Congress, but then the Vietnam War overwhelmed him. In practice, such leadership is extremely difficult to sustain.

Truman was very effective with Congress; he knew the Senate's ways, and could work equally well with leaders of the House; when he put through a telephone call to a Senator or Congressman, as he often did, he could be quite as persuasive as Wilson, FDR, or LBJ. Unlike those other Presidents, he did not like to push his programs publicly, and maintained that the Cabinet departments and agencies should rely on their own presentations to Congress; but, like other strong Presidents, he found himself almost powerless to push legislation when Congress, in hesitation or recalcitrance, was reflecting the mood of the country. When the nation wanted strong leadership, Congress usually wanted it too, and great rushes of legislation could go through. Then the popular support slowed and legislation with it. The national mood in 1945–50 was sluggish; the country wanted peace and quiet after World War II.

Truman did try mightily to change one national program that he knew to be wrong: the agricultural support program, which he wanted to convert to what he described as the Brannan Plan, after his extremely talented Secretary of Agriculture, Charles F. Brannan. Brannan faced an immense problem in the agricultural support program, a crazy-quilt of fixed prices and foolish measures that helped all farmers, but mostly the big ones. The Brannan Plan proposed direct subsidies rather than the prevailing complex arrangement of government loans and purchase agreements, and it proposed marketing agreements, pledging the individual farmer to produce no more than agreed—or at least to market no more. The plan unfortunately failed. Congress—conservative Republicans and Democrats alike—preferred to let farm prices fall, even if (as Brannan realized) such prices would encourage ruinous overproduction. And the idea of direct payments was too socialistic for many Americans of that time, who preferred disguised payments.

In the early 1950s, Truman favored an equally forward-looking proposal for management of the national economy, a plan to allow a hands-off policy with the economy in the place of strict price controls. The economic indices had been almost stationary from 1945 to 1950, with personal incomes dropping a bit. The Truman administration in its first years had received little criticism for what in later times would have been considered a poor economic performance, since in other ways the reconversion had gone so smoothly. But the Korean War called attention to this lack of growth because of the inflation that occurred from June 1950, through February 1951, when the cost-of-living index rose at an annual rate of 12 percent. The inflation appeared unstoppable. Conservative economists such as the President's former chairman of the Council of Economic Advisers, Dr. Edwin A. Nourse, counseled price controls and rationing, but Nourse's ebullient successor, Leon Keyserling, called for expanding the economy. Keyserling told a Senate committee, "We'll never be able to out-control the Russians, but we can out-produce them." He said to the President that with the right sort of encouragement—no controls, tax breaks, government credits, low interest rates—businessmen would create new plants, production would rise astronomically, and everything would be all right, perhaps without the slightest inflation. Keyserling's opponents charged that he was trying to sweep the possibility of inflation under the rug, that a combination of price controls and rationing was in reality the only workable course.

The argument came to an end in midsummer 1951, when it became evident that the inflation had stopped. After February, prices had risen hardly at all. Scare buying at the beginning of the war and during the Chinese intervention had probably produced the inflation.

However, what happened during the full course of the Korean War was a vindication of Keyserling and others such as Sam Rayburn, who had counseled the President against price controls, for without serious strictures the GNP began to rise. In 1948 it had been $285 billion; by the end of 1952 it reached (in stable dollars) $350 billion. From all appearances, a relatively hands-off management of the economy during the war had allowed it to take off, and Keyserling seems also to have been right in believing that, within reasonable limits, price increases did not matter. Many years later his point was proven: American production doubled from 1950 to 1965 under steady prices. It doubled again from 1965 to 1980 under inflating prices.

For the Truman administration to get through the Korean War without some labor troubles at home was impossible but, fortunately, such problems were fewer in 1950–53 than in previous years, certainly than in 1946, when it seemed that every second American worker was out on strike. The principal labor trouble during the Korean War was the steel strike of 1952, in which the steel unions demanded higher wages and the steel managers asked for higher prices. The companies insisted upon increases of $10 to $12 per ton. Truman's experts on the White

House staff and within the Department of Labor analyzed Big Steel's demands and believed that $2.50 to $4 per ton would suffice. It seemed possible to negotiate a settlement, and labor was tractable. Workers stayed on the job for more than eighty days, despite lack of a contract, but no agreement was reached. The President then had to decide whether to invoke the Taft-Hartley Act, which would have forced an arbitration, or to seize the mills, which seemed preferable, since the steel managers remained adamant. He settled on seizing the mills, and one move led quickly to countermoves. Seizure by Secretary of Commerce Charles Sawyer was met with Big Steel's resort to a federal judge, who ruled against the government, followed by confirmation of the lower court's judgment by the Supreme Court on June 2.

The Supreme Court's majority decision in *Youngstown Sheet and Tube Company v. Sawyer* defeated the President's attempt to hold down steel prices, which usually served as indices for prices of other heavy manufactures. In this respect it was an added rebuff for President Truman in the middle of the Korean War. More importantly, it made a lasting constitutional point: that the President had exceeded his authority by seizing the mills. The verdict in the 1952 court action, together with that in *United States v. Nixon* (1974), was to rank as one of the two basic decisions limiting presidential power, and was to mean much for the future of American democracy. Ironically, it was invoked against one of the most fervent democrats ever to occupy the White House.

THE OUTCOME OF the steel strike was thoroughly disagreeable to Truman. Nor could he find solace in public opinion, because during his second term that was distorted by another development, next to which the steel decision was hardly worthy of note. This was the manner in which the Republican Party criticized his every move and those of his assistants in 1950–53, talking about "communism in government," and holding a veritable trial by accusation. Apparently taking the country into the Korean War didn't constitute proof enough of Truman's anticommunism. To be sure, most of the critics did not accuse the President of being a traitor, but by going for individuals within his administration, and especially Secretary of State Acheson, whom Senator Joseph R. McCarthy of Wisconsin accused of harboring communists within his department, they also tried to make a case against the President himself.

The allegation of "communism in government" had been building up for several years prior to early 1950, when McCarthy told the Republican Women's Club of Wheeling, West Virginia, that he had in his hand a list of the names of 205 communists in the State Department. Not long thereafter came the opening of the Korean War, the congressional elections of November 1950, and the dismissal of MacArthur in April 1951, which allowed the most preposterous charges of Red subversion to gain undeserved attention.

With the smoke *was* fire—there were indeed Soviet spies at work in the United States, but the ones who were the real threats did not surface. Instead, public attention centered on one of the least important of the spy cases, the accusations of espionage made against the New Deal lawyer and State Department official, Alger Hiss, by Elizabeth T. Bentley and Whittaker Chambers, two ex-communists who admitted that they themselves had been spies. Shielded by the three-year statute of limitations for espionage, they made their accusations against Hiss in a long-drawn-out testimony that began in private in 1946 and erupted into public notice in 1948. Two trials (the first of which resulted in a hung jury) brought Hiss's conviction in January 1950, on counts of perjury (denying having given classified State Department documents to Chambers, and having testified that he did not know Chambers). Everything, however, that came out in the trial was from the 1930s and was hardly useful for catching spies in more recent years. As the case wound toward conviction, the President in a press conference agreed with a reporter's phrase that it constituted "simply a red herring," an excuse for the Republicans in Congress to keep from doing what they ought to do; he thereby seemed to have said it himself and Republicans were furious. Secretary Acheson had known Hiss and admired him, and told reporters that he refused to turn his back on him. After Hiss's conviction Acheson privately offered the President his resignation, but Truman refused it, saying that in 1945 he had himself—as Vice President—braved criticism when he attended the funeral of Tom Pendergast, "a friendless old man just out of the penitentiary."

Attention fastened on the bizarre Hiss trial, and the conviction of a man whose guilt was never proved beyond doubt, even to the present day. It might have turned instead to real spy cases. Notable examples were: the defection of a Russian cipher clerk, Igor Gouzenko, from the Soviet Embassy in Ottawa late in 1945, that revealed the existence of a wartime Russian spy ring operating within the United States, seeking out information on nuclear matters; and the confession, early in February 1950, of a naturalized British nuclear physicist, Klaus Fuchs, who had told the Russians everything he knew—which was a great deal—and his incrimination of American citizens David Greenglass and Julius and Ethel Rosenberg—the latter two, husband and wife, executed in 1953. Especially damaging were four Britons—Donald Maclean, Guy Burgess, Harold A. R. (Kim) Philby, and Anthony Blunt; the existence of the British spy ring and of its infiltration of the Central Intelligence Agency and the Atomic Energy Commission did not become known until 1959, Philby's part in it only in 1963, and Blunt's not until 1980. By the time of Blunt's unmasking, Maclean, Burgess, and Philby had long since fled to the Soviet Union. The sham of that earlier national spy hunt is obvious in its overlooking of these men's activities.

Unsuspecting where the real work of communism was being done, the critics of the Truman administration made what they could of smaller matters and filled in the details with exaggeration, such as the GOP pledge, in the 1946 elections, to "clean the communists and fellow travelers out of the government." They wanted a statutory definition of loyalty, which Truman rightly suspected might become the basis for a witch-hunt. After the elections he established a Temporary Commission on Employee Loyalty, accepted its recommendations, and on March 2, 1947, issued Executive Order 935, which provided for a Federal Employee Loyalty Program. It produced at least a name check of every federal employee and potential employee, after which, in case of derogatory information, the case was referred to a loyalty board. By mid-1952 more than four million persons had undergone at least a routine check. As a result, charges were placed against 9,077 people, 2,961 received formal hearings, and of these only 378 were either dismissed from jobs or denied employment—0.002 percent of all those checked. No case of espionage was found. Meanwhile, the Department of Defense held its own investigation of civilian employees working for firms with defense contracts, and fired people without the benefit of hearings. The U.S. Immigration Service screened immigrants, and in a notable instance held a war bride named Ellen Knauff on Ellis Island for more than three years.

In the early years after World War II, the Democratic Party managed to avoid accusations of communist leanings, which tended to be directed at the Progressive Party of Henry Wallace; but after the Progressives' demise in 1948 the Democrats began to suffer. Announcement of a Soviet nuclear explosion in the autumn of 1949, the simultaneous fall of the Nationalist government of Chiang Kai-shek in China, the Hiss trials, and especially the Korean War made anticommunism a rallying cry. Senator McCarthy in fact came late to the crusade, and seems to have gotten the idea of anticommunism from Father Edmund A. Walsh, vice president of Georgetown University, who advised him to go after traitors in high places. The Senator wasted no time. "The government is full of communists," he said. "The thing to do is to hammer at them." He hammered first in Wheeling, and then flew out to Nevada for a second speech, in which the number of State Department communists dropped from 205 to 81, the figure he subsequently quoted in the Senate. He sent telegrams to Washington but refused to reveal the names of the alleged communists. President Truman was furious and wrote out a letter that, unfortunately, he did not send:

My Dear Senator:

I read your telegram of February eleventh from Reno, Nevada, with a great deal of interest and this is the first time in my experience, and I was ten years in the Senate, that I ever heard of a Senator trying to discredit his own government before the world. You know that isn't done by honest public officials. Your telegram is not only not true and an insolent approach . . . but it shows conclusively that you are not even fit to have a hand in the operation of the government of the United States. . . .

If the President early in 1950 held back from sending this letter, he did not reserve judgment on McCarthy in other ways. About the time he wrote the letter, he told a press conference that the Senator's accusations contained "not a word of truth." At the end of March he told reporters that McCarthy and his supporters were the "greatest asset the Kremlin had." When Senator Robert A. Taft of Ohio responded that Truman had libeled McCarthy, the President asked a reporter, "Do you think that is possible?" He advised the Federal Bar Association that "We are not going to turn the United States into a rightwing totalitarian country in order to deal with a leftwing totalitarian threat. . . . We are going to keep the Bill of Rights on the books." Privately he wrote a Missouri friend: "My main effort is to prevent honest people from being persecuted and from unnecessarily losing their reputations by attacks such as that blatherskite from Wisconsin puts on."

But the President, however outspoken, was too late to stop his wily opponent. For a time the Senator seemed unassailable. His colleagues in the Upper House organized an investigating committee under Millard E. Tydings of Maryland, and its findings, hostile to McCarthy, were voted on purely according to party loyalty; the Senate vote was forty-five Democrats in favor and thirty-seven Republicans against, effectively making a mockery of the committee's findings. Senator McCarran of Nevada, a renegade Democrat whom Truman despised, assembled as a bill a grab-bag of confused stipulations pertaining to communists and to internal security; known as the Internal Security Bill, it was passed over Truman's veto, with only forty-eight House members and ten Senators sustaining the President.

In the 1950 congressional elections Tydings lost his Senate seat, as did the moderate Democratic majority leader, Scott W. Lucas, who was replaced in Illinois by the conservative Everett M. Dirksen. In California, a Senate seat went to Representative Richard M. Nixon, who had campaigned scurrilously against his Democratic opponent, Helen Gahagan Douglas. From that point onward, through the remainder of Truman's presidency, McCarthyism became the dominant force within the Republican Party, and was defeated only after a Republican President, Eisenhower, in 1953–54 turned the full power of his massive popularity against McCarthy and galvanized enough Senators of his own party to join with the Democrats in voting to "condemn" him.

In the final year of the Truman administration, the harried President—with the Korean War still unsettled, and with the economy troubled by the steel strike—found himself facing one last major challenge: to find a suitable person for nomination as the Democratic presidential candidate and then to do everything possible to secure his election. He didn't see a truly promising choice of candidate, but his expectations of any future President were high. In February 1952, he made a list of the President's duties, perhaps partially to assess the pressures on himself, and also to help him think about a possible successor.

1. By the Constitution, he is the [chief] executive of the government.
2. By the Constitution, he is the commander in chief of the armed forces.

3. By the Constitution, he is the responsible head of foreign policy and with the help of his Secretary of State implements foreign policy.

4. He is the leader of his party, makes and carries out the party platform as best he can.

5. He is the social head of the state. He entertains visiting heads of state.

6. He is the number-one public relations man of the government. He spends a lot of time persuading people to do what they should do without persuasion.

7. He has more duties and powers than a Roman emperor, a general, a Hitler or a Mussolini; but he never uses those powers or prerogatives, because he is a democrat (with a little "d") and because he believes in the Magna Carta and the Bill of Rights. But first he believes in the XXth chapter of Exodus, the Vth chapter of Deuteronomy, and the V, VI, and VIIth chapters of the Gospel according to St. Matthew.

8. He should be a Cincinnatus, Marcus Aurelius Antoninus, a Cato, Washington, Jefferson and Jackson all in one. I fear that there is no such man. But if we have one who tries to do what is right because it is right, the greatest republic in the history of the world will survive.

Later, it became clear that 1952 was not to be a Democratic year, that the Republicans were going to win with Eisenhower as their presidential candidate. Until the Republican convention was held in the summer, however, Truman believed that Senator Taft would be the GOP nominee, despite Eisenhower's decision in the previous January that he, the general, was in fact a Republican, and despite the mounting of a campaign by his friends to secure his nomination. "Taft has control of the organization," the President wrote, "and will no doubt seat enough delegates to have himself nominated." Taft was a tactless, cold, sanctimonious rightwinger known as Mr. Republican. He had a genius for taking false positions; it was said that he had the best mind in the Senate until he made it up. He would have been a pushover for any Democratic candidate in 1952.

The President's great trouble with the approaching campaign was the reluctance of Governor Adlai Stevenson of Illinois, whom Truman asked in January to be the Democratic standard bearer. Stevenson refused, saying that he had promised the voters of Illinois that he would seek another term as governor and hence could not make himself available as part of a national ticket. Truman could not understand Stevenson's diffidence. In March, however, he began to come to terms with it. Having already declared himself to be out of the race, the President—who was sixty-eight that year—even toyed with the possibility of getting back in; at one point he asked his appointments secretary, Matthew J. Connelly, "Matt, do you think the old man will have to run again?" By way of reply, Connelly pointed to Mrs. Truman's picture behind the presidential desk and asked, "Would *you* do that to her?" The President was silent for a moment. "You know," he mused, "if anything happened to her what would happen to me?" Connelly said, "All right. I think you've thought about it."

Two weeks before the convention, with Stevenson still coy, the President agreed with some misgivings to support seventy-four-year-old Vice President Barkley for the presidential nomination. When the convention opened in Chicago, Stevenson made an eloquent speech of welcome:

> Where we have erred, let there be no denial; where we have wronged the public trust, let there be no excuses. Self-criticism is the secret weapon of democracy, and candor and confession are good for the political soul. But we will never appease, nor will we apologize for our leadership in the great events of this critical century from Woodrow Wilson to Harry Truman.

Shortly afterward, he called the White House, said his friends wanted to nominate him, and would Truman object? "Well, I blew up," the President remembered years later, "and talked to him in language I think he'd never heard before . . ." Following his initial angry reaction, however, Truman made it clear that he would not be embarrassed if at this late stage Stevenson agreed to seek the nomination. The first two ballots were inconclusive, with Senator Estes Kefauver of Tennessee leading, but after Vice President Barkley withdrew, switched votes gave Stevenson the nomination.

In the ensuing campaign against a Republican candidate whom the Democrats described forlornly as a national monument, Stevenson did his best, but he refused all coaching from the man whom he had compared with Woodrow Wilson. Truman never forgot the experience—"He didn't know anything about national politics and didn't want to learn." The Democratic candidate replaced Truman's able chairman of the national committee with an inexperienced Chicago lawyer, then said he would run the campaign not from Washington, D.C., but from Springfield, Ill. Soon Truman was trying his hand at a pained letter, which he did not send: ". . . it seems to me that the Democratic candidate is above associating with the lowly President of the United States." He added that he would stay out of the campaign; he would go out to Montana to dedicate the Hungry Horse Dam, "make a public power speech, get in a plane and come back to Washington and stay there."

Shortly afterward, Stevenson, who was not as quick on his feet as his friends believed, received from the *Oregon Journal* a series of questions. One of these the newspaper called the "oft-heard question": "Can Stevenson really clean up the mess in Washington?" Republican campaigners had been speaking by a formula recommended from their speakers' bureau; they called it K^1C^2 (Korea, communism, and corruption), and the *Oregon Journal*'s question underscored it. With no thought at all, the candidate answered the query by repeating its phraseology: "As to whether I can clean up the mess in Washington . . ." He then compounded his error by saying, "As you well know, I did not want the nomination and received it without commitments to anyone about anything—including President Truman." On learning of this, Truman penned another message, also unsent:

My dear Governor:

Your letter to Oregon is a surprising document. . . . It seems to me that the presidential nominee and his running mate are trying to beat the Democratic President instead of the Republicans and the General of the Army who heads their ticket.

There is no mess in Washington except the sabotage press in the nature of Bertie McCormick's *Times-Herald* and the anemic Roy Howard's snotty little *News*.

The Dixiecrats and the Taft Republicans . . . make the only mess in the national scene.

You seem to be running on their record and not on the forward-looking record of the Democratic administration . . .

You fired and balled up the Democratic committee organization that I've been creating over the last four years. I'm telling you to take your crackpots, your high socialites with their noses in the air, run your campaign and win if you can. . . .

Nevertheless, for a man who had introduced whistle-stopping, a new word in the American political lexicon, and who believed the Democratic Party to be the party of the people and the Republican Party the organization of the economic royalists, it was impossible to stay on the sidelines. Despite a marked lack of enthusiasm from Stevenson supporters, the President got out on the hustings at the end of September, undertaking a whistle-stop tour even more arduous than he had made in 1948.

The resulting oratory at least enlivened the campaign. Truman dutifully eulogized Stevenson and, with considerably more vigor, defended the New and Fair Deals. He criticized the negative stance of the Republicans in Congress in restricting immigration and civil rights. Then he got down to business, excoriating Republican opponents in his inimitable way. "Moral pigmies," he termed Senator McCarthy and Senator William E. Jenner of Indiana, who had accused General Marshall of being a living lie and a front man for traitors. "Nothing more contemptible has ever occurred in the long history of human spite and envy." Then he went for Eisenhower who, he announced pointedly, had acted on the principle of the communists and fascists—that the end justified the means. "Finding out what manner of man he is," said the President of the United States, about the Republican presidential candidate, "has been to me, my friends, a most sad experience." Long afterward, he remembered that day in which he "skinned" Eisenhower "from the crown of his head to the heel of his foot and he might have felt that that was a personal matter."

About that time, too, Truman read the remarks of the Republican vice-presidential candidate, Senator Nixon, offered in Texas, that the President himself was a traitor. "I made the statement after that that if George Marshall and myself were traitors, the country was in a helluva fix." The Republicans desperately dispatched a truth squad to follow Truman around. In a Columbus Day speech in New York City, the irrepressible President wondered aloud if the great navigator had once been followed by a truth squad proclaiming incessantly that the world was flat.

After the Republicans won, the President glumly analyzed the campaign. "Propaganda, character assassination, and glamor," he decided, had overshadowed hard facts. But the Democrat in the White House had fought to the end for what he believed to be right.

The retired President in his office at the Harry S. Truman Library, 1959. Compiling his memoirs became Truman's top priority after leaving the White House.

HOME FROM THE HILL

INDEPENDENCE
The HOME OF
HARRY S. TRUMAN
33rd PRESIDENT
OF THE
UNITED STATES

A happy retirement

Back in Independence, the former Chief Executive could enjoy a privilege he had not had in years—the freedom to set out on an early-morning constitutional alone. Well, almost alone. A photographer went along to take his picture on January 25, 1953 (*left*). Like anyone else in town, the ex-President had to keep after the mechanic when his car was in for repair (*right*). Home, of course, was the Victorian house at 219 North Delaware, which Bess's Grandfather Gates had built nearly a century before. The Trumans posed for a formal portrait in the south parlor in 1954.

Politics as usual

A lifelong Democrat, Truman could never get politics out of his bloodstream. At the Democratic national convention of 1956, held again in Chicago, the former president, seen holding the Missouri standard, made it obvious that he was thoroughly relishing the experience. Dissatisfied with Adlai Stevenson's lack of leadership, Truman backed Averell Harriman for the presidential nomination that year, but the convention stuck with Stevenson. Truman dutifully went through the ritual motions of congratulating the party's preferred candidate (*below*), but there clearly was no love lost between the two men.

Stevenson was defeated by an even wider margin in 1956 than in 1952, but in 1960—after eight years of Republican rule—the Democrats won the election with John F. Kennedy. The new President lost no time in inviting Truman back to the White House. The two are pictured in the Oval Office the day after JFK's inauguration, January 21, 1961. Four years later, another Democratic President, Lyndon B. Johnson, journeyed to Independence to sign the Medicare Bill in the Truman Library, July 30, 1965, with the former President, Vice President Hubert Humphrey, and Mrs. Johnson and Mrs. Truman in attendance. The aims of the Fair Deal, enunciated by Truman in 1949, were at last being realized.

Grandchildren

Margaret was married in Independence on April 21, 1956, to Clifton Daniel, an editor on the *New York Times*. The first of their four sons, Clifton Truman Daniel ("Kif"), was born the following year, and when the Daniels came to Independence for a Christmas visit in 1959, Harry and Bess were naturally at the station to greet their first grandchild (*below, left*). On that same visit, grandpa took Kif on a tour of the Truman Library.

A year later, the grandparents came to New York to babysit while their daughter and son-in-law took a trip to Europe. From the window of the Daniels' apartment, a beaming Harry poses with Kif and year-old William Wallace Daniel for the benefit of photographers on the sidewalk (*above*). By 1968 there were four grandchildren: Kif, Will, Harrison, and Thomas Daniel. In March of that year they came to Key West to visit their now visibly aging grandfather (*right*).

The Library

The Harry S. Truman Library, housing all the presidential papers and much other memorabilia, was built on a site just a few blocks from the family home at 219 North Delaware. Truman threw himself into the project body and soul. He helped raise the money for its construction, broke the first ground (*opposite, above left*), and even gave Thomas Hart Benton a hand by painting a few daubs for his mural "Independence and the Opening of the West" in the lobby. At the dedication ceremony on July 6, 1957, the chief speaker was one of Truman's favorite people, Eleanor Roosevelt. The same description hardly applied to Richard Nixon, but he was the elected President of the United States, and as such deserved the Trumans' hospitality when he and his wife Pat visited the library in March 1969.

Octogenarian

For his eightieth birthday, May 8, 1964, the former President was invited to address the Senate. He is shown (*above*) being greeted by Senators Mike Mansfield and Hubert Humphrey (who would be elected Vice President later that year). In the event, Truman was so overcome with emotion that he could not deliver his speech when introduced in the Senate chamber. It was an indication of his increasing frailty. Thereafter Truman aged quickly. Within three years he had become a very old man; he is shown (*left*) on the front porch of 219 North Delaware, watching the Shrine parade. Though he still took frequent walks along the streets of Independence, he was always in the company of his bodyguard, Mike Westwood. On what was to be his final visit to Key West, in March 1968, the former commander-in-chief inspected the naval base there for the last time. Three years later, in early 1971, Thomas Hart Benton came to Truman's home to sketch the gnarled features of a man whom few Americans would recognize as the once jaunty Harry.

Doing what comes naturally. Harry and Bess cast their votes in the Democratic primary, April 17, 1970.

ONE OF HARRY TRUMAN'S last complaints about the pressures of the presidency was made in a letter he wrote to his cousin Ethel Noland. "It bears down on a country boy. But I'm coming home January 20, 1953." The months after the 1952 election were spent in looking homeward and in making the necessary arrangements for the transition to the incoming Republican administration. Late in November, Truman invited President-elect Eisenhower to the White House to talk over the change of leadership. He set up the meeting partly as a gesture of goodwill. Certainly the campaign had been unfriendly, but Truman always believed that anyone in public office needed the hide of a rhinoceros and should never take continuing offense at anything said in the heat of campaigning. The President was willing to forget.

He came in with "a chip on his shoulder," wrote Truman in his diary after Eisenhower's initial White House visit. Eisenhower was unwilling to be more than coldly polite. Although Truman believed he had covered most topics, from policy to an appointments secretary, he later wrote a memo to himself that the information "went into one ear and out the other." Truman worried. He knew that twenty years before, in 1932–33, the presidency had changed hands with hardly any discussion between the outgoing Republican, Herbert Hoover, and the incoming Democrat, Franklin D. Roosevelt. Roosevelt had rejected Hoover's overtures, and meanwhile the country's economy reached its lowest point in the Great Depression. No problem so pressing looked likely in 1952–53, but it seemed to Truman only prudent that there be as smooth a transition as possible.

During discussions in the Oval Office and the Cabinet Room (where Truman had called together his entire Cabinet), Eisenhower acted as if the presidency would be something of a lark, and let it be known that he would handle it just as he had the U.S. Army. Truman knew otherwise. "He'll sit right here, and he'll say do this, do that! And nothing will happen. Poor Ike—it won't be a bit like the army. He'll find it very frustrating." The distress of the meetings was compounded for Truman by the appearance of Eisenhower's future "chief of staff," Governor Sherman Adams of New Hampshire, who soon had the White House staff in a state of turmoil. Finally Truman, his patience exhausted, told him to go out into the middle of Pennsylvania Avenue and sit down.

The strain of the transition was topped off by the inaugural festivities when the Eisenhowers refused the traditional invitation to lunch with the outgoing First Family prior to the ceremony. Then, as the President and President-elect rode in a limousine the mile from the White House to the Capitol, Ike reflected aloud that he had not come to the 1948 inauguration because he did not want to attract attention away from the President. "You were not here in 1948 because I did not send for you," Truman replied. "But if I had sent for you, you would have come." As they went to the sergeant-at-arms' office at the Capitol to wait for the ceremony to start, the President-elect said, "I wonder who is responsible for my son John being ordered to Washington from Korea? I wonder who is trying to embarrass me?" Truman had ordered the President-elect's son home for his father's inauguration as a courtesy, and was astonished at Eisenhower's remark. "The President of the United States ordered your son to attend your inauguration," he said. "If you think somebody was trying to embarrass you by this order, then the President assumes full responsibility."

Despite stiff relations with his successor, Truman found that his last days in the White House held some happy times. The family was together for once, gathered partly for the social responsibilities the waning of an administration required, and partly to be with Mrs. Wallace, Bess's mother, who had fallen into her final illness. Mother Wallace died in December; her passing sealed for the family their sense that directions were truly changing for history and for the Trumans.

When, after the inauguration, the family left for Union Station to begin the trip back to private life, they were surprised at the size of the crowd. By the time they reached the station they were dumbfounded; police had to form a flying wedge to get them to the railroad car. Thousands cheered and waved as Harry Truman stepped out on the familiar little platform at the back of the train and said, "This is the greatest demonstration that any man could have, because I'm just Mr. Truman, private citizen now. This is the first time you have ever sent me home in a blaze of glory. . . . I'll never forget it if I live to be a hundred."

All along the route, as the train rocked toward Independence and home, crowds gathered in the chill January air to stand and wave as the cars sped by. When the train reached Independence at eight-fifteen the next evening, ten thousand people were gathered at the station and another five thousand waited outside the Delaware Street house. "Mrs. T. and I were overcome," Truman noted in his diary. "It was the payoff for thirty years of hell and hard work."

The Delaware Street house had changed hardly at all since Grandfather Gates had built it after the Civil War. In 1950 the Trumans widened the back porch by a few feet, but otherwise they had done almost nothing to it. Their privacy was protected by the sizable yard in front and to the north side, the alley to the south; surrounding the house and barn-like garage at back was a wrought-iron fence put up in 1949 at a cost of $5,400 to protect the family from the public. Some years later, in the 1960s, when presidential security became a serious matter, the federal government installed alarms and a closed-circuit television security system, at a cost of $22,000, and a round-the-clock team of Secret Service men was stationed in a little bungalow across the street on the corner of Delaware and Truman Road. When tourists approached the iron gate in front of the house and without thought asked each other how they might get inside the fence, a sepulchral voice would answer from a box next to the gate. Connected to the duty man in the front room of the bungalow, the box told visitors that the Trumans wanted to have their privacy respected.

The repeated attempts to invade that privacy made life back in Independence more open to public scrutiny than the Trumans would have wished, but they were philosophical if not resigned to it, as long as the house behind the fence was relatively safe from tourists wanting mementos. Truman observed, "We are going to leave that fence there, not because we like it, but it's just the American way to take souvenirs. It was said in the First World War that the French fought for their country, the British fought for freedom of the seas, and the Americans fought for souvenirs." In some cases, however, the fence wasn't enough to give the ex-President the level of quiet he desired. One day he said to a friend that "a lot of folks want their sons to be President. You'd better pray that neither one of your boys ever make it because you can't ever be your own man again. You can't sit in the sun like other old men do." Another time, he told a reporter, "I still don't feel like a completely private citizen and I don't suppose I ever will. It's still almost impossible to do as other people do, even though I've tried."

Still, simple pleasures abounded, and those had always been the pleasures that suited Truman best. The squirrels and pigeons in the Delaware Street yard intrigued him more than some ambassadors ever had. When, in 1955, he had to fly to San Francisco for the tenth anniversary of the conference that drew up the U.N. Charter, Truman made this entry in his diary: "Bess was at the window waving goodbye to me, the old yard rabbit was looking at me as were two neighborhood cats— a black one and a yellow one from under the spirea bushes at the back door. Pigeons, jay birds, robins, a thrush and a catbird were on hand for a drink and a flutter in the birdbath."

That year, Mrs. Katie Louchheim of the Democratic national committee telephoned the Truman house, hoping to speak to Mrs. Truman. Expecting to be answered by a maid, she got the President instead. "Just a minute and I'll call the Boss," he said. "She's getting dinner." Meals in Missouri were like the ones he had eaten privately at the White House when Bess was there to oversee; it was one carry-over from public to private life that remained unchanged. He liked roast beef and browned or baked potatoes, spinach or green beans, with custard pie or fresh fruit for dessert. For a beverage he always had iced tea. He ate a soft-boiled egg for breakfast, a sandwich for lunch. There were no footmen and no finger bowls, and Harry Truman thought it was grand.

At the outset of his retirement Truman kept an office downtown in Kansas City in the Federal Reserve building, a convenient place to meet visitors and handle correspondence. However, at lunchtime he was ten miles from home, and finding a place to eat was a problem. He tried the Pickwick Hotel coffee shop, a favorite haunt from years before. The waitress came over in offhand fashion, then—on recognizing him—blanched, blushed, shook the President's hand, and thereby called attention to his presence. Soon he was busy signing autographs for every lunch patron there and could hardly eat his own meal. Tom Evans then arranged for him to eat at the Kansas City Club, where he went at first uncertainly, as he knew the club to be a stronghold of conservative Republicans. There was an uproar, but it was entirely in his favor—the rockribbed conservatives lined up to shake his hand, welcoming him with enthusiasm, delighted to have him. Soon they elected him not merely to the club but to the 822 Club, the oldest and most exclusive inner group of the Kansas City Club. There he usually ate, until in 1957 the Truman Library opened in Independence and he had the wonderful convenience of a suite of offices three blocks from the North Delaware house and lunch at home.

In the years from 1957 until the mid-1960s, the President seldom varied his routine. He arose around five or five-thirty and went downstairs, took his walk, and worked on mail and read the papers. At seven or seven-fifteen Bess came down and got breakfast. About a quarter to eight he drove to the library, dealt with more mail, and dictated forty or fifty letters. Home for lunch at eleven-thirty, and back at the library at one or one-thirty. Then he would return to the house for a nap. About five-thirty or six Bess prepared dinner. After dinner he went through documents, such as the *Congressional Record*, which he read avidly, and sometimes he and Mrs. Truman watched television. Then to bed at nine-thirty or ten.

As his routine smoothed out during the 1950s and early 1960s, the retired President's energy seldom flagged—indeed he was seriously ill only once, with a gall bladder attack and operation in 1954—and he took up new tasks that would have exhausted many younger men. The indomitable Truman spirit required tasks at hand, important tasks; but even in retirement, important tasks to Truman were for other rewards than money. Of course he had plenty of opportunities to earn money in positions that would have required little of him. A chain of clothing stores wanted him as its vice president at a six-figure salary. A sewing machine company asked him to be chairman of the board, also at six figures, with no work except appearances in public ceremonies. The chief executive of a motion picture company tried to interest him in a merger of several producing companies, with a fabulous salary. Several oil companies thought he would be a good man just to have around—one proposal, with an eight-year contract, required only an hour's work a day, and guaranteed over a half million dollars. In every case the President would listen to the pitch men and then chuck the proposals as if they never had been made. He then designed his own workload, which consisted of three main enterprises.

THE FIRST OF TRUMAN'S principal activities in retirement was writing his memoirs; these were published by Doubleday in two volumes in 1955–56 under the titles of *Year of Decisions* and *Years of Trial and Hope*. The President had determined not to let someone else account for his administration to posterity. He decided that the history of the mid-twentieth century would have no false chronicling. "It is the habit of some of these historians to think for the President after he's dead," he said, "and I want to fix things so they'll have to take my thoughts instead of their own." Or, as he advised an assistant even before his administration was over:

> The lies are beginning to be solidified and made into historical "facts." Let's head them off now while we can. The truth is all I want for history. If I appear in a bad light when we have the truth that's just too bad. We must take it. But I don't want a pack of lying, so-called historians to do to Roosevelt and to me what the New Englanders did to Jefferson and Jackson.

Truman brought in assistants and got to work on what proved to be a huge memoir. His initial helpers were far from talented, and the result was bulky and very badly proportioned (one year, 1945–46, in the first volume, the rest of the administration in the second). It was not well written; his own clear prose would have been better left alone. Still, the Truman personality shone through the murk, and there was no mistaking his defense of everything he did, from his way of ending the war in Europe and the Far East through the formative measures of a new policy for Western Europe to the Korean War and the dismissal of General MacArthur. The work sold well, especially in Kansas City; at the autographing party at the Muehlebach Hotel the retired President signed nearly four thousand copies of the first volume at a rate of nine or ten a minute.

The second enterprise of the retirement years was the construction of the Harry S. Truman Library. After first considering that he might put the library on the campus of the University of Kansas City (later the University of Missouri in Kansas City), or near Grandview on the family farm, he decided on a site north of the Delaware Street house. There the building went up, a half-circle, single-story structure of Indiana limestone, with contemporary lines quite unlike the Georgian courthouse on the Independence square or the art deco courthouse in Kansas City that Truman admired. Initially the modernity of the design bothered him, but he came to accept it as a necessary result of changing tastes, and eventually enjoyed the building with its museum in the front, administrative offices and his own private suite at rear. There he worked in a book-lined office that looked out on the courtyard, with his presidential private secretary Rose Conway in a little office next door where she could type the answers to the interminable flow of inquiring letters.

The answers cost him $40,000 a year in secretarial salaries, stationery, and stamps. Congress in 1957 passed the Retired Presidents Act that provided for office help and, if necessary, rental of office space; Truman's friend Sam Rayburn got the act through after the cost of being a retired public figure had threatened literally to bankrupt the principal citizen of Independence. The cost of building the library was covered by donations, and much of the money came from fund-raising dinners at which Truman spoke. In 1957 the library was dedicated to the people of the United States.

About the same time the library was finished, Truman's life found a new dimension full of joy for him and Bess. Margaret married Clifton Daniel, an editor of the *New York Times*, in 1956, and her parents were thrilled. Later, Margaret observed that her husband rapidly achieved more influence with her parents than she had ever had, persuading the stubborn Trumans to changing their minds on occasion, an activity neither Bess nor Harry had ever been famous for. In 1957, the Daniels' first son was born. In time the President had four grandsons, who delighted him the rest of his life. He took them strolling on his morning walks, read them the Greek historian Thucydides, and fished with them at Key West. A new generation was for Truman the fulfillment of a life devoted to both family and the future of his country.

Meanwhile, the ex-President made himself available for speeches in support of the Democratic Party, against the GOP of Dwight D. Eisenhower. Part of Truman's Democratic actions consisted of simply using his wits against his less clever opponents. One occasion arose when the Republican national committee suggested that the Democratic Party be renamed the "Democrat Party." The newscaster of the local NBC television station in Kansas City, Randall Jessee, knew that this proposal would get a rise out of the former President, and rigged his television camera in the Kansas City parking lot that Truman then was using, next to the Federal Reserve building, and waited for his quarry. Soon along came HST, driving the car himself.

"Hi, Randall," said Truman, "what do you want to know this morning?"

"Well, Mr. President," was the response, "NBC would like to know what you think of the move by the Republican national committee to force the changing of the name of your party from Democratic Party to Democrat Party."

"I think that's just fine, Randall," was the snappy response. "Providing, of course, they let us change the name of their party to the Publican Party. You know, in the Bible those publicans and big-money boys didn't come off too well!"

When Truman traveled to make speeches, he liked to say that each time he came back to Independence he was "dragging a few Republican carcasses" behind him. The speeches were hardhitting, especially against Publicans he disliked, such as Richard M. Nixon who, after serving for two terms as Vice President under Eisenhower had failed in his bid for the presidency in the 1960 election. When Nixon attempted a comeback in 1962, by running for governor of California, Truman decided to make a special trip out West to get him. In preparation for what must have been a rousing address, the former Democratic President on the evening of his talk scrawled on a scrap of paper: "The people shut the *front* door on him. Watch out that they don't sneak him in through the *back* door." And on an envelope: "Fine man [Governor Pat Brown]. Clean fight. Character assassin and dirty name-calling. Choice between Brown good governor and a kindly man and the opposite in a mean, nasty fellow." And on another envelope:

That fellow couldn't get into the front door of the White House. Now he's trying to sneak in over the transom. Russian visit [of Nixon]. The Russian people wanted to learn something from him but Khrushchev taught him something. Khrushchev has been threatening to bury the free world and now that fellow [Nixon] boasts that he will bury the Democratic Party and its leaders here in California. Didn't come here to tell California what to do—but what not to do to the detriment of the great state. But the situation that has developed in California has importance outside your borders. It affects the whole nation. An effort is underway to revive the man's political future. I am here to help prevent it.

In the course of all these activities, conducted mostly during the time of Democratic low fortunes in the 1950s, Truman also enjoyed himself on university campuses where, contrary to his earlier custom, which had been to decline honorary degrees, he now accepted them happily. In all, Truman received twenty-two honorary degrees, counting the initial degree at Grinnell College in Iowa where he had gone to speak without any thought of being honored, and the second at George Washington University where he had spoken because he wanted to be on the same platform as his daughter Margaret when she graduated.

On a trip to Europe in the summer of 1956, Truman received a degree from Oxford. When undergraduates saw him appear in a red gown and Henry VIII hat, they were so pleased that they started cheering and chanting "Give 'em hell, Harricum!" Randall Jessee liked to tell a story about Truman and "the king's hat" received at Oxford, and it shows the enchanting way in which the retired President treated young and old, whoever came his way. After Truman returned from Europe, his friend Jessee arranged to show the excess NBC newsreel footage of the trip to the Trumans in the Delaware Street house. After the showing, the President and Mrs. Truman and the Jessee family, including their four-year-old daughter, ate ice cream in the backyard. Jessee had instructed his daughter carefully to address Mr. Truman as "Mr. President." She therefore went up to him and said, "Mr. President, you sure looked funny in that king's hat!"

Her father said, "Now, Janet, you mustn't ever say the President looks funny. Presidents just don't look funny!"

"All right," said Janet, who went back to Truman and said, "Mr. President, you sure looked silly in that king's hat!"

Truman excused himself and went into the house for a few minutes. When he came out he was dressed in his Oxford cap and gown. He picked Janet up in his arms and said to her, "Any little girl who is so interested in the robes of Oxford should be able to say she's seen the real thing!"

POLITICS WAS TRUMAN's life's blood, and the political scene during the 1950s distressed him. His relations with Eisenhower were virtually nonexistent; he never entered the White House during the eight years of Eisenhower's presidency. At one time Eisenhower came to Kansas City and Truman phoned him at the Muehlebach Hotel to pay his respects. However, an underling took the call, and Eisenhower never returned it. Truman felt certain that the slight was intended.

The 1950s were doubly difficult for Truman politically, in that Democratic counsels did not welcome the retired President's advice. Adlai Stevenson controlled the party and Truman's irritation with Stevenson in 1952 was unforgotten. At the beginning of the 1956 convention the man of Independence came to Chicago wearing a big

Harriman button, and championed Averell Harriman in his usual way, which was to blacken the name of his opponent. He pushed his pro-Harriman, anti-Stevenson views long after it was clear that Harriman was going to lose. For the only time in his life the Trumans' long-time friend Tom Evans, who was present, saw Bess in tears. "Tom, can't you do something to stop Harry?" she pleaded. "He's making a fool of himself." Wisely, Tom stayed out of the matter.

In 1960 the President again bet on the wrong horse, Lyndon B. Johnson, and wrote friends that the danger of young John F. Kennedy was not the Massachusetts Senator's Catholicism but his economic royalist father, Joseph P. Kennedy—it was "not a case of the Pope, but the Pop." When Kennedy won the nomination, Truman warned Johnson in strongest terms not to take the vice-presidential place on the ticket. Gradually, however, he warmed to Kennedy, and to Johnson's participation, and visited the White House the day after Kennedy took office. At the time of the assassination in 1963, he was unable to make a statement; he was so shocked he went to bed.

Interestingly, it was on the occasion of the Kennedy funeral that Truman at last made up with Eisenhower, whom he had so admired years earlier when the President of the 1950s had been General Eisenhower of the 1940s. At the time of the funeral the former Missouri President stayed at Blair House, and a message came through in garbled form, supposedly from President Eisenhower, to the effect that he wanted to know if he could pick up President Truman and Margaret (Bess had remained in Independence) to go to the ceremony. Admiral Robert L. Dennison, who had been Truman's naval aide in the White House, was present at Blair House, heard of the message from a butler or perhaps a Secret Service man, and found it difficult to believe. He nonetheless called the Statler Hotel and got through to Eisenhower.

"Thank God, I've got you on the phone," said Ike, "I don't seem to be able to get through to anybody."

"What can I do for you?" asked Dennison.

"All I want to know," said Eisenhower, "is whether Mamie and I could stop by to pick up President Truman and Margaret to go to the cathedral. I don't intend to go to the graveside and I don't suppose President Truman does either."

"Well, General," said Dennison, "I'll call you back."

"Well, that's no problem," said Ike. "I'll hold the phone."

Dennison told him that Truman was right there, asked him, and he replied, "Certainly."

President and Mrs. Eisenhower duly took the Trumans to the funeral, and after the ceremony went back to Blair House. Truman asked the Eisenhowers if they would like to come in and have a drink or cup of coffee, and they accepted. Soon the two men were talking animatedly. Dennison recalled that "They just kept on having another drink and talking. I thought it would never end, but it was *really* heartwarming because they completely buried the hatchet and you'd think there had never been any differences between them . . ."

Truman much appreciated Kennedy's successor, Johnson, although the Texan President received very little advice from Missouri because Truman's health was rapidly worsening. In 1968, Vice President Hubert Humphrey and Senator Edmund Muskie, Democratic candidates for President and Vice President, called dutifully at the Truman house in Independence. Humphrey does not seem to have gained much from the visit, but to the Lincolnesque Muskie, Truman gave memorable advice. "Tell the truth," said the old man. When the Senator replied that his way of telling the truth was not the same as Truman's, the retired President said, "Be yourself."

Meanwhile, by the mid-1960s, old age at last had caught up with Harry Truman. For a long time he had resisted the old lady he called Anno Domini to friends. He told them she was chasing him, but as late as 1963 he still refused to be called a "senior citizen." He wrote to an old friend: "I still get around and when I get to be a 'senior citizen' I hope they will put me in a pine box and cover me up."

In 1964 he stumbled in the upstairs bathroom of the Independence house, striking his head against the sink, but he appeared to recover. Then a combination of physical failures that sometimes assail previously strong men and women almost at once seemed to attack him in a frightening wave. He lost weight rapidly. His hearing deteriorated. His eyes, once so luminous, glazed over with fatigue or illness or whatever it is that takes away the sparkle. His false teeth fitted badly, and when he thought no one was looking he would take them out, which made him appear even more aged.

The problem of his teeth amused him, and he could laugh at himself about the vanity involved. One day he and Police Officer Mike Westwood, his Independence bodyguard, stopped at George Miller's barbershop around the corner from Delaware Street, and only after Truman got into the chair did he realize he had left the teeth at home. A photographer happened by, and the toothless Truman, Mike, and the barber all posed, in and around the chair, with no one's grin wider than the President's. Miller received a print from the photographer and it hangs in honor even today near the door of his shop.

The President's sister Mary said of him in these declining years that "He doesn't look a thing like he used to. He always had a full face and always looked so well. He takes a miserable picture now, he's so thin. And he's always taken such a nice picture." But the artist Thomas Hart Benton, who painted him in 1971, disagreed. Benton sketched him in a chair in the little library off the north parlor, the room with three sides covered by shelves filled with books. The old President sat slumped in a chair before a small table piled with books; alongside him was a stack of books on which he rested his arthritic arm; he held a book in his gnarled fingers, reading as Benton sketched him. Benton liked what he saw. "He's a skull now," he said, "You can see the man without the jowls and the fat. He has no need to put on an act, any kind of public act. So he relaxes now. He's a very interesting old man."

HARRY S. TRUMAN died on the day after Christmas 1972, in his eighty-ninth year. In remembering him, the main lines of his private self and public life become evident. In every endeavor, he sought clarity and effectiveness. Often the understanding he needed came to him through hard work. He learned through books all his life, and in his political career through testimonies and hearings, the *Congressional Record*, and documentary annexes. He always consulted people, both neighbors and statesmen, in his search for the truth he believed lay beneath all appearance of confusion. Whatever his sources, he queried them thoughtfully and tried to turn the benefit of their experience to his own. He never tried to guess or bluff his way through important tasks and questions, in personal or public life.

Shortly after his return to Independence, he wrote a long reflection on politics and his own career. In it he observed:

> It takes a lifetime of the hardest kind of work and study to become a successful politician. . . .
>
> A great politician is known by the service he renders. He doesn't have to become President or governor or the head of his city or county

to be a great politician. There are mayors of villages, county attorneys, county commissioners or supervisors who render just as great service locally as do the heads of governments.

No young man should go into politics if he wants to get rich or if he expects an adequate reward for his services. An honest public servant can't become rich in politics. He can only attain greatness and satisfaction by service.

When a man with analytical ability reaches high office, the results can be formidable if the official also has the nerve to make up his mind. Harry Truman began his tenure as President with some of the hardest decisions any leader of the Western world has ever had to make; having made them, he then stood by them.

A President needs more than analytical skill and decisiveness—he must be a consummate administrator. Truman's innate administrative talents were obvious from the time he joined the army in 1917; by the time he was President he knew how to use the skills of everyone involved to reach a common goal. He pulled the appropriate administrative levers with his White House staff and his Cabinet, and even with the Congress as successfully as could be expected during the upheavals of a postwar period and a new war. But great administrators cannot be great Presidents without depth of character. Truman was reviled in the press for so many of his traits—even more than his actions—but his life in retrospect is one of exemplary morality. Without it he would have amounted to very little as President.

In a time when public officials appear too often to be the creations of public relations agencies and political committees, Truman's moral commitment calls out in appealing fashion. He demanded from the Republic not a morality someone coached him to preach, but the one he lived by himself. "Do as you would be done by" and "The buck stops here" probably took complementary places in his mind as rules for both public and private life, and he believed in each person's taking final responsibility for his obligations to the community at large. In line with this, he demanded honesty at every level. He never tolerated the notion that public morality is somehow different from private.

He was steadfast in his relationships, professional and personal. Nothing shows this more fully than his lifelong devotion to his family and his marriage to Bess. He had a capacity to respect the needs of others even when they conflicted with his own. In his private life, he endured great loneliness because of his wife's preference to be away from Washington; but his admiration for her and his affection never slackened. In professional life, he made allowances for the wishes of others when they thwarted his own, so long as he could see there was neither dishonesty nor threat to public welfare involved.

His defects were linked to his qualities in the way that character flaws can come from an excess of what otherwise would be considered a strength. For example, Truman's steadfastness and loyalty may have carried too far in friendships. He stood by friends, believing them innocent until proven guilty; even guilty ones could still have a measure of his loyalty. His own political career was marked by difficult times, and he refused to forget the friends who stood by him then.

The quirks and quips that gave the press a field day throughout his presidency seem less defects now than a refreshing naturalness. Harry Truman was a farm-boy President who had come up the hard way through the army and though years as a local official. His only real polish was a certain natural grace and a beguiling smile, the courtliness that a Southern upbringing used to impose on young men, and the attempts of a good-hearted person to put others at ease. But he had a reserve of salty language, and a ready wit. He could say things that were too quotable. Sophisticates saw him as gauche and uninstructed; they were embarrassed by a President who would play the piano in public—and so obviously enjoy himself. Now his owlish spectacles and rumpled suits, his simple habits and fatherly pride, his passion for history, his pungent humor, his love for Bess all are part of a charm that reminds us that a good President and a good person can be one.

In 1962, Arthur M. Schlesinger, Sr., of Harvard University surveyed seventy-five leading historians, and Truman's name appeared ninth on a list of American Presidents, below five classed as "great" and with six viewed as "near great." In a survey of 1981, Steve Neal of the Chicago *Tribune* found that a somewhat similar group of respondents advanced Truman to eighth, ahead of Polk, preceded only by Lincoln, Washington, Franklin D. Roosevelt, Wilson, Jefferson, Jackson, and Theodore Roosevelt. Whether he would emerge as a great President was a question that never bothered Harry Truman, who told a television producer in the early 1960s that he would not say he was in the great class, but that he had a great time trying to be great.

ACKNOWLEDGMENTS

Of the many individuals who assisted with the preparation of this book, I am first of all indebted to Jane Mobley, whose participation in the drafting of the text was invaluable. Christie Cater of the Kansas City *Star* read the early chapters and forthrightly told Jane and me what aspects readers would find uninteresting—and these passages we took out.

Roland Gelatt conceived this book as a successor to Joseph Alsop's *FDR: A Centenary Remembrance* (1982). He watched over the project from the beginning, compiled the picture sections, and wrote the captions.

The staff of the Harry S. Truman Library in Independence assisted me in every possible way. Dr. Benedict K. Zobrist, the director, and his devoted assistants could not have been more cooperative or forthcoming. My special thanks go to Pauline Testerman and Niel M. Johnson in the audiovisual archive, and to Elizabeth Safly, who made the library search room such an efficient and enjoyable place to work in.

R.H.F.

Picture credits

The majority of the illustrations, including all those not specifically credited, were provided by the Harry S. Truman Library in Independence, Missouri, and are hereby gratefully acknowledged. Items noted below came either from the Library's archives or directly from the sources named, and are identified by page numbers. The following abbreviations are used where necessary:
a = above; *al* = above left; *ar* = above right; *bl* = below left; *br* = below right; *c* = center; *cl* = center left; *l* = left.

Photographs
Baroff, Scranton, Pa. 167*al*
Battery F, 129th Field Artillery Regiment 232*al*
Bundesbildstelle, Bonn 151
Marion Carpenter, St. Paul, Minn. 128
William J. Curtis 12*cl*
Al Fairweather, New York 163*b*

George Fuller Green/Native Sons of Kansas City 14*b*
Historical Picture Services, Inc., Chicago 68*bl*, 69, 158*b*
Imperial War Museum, London 126
Independence, Mo., School District 13*a*
Jackson County Historical Society, Independence, Mo. 15*a*, 60–1, 62, 63*b*, 159*b*
Randall Jessee, Kansas City 235*b*
Kansas City *Journal-Post* 59*a*, 72
Kansas City *Star* 15*b*, 16*a*, 66, 68*a*, 71*a*, 227*b*, 232*b*, 234*b*, 235*al*, 236
Rene Laursen, Irvine, Cal. 2–3
National Park Service/Abbie Rowe 116–7, 162, 229*a*
Norristown, Pa., *Times Herald* 165*b*
Oklahoma City *Times* 167*ar*
Philadelphia *Inquirer* 164*a*
Photoworld, New York 115, 159*a*
Popperfoto, London 122*b*, 123
RLDS Church, Independence, Mo. 226*b*
St. Louis *Post-Dispatch* 71*b*, 96*a*
Terry Savage, St. Louis 150
Edwin Saxton Photo 58–9
Edmund Trissell, Kettering, Ohio 63*a*
United Press International, New York 55, 68*bl*, 91*b*, 94–5, 96*b*, 98, 111, 114*b*, 118*br*, 119, 120*l*, 120–1*b*, 149, 157*r*, 158*ar*, 158*b*, 163*a*, 164*b*, 166*a*, 198*l*, 199*al*, 199*b*, 200*b*, 202, 203*a*, 204*a*, 228*a*, 231*a*
U.S. Air Force 199*ar*
U.S. Army 12*b*, 127*b*, 200*a*
U.S. Navy 122*a*, 124, 160–1
James Waddleton, Smyrna, Ga. 227*a*
Washington *Post* 97*b*, 118*l*
Wide World Photos, New York 93*a*, 113, 152*a*, 197, 201*a*, 204–5*b*, 205*a*, 206, 226*a*, 234*a*

Cartoons
Cal Alley/Kansas City *Journal-Post* 91*a*
Berryman/Martin Luther King Library, Washington, D.C. 112*b*
Burck/Field Enterprises, Inc. 201*b*
Gib Crockett/Library of Congress 157*al*
Ding/St. Louis *Globe Democrat* 203*bl*
D.R. Fitzpatrick/St. Louis *Post-Dispatch* 89*al*, 92*b*
Shoemaker/Library of Congress 158*al*
H. M. Talburt/Scripps Howard Newspapers 165*ar*, 205*b*

NOTES ON THE TEXT

Page numbers are shown in bold type. Except where otherwise indicated, the documentary sources are items in the possession of the Harry S. Truman Library, Independence, Mo. (abbreviated "TL"). Classifications occurring frequently are: Family Correspondence File ("FCF"); President's Secretary's Files ("PSF"); and Post-Presidential Files ("PPF"). In addition, quotations are taken from the Library's transcripts of various oral history interviews, and from the vast collection of miscellanea stored in the Library's special vertical file. The present book quotes only from such materials in the Library as have been dedicated to the public. Titles of published works and bibliographical details are cited in full only at the first mention.

30 "You know—horse trading . . . hardest to know." Harry S. Truman to Bess Wallace, Feb. 16, 1911, FCF, box 1; Robert H. Ferrell (ed.), *Dear Bess: The Letters from Harry Truman to Bess Truman, 1910–1959* (New York: Norton, 1983), pp. 23–4.
33 "I certainly did . . . the dish." FCF, box 1; *ibid.*, p. 23.
34 "I had to milk . . . turn on a gadget." Remarks made in Philadelphia in the Girard College Chapel, May 20, 1948, *Public Papers of the Presidents of the United States: Harry S. Truman, 1948* (Washington, D.C.: Government Printing Office, 1964), p. 265.
"I can remember . . . payday since." Harry S. Truman to Margaret Truman, June 23, 1941, FCF, box 10.
35 "We all had . . . we knew." Mary Paxton Keeley oral history interview, July 12, 1966, p. 30.
"Elmer, why . . . too well." *Loc. cit.*
36 "I am very glad . . . went to school." Letter of Dec. 31, 1910, FCF, box 1; *Dear Bess*, pp. 18–19.
36–7 "*Everybody's* . . . farm publications." Letter of Jan. 10, 1911, FCF, box 1; *ibid.*, p. 19.
"I have been reading . . . Christendom." FCF, box 1; *ibid.*, p. 20.
38 "I don't think . . . one of them." FCF, box 1; *ibid.*, p. 19.
39 "didn't know how . . . coal oil lamp." Harry S. Truman to Margaret, May 13, 1944; Margaret Truman (ed.), *Letters from Father: The Truman Family's Personal Correspondence* (New York: Arbor House, 1981), p. 52.
40 "all about . . . back to us." Edwin H. Green, in Edward R. Schauffler, *Harry Truman: Son of the Soil* (Kansas City, Mo.: Schauffler, 1947), p. 26.
41 "I have some cousins . . . am sorry." Letter of Jan. 10, 1911, FCF, box 1; *Dear Bess*, p. 20.
"Harry, this . . . here again." PSF, box 298; "Autobiographical Sketch," Robert H. Ferrell (ed.), *The Autobiography of Harry S. Truman* (Boulder, Col.: Colorado Associated University Press, 1980), p. 28.
42 "I suppose . . . as possible." Letter of Jan. 10, 1911, FCF, box 1; *Dear Bess*, p. 20.
43 "We had riding plows . . . miles an hour." Draft speech, Feb. 17, 1959, PPF, Invitations File, box 81, "Massman Rockhurst."
"along in September . . . threshed." *Loc. cit.*
"sown on . . . be harvested." *Loc. cit.*
"fall plowing . . . all crops." *Loc. cit.*
45 "I guess . . . always was." Letter of July 12, 1911, FCF, box 1; *Dear Bess*, pp. 40–1.
45–6 "I have been . . . is something." FCF, box 1; *ibid.*, p. 40.

46 "Go over . . . killed himself." Mary Paxton Keeley oral history interview, p. 40.
47 "with something . . . of light." Margaret Truman, *Harry S. Truman* (New York: Morrow, 1973), p. 55.
"water and potatoes . . . blest that way." Letter of June 22, 1911, FCF, box 1; *Dear Bess*, p. 39.
"You see . . . nor ever will." Letter of July 12, 1911, FCF, box 1; *Dear Bess*, p. 40.
49 "I am generally . . . national bank." Letter of Nov. 26, 1917, FCF, box 3.
"They say I have . . . has one." Letter of Dec. 14, 1917, FCF, box 3; *Dear Bess*, p. 238.
49–50 "made me take off . . . canteen a while . . ." Letter of Dec. 11, 1917, FCF, box 3.
50 "and then we gave . . . at all." Vere C. Leigh oral history interview, Mar. 4, 1970, pp. 10–11.
"Run, boys, . . . on us!" Jonathan Daniels, *The Man of Independence* (Philadelphia: Lippincott, 1950), p. 96.
"It took . . . right around." Alfred Steinberg, *The Man from Missouri: The Life and Times of Harry S. Truman* (New York: Putnam, 1962), p. 46.
51 "You can take . . . that horse." James J. Doherty, vertical file, TL.
"We'll . . . Harry." Vertical file, TL.
"You could turn . . . drunk." Kansas City *Star*, Nov. 12, 1980; vertical file, TL.
"Won't you . . . thirty minutes." Letter of Nov. 24, 1917, FCF, box 3; *Dear Bess*, p. 238.
52 "Call her . . . loves you." Harry S. Truman, *Memoirs: Year of Decisions* (New York: Doubleday, 1955), p. 129. In a letter to Bess of Mar. 21, 1918, FCF, box 4 (*Dear Bess*, p. 252), Truman says he called at five o'clock rather than four as stated in the memoirs. "Remember how . . . showed up?" Letter of June 27, 1943, FCF, box 8.
"A wedding . . . cathedral candles." Independence *Examiner*, June 28, 1919; vertical file, TL. The fact that the marriage took place in the Trinity Episcopal Church, rather than the Presbyterian, deserves some explanation: a family connection existed because, after Grandfather Gates died in 1918, his widow (who in her youth had been Elizabeth Emery of Raunds, a village in Northamptonshire, England) had returned to the Protestant fold. In Independence at the turn of the century (see p. 33), the Episcopal Church had not featured in the social hierarchy of the town because its parish was so small.
53 "These will cost . . . that much." Diary of Eben Ayers, Sept. 4, 1948, TL.
74 "George, you didn't miss much." Alfred Steinberg, *op. cit.* p. 223.
"I recall . . . to death!" Taped interview, Oct.

23, 1959, PPF, "Mr. Citizen" File, box 2.
"My whole political career . . . associates." Jonathan Daniels, *op. cit.*, p. 90.
76 "I told you . . . the business." Tom Evans oral history interview, 1962–63, p. 178.
78 "Mr. Truman . . . of Missouri." Jonathan Daniels, *op. cit.*, p. 170.
82 "The difficulty . . . 'be damned.'" Box 5, Draft File, Speech File, "Statement to Railroad Leaders Conference on Proposed Pay Cut to Labor—October 12, 1938." For the speech of Dec. 20, 1937, see 75th Cong., 2d Sess., *Congressional Record*, pp. 1912–25.
82–3 "Some of the . . . real artists." Speech of June 3, 1937, 75th Cong., 1st Sess., *Congressional Record*, pp. 5271–2. For this earlier speech see pp. 5271–5.
83 "the highest . . . with shame!" Speech of Dec. 20, 1937, 75th Cong., 2d Sess., *Congressional Record*, p. 1920.
83–4 "I believe . . . 7 million people." *Ibid.*, p. 1923.
84 "No one ever . . . His teachings." *Loc. cit.*
84–5 "is one of the . . . but talk." Letter of July 26, 1935, FCF, box 6; *Dear Bess*, p. 374.
100 "Tell them . . . to run." Margaret Truman, *Harry S. Truman*, p. 120.
"Go down . . . mine." Tom Evans oral history interview, pp. 250–1.
101 "three dollars and a quarter." Harry H. Vaughan oral history interview, Jan. 14, 1963, p. 31.
"Truman . . . federal post . . ." Eugene F. Schmidtlein, "Truman the Senator," doctoral dissertation, University of Missouri, 1962, p. 212.
"I believe . . . shanties and tenements." Alfred Steinberg, *op. cit.*, p. 171.
105 "yes . . . didn't I?" Cabell Phillips, *The Truman Presidency: The History of a Triumphant Succession* (New York: Macmillan, 1966), p. 37.
"my mother . . . to it." *Souvenir: Margaret Truman's Own Story* (New York: McGraw-Hill, 1956), p. 73.
"always enter . . . Missouri." Letter to Mrs. Martha Ellen Truman and Mary Jane Truman, Apr. 11, 1945, PPF, Memoirs File, box 47; Robert H. Ferrell (ed.), *Off the Record: The Private Papers of Harry S. Truman* (New York: Harper and Row, 1980), p. 13.
106 "I have no ambitions . . . the creek." Letter of Jan. 21, 1944; Easley Papers, TL.
107 "Wallace knew . . . in politics knew . . ." Matthew J. Connelly oral history interview, Nov. 30, 1967, pp. 114–5.
"It is funny . . . at sixty." Margaret Truman (ed.), *Letters from Father*, p. 55.
108 "Harry, the President . . . nominate me." Jonathan Daniels, *op. cit.*, p. 244.

"Bob, it's Truman. FDR." Memorandum, Jan. 1950, PSF, box 334, "Longhand Notes, Undated." *Autobiography*, p. 89.

108–9 "Well, I don't want . . . can't take on a campaign." Tom Evans oral history interview, pp. 335–7.

109 "Well, you tell him . . . that's his responsibility." Memorandum, Jan. 1950, PSF, box 334, "Longhand Notes, Undated." *Autobiography*, p. 90.

"Well, I just think . . . I'll do it." Tom Evans oral history interview, p. 356.

110 "Harry . . . my future." Diary of Vic Housholder, recording a visit to the White House, Feb. 7–8, 1947; Housholder Papers, TL.

"He's still . . . keen as a briar," Margaret Truman, *Harry S. Truman*, p. 185.

"to put a clamp . . . mental balance." Letter to Thomas Van Sant, Nov. 28, 1944; Van Sant Papers, TL.

"And I stayed . . . was out." Harry Easley oral history interview, Aug. 24, 1967, pp. 98–9.

129 "If ever . . . that man." Letter to Mrs. Emmy Southern, May 13, 1945, PSF, box 322, "S." *Off the Record*, p. 23.

"some times . . . one of them." Letter of Jan. 10, 1911, FCF, box 1; *Dear Bess*, p. 19.

130 ". . . is always here . . . start over." Letter of Apr. 11, 1945, PPF, Memoirs File, box 47; *Off the Record*, pp. 13–14.

131 "Turn on . . . I'll introduce." Letter of Apr. 12, 1945, to Mrs. Martha Ellen Truman and Mary Jane Truman; Harry S. Truman, *Year of Decisions*, p. 6.

"maybe the President . . . Warm Springs." Diary, Apr. 12, 1945, PSF, Presidential Appointments File, box 82; *Off the Record*, p. 15.

"The President is dead . . . the situation." *Loc. cit.*

132 "Let me speak to your mother." Margaret Truman, *Souvenir*, p. 83.

"They had had a turkey dinner . . . worry any more." Diary, Apr. 12, 1945, PSF, Presidential Appointments File, box 82, *Off the Record*, p. 16.

133 "I did not know . . . to think about . . ." *Loc. cit.*

"I was the driver . . . once more." Letter of June 20, 1945, FCF, box 9.

133–4 "I've got to lunch with the Limey King . . ." Letter of July 31, 1945, FCF, box 9; *Dear Bess*, p. 523.

136 "Thanks for the ten . . . send it back." Letter of Aug. 19, 1946. FCF, box 9; *Dear Bess*, p. 529.

"Don't tell her . . . chance . . ." Letter of Aug. 12, 1946, FCF, box 9; *Dear Bess*, p. 530.

137 "I have always . . . future time." PPF, Memoirs File, box 32; *Autobiography*, p. 116.

138 "I acquired . . . procrastination." Cabell Phillips, *op. cit.*, p. 131.

139 "For even five seconds. . . . been his.'" Margaret Truman, *Harry S. Truman*, pp. 202–3.

"this is a lonesome place." Letter of June 3, 1945, FCF, box 9.

"Broke and . . . War End." Letter of June 28, 1957, FCF, box 9; *Dear Bess*, p. 568.

139–40 "It seems . . . reputation." Letter of Sept. 13, 1946, FCF, box 9; *Dear Bess*, p. 536.

140 "I'd rather be anything than President." Letter of Sept. 21, 1946, FCF, box 9; *Dear Bess*, p. 539.

"If you will study . . . the country." PSF, "Undated," box 333; *Autobiography*, p. 116.

142 "The dramatic postwar . . . by the West."

Paul Fussell, "Hiroshima: A Soldier's View," *New Republic*, Aug. 22/29, 1981, p. 28.

145 "We have discovered . . . save lives." Diary, July 25, 1945, PSF, box 322, "Ross, Mr. and Mrs. Charles G." *Off the Record*, p. 55–6.

146 "I know FDR . . . $2 billion." Jonathan Daniels, *op. cit.*, p. 281.

"All this uproar . . . end the war." Harry S. Truman, *Truman Speaks* (New York: Columbia University Press, 1960), pp. 73, 67.

"I hope . . . any of it." Diary, July 16, 1945, PSF, box 322, "Ross, Mr. and Mrs. Charles G." *Off the Record*, p. 50.

147 "My office force . . . to death." Letter of June 6, 1945, FCF, box 9; *Dear Bess*, pp. 514–5.

"Mrs. Roosevelt . . . that way." Margaret Truman, *Harry S. Truman*, p. 246.

148 "gauntlet of guards," *Ibid.*, p. 245.

"I'm always . . . no fun." Diary, June 1, 1945, PSF, box 333, 1945; *Off the Record*, p. 40.

"I sit here . . . work done." Letter of June 12, 1945, FCF, box 9; *Dear Bess*, pp. 515–6.

"lonesome a hole . . . sure as shootin'." Letter of Sept. 9, 1946, FCF, box 9.

169 "just a country jake who works at the job." Margaret Truman (ed.) *Letters from Father*, p. 35.

"overshadowed . . . destroying the other." Cabell Phillips, New York *Times*, Dec. 31, 1972, in *Harry S. Truman, Late a President of the United States: Memorial Tributes Delivered in Congress* (Washington, D.C.: Government Printing Office, 1973), p. 260.

"Oh, Almighty . . . amen." Aug. 15, 1950, PSF, box 334; *Off the Record*, p. 188.

170 "I was always . . . to be done." Taped interview, Sept. 10, 1959, PPF, "Mr. Citizen" File, box 2.

"I call it . . . the correct one." Taped interview, Nov. 16, 1959, PPF, "Mr. Citizen" File, box 2.

171 "cease his gallivantin' around." Letter of Jan. 20, 1919; Noland Papers, TL.

172 "I used to get in . . . knew that," Taped interview, Sept. 10, 1959, PPF, "Mr. Citizen" File, box 2.

"never go off . . . expert in explosives." Harry S. Truman, *Year of Decisions*, p. 11.

172–3 "began to tell . . . foreign minister." Diary, Apr. 17(?), 1948, PSF, box 48; *Off the Record*, p. 131.

173 "I told Harry . . . to Russia . . ." Diary, May 19, 1945, Presidential Appointments File, box 82; *Off the Record*, p. 31.

"The American army . . . plead . . ." W. S. Churchill, *Triumph and Tragedy* (Boston: Houghton Mifflin, 1953), p. 602.

"I had the kindliest . . . broken." Draft speech, Apr. 17(?), 1948, PSF, box 48; *Off the Record*, p. 132.

174 "I'm not afraid . . . special privilege." Diary, June 7, 1945, PSF, box 333; *Off the Record*, p. 44.

"just police government . . . lower levels." Diary, July 26, 1945, PSF, box 322, "Ross, Mr. and Mrs. Charles G." *Off the Record*, p. 57.

"Propaganda seems . . . the Russians . . ." Diary, PSF, box 333; *Off the Record*, p. 45.

"In all the history . . . if it comes." Draft speech, Apr. 17(?), 1948, PSF, box 48; *Off the Record*, p. 133.

175 "Unless Russia . . . the Soviets." Letter of Jan. 5, 1946, PSF, box 333, 1946; *Off the Record*, p. 80.

"Dear Winnie. . . . introduce you." Harry H. Vaughan oral history interview, Jan. 16, 1963, pp. 138–9.

176 "Well, General, . . . Fulton, Sahara." Margaret Truman, *Harry S. Truman*, p. 311.

"I am not yet . . . speech." *Ibid*, p. 312.

179 "wouldn't give you . . . chances." Eugene Davidson, *The Death and Life of Germany* (New York: Knopf, 1959), pp. 202–3.

"Have a terrific day. . . . close to war." PPF, Memoirs File, box 3; *Off the Record*, pp. 148–9.

"During our . . . at any time." Diary of Eben Ayers, TL.

180 "Could you . . . 'We didn't have them.'" Taped interview, Sept. 9, 1959, PPF, "Mr. Citizen" File, box 2.

"There are liars . . . loyal support." Diary, Nov. 30, 1950, PSF, box 333; *Off the Record*, p. 201.

180–1 "We are faced . . . from it—but— . . ." Diary, May 7, 1948, PPF, Memoirs File, box 3; *Off the Record*, p. 134.

"I'm going home . . . I hope?" Letter to Stanley Woodward, June 24, 1950; papers of Stanley Woodward, box 1, TL. Margaret Truman, *Harry S. Truman*, p. 453.

183 "Bess and Margaret . . . I know." Diary, July 31, 1948, PPF, Memoirs File, box 3; *Off the Record*, p. 145.

183–4 "Well, I'm here . . . will be done." Letter of Dec. 28, 1945, PSF, Desk File, box 309; *Off the Record*, pp. 75–6.

184–5 "Had dinner . . . What a life!" Diary, Nov. 1, 1949, PSF, box 278; *Off the Record*, pp. 168–9.

186 "I've just read . . . four-ulcer pay.'" Robert J. Donovan, *Tumultuous Years: The Presidency of Harry S. Truman, 1949–1953* (New York: Norton, 1982), p. 312.

190 "I've got to . . . implement it." Margaret Truman, *Harry S. Truman*, p. 392.

191 "My forebears . . . like this." *Loc. cit*

191–2 "I am going . . . in a good cause." PSF, box 306, "c." *Off the Record*, pp. 146–7.

192 "When I was . . . doing things." *New York Times*, Apr. 28, 1955; vertical file, TL.

194 "You remember . . . eats oats." Address at the state fairgrounds, Raleigh, N.C., Oct. 19, 1948; *Public Papers of the Presidents of the United States: Harry S. Truman, 1948*, pp. 823–4.

"Give 'em hell, Harry! . . . it was hell." Taped interview, Oct. 22, 1959, PPF, "Mr. Citizen" File, box 2.

195 "Vote . . . special privilege." Richard O. Davies, "Whistle-Stopping through Ohio," *Ohio History*, vol. 71 (1962), p. 121.

"It now looks . . . prevent that." Margaret Truman, *Harry S. Truman*, pp. 19–20.

208 "To organize . . . follow them." Diary, Feb. 26, 1952, PSF, box 333; *Off the Record*, pp. 241–2.

209 "By God, . . . have it!" James E. Webb to John W. Snyder, Apr. 27, 1975; Webb Papers, TL.

211 "Mr. Prima Donna . . . God right off." Diary, June 17, 1945, PSF, box 333; *Off the Record*, p. 47.

212 "Harry, . . . our policemen!" Margaret Truman, *Harry S. Truman*, p. 488.

"A President . . . these things." *Loc. cit.*

"The grand guards . . . why worry." Letter of Nov. 17, 1950, Noland Papers; *Off the Record*, p. 199.

215 "We'll never . . . out-produce them." Alonzo L. Hamby, *Beyond the New Deal: Harry S. Truman and American Liberalism* (New York: Columbia University Press, 1973), p. 447.

219 "The government . . . hammer at them." Eric F. Goldman, *The Crucial Decade* (New York: Knopf, 1956), p. 140.

"My dear Senator: . . . the United States."
Letter of Feb. 11(?), 1950, PSF, box 128,
"McCarthy, Joseph." *Off the Record*, p. 172.
"not a word . . . that is possible?" Alonzo L.
Hamby, *op. cit.*, pp. 396–7.
219–20 "My main effort . . . puts on." Letter
to Thomas H. Van Sant, Feb. 12, 1952, Van
Sant Papers, TL.
220–1 "1. By the Constitution . . . will
survive." Diary, Feb. 18, 1952, PSF, box 333;
Off the Record, p. 239.
221 "Taft has control . . . nominated."
Memorandum of July 6, 1952, PSF, box 333;
Off the Record, p. 259.
222 "Matt . . . about it." Matthew J.
Connelly oral history interview, pp. 421–2.
"Well, I blew up . . . heard before . . ." Taped
interview, Sept. 9, 1959, PPF, "Mr. Citizen"
File, box 2.
"He didn't know . . . learn." Taped
interview, Oct. 21, 1959, PPF, "Mr. Citizen"
File, box 2.
223 "it seems . . . stay there." Letter of early
Aug. 1952, PSF, box 333; *Off the Record*,
p. 267.
"As to whether . . . President Truman." *New
York Times*, Aug. 16, 1952.
"My dear Governor: . . . win if you can."
Letter of late Aug. 1952, PSF, box 334; *Off
the Record*, p. 268.
224 "moral pigmies . . . Nothing more . . . sad
experience." Address at Colorado Springs,
Col., Oct. 7, 1952; *Public Papers of the
Presidents of the United States: Harry S.
Truman, 1952–53* (Washington, D.C.:

Government Printing Office, 1966), p. 740.
"from the crown . . . personal matter."
Taped interview, Oct. 21, 1959, PPF, "Mr.
Citizen" File, box 2.
"I made . . . helluva fix." Taped interview,
Sept. 9, 1959, PPF, "Mr. Citizen" File, box 2.
237 "It bears down . . . 1953." Letter of Jan.
2, 1953, Noland Papers, TL; *Off the Record*,
p. 287.
"a chip on his shoulder . . . the other." Nov.
20, 1952, PSF, box 333; *Off the Record*,
pp. 274–5.
"He'll sit . . . very frustrating." Margaret
Truman, *Harry S. Truman*, pp. 551–2.
238 "You were not here . . . would have
come." *Ibid.*, p. 557.
"I wonder . . . full responsibility." *Loc. cit.*
"This is the greatest . . . a hundred." *Ibid.*,
p. 558.
239 "Mrs. T. . . . hard work." Diary, Jan. 21,
1953, PSF, box 278; *Off the Record*, p. 288.
"We are going . . . souvenirs." Margaret
Truman, *Harry S. Truman*, p. 560.
"a lot of folks . . . old men do." Randall
Jessee, "The 'Most Secure Man,'" in
Missouri Life, Jan.–Feb. 1976; vertical file,
TL.
"I still don't feel . . . I've tried." Wabash
(Ind.) *Plain Dealer*, May 8, 1972.
240 "Bess was . . . birdbath." Diary, June 24,
1955, PPF, Trip File, box 6, "San Francisco."
Off the Record, pp. 315–6.
"Just a minute . . . dinner." Kansas City
Times, Sept. 6, 1973; vertical file, TL.
241 "It is the habit . . . their own." Television

interview with David Susskind, 1962.
242 "The lies . . . Jefferson and Jackson." To
George Elsey(?), Feb. 15, 1950, PSF. In the
mid- and latter nineteenth century, the
history of the United States was written
largely by New Englanders of Whig and
Republican instincts, men who disliked the
founders of the Democratic Party—Jefferson
and Jackson.
243–4 "Hi, Randall . . . too well." Randall
Jessee, *op. cit.*
244 "The people . . . prevent it." Notes for
speech of Sept. 11, 1962, PPF, Trip File, box
32, "San Francisco." *Off the Record*,
pp. 405–406n.
245 "Mr. President . . . real thing!" Randall
Jessee, *op. cit.*
246 "Tom, can't you . . . himself." Tom
Evans oral history interview, p. 687.
246–7 "Thank God . . . between them."
Robert L. Dennison oral history interview,
pp. 207ff.
247 "Tell the truth. . . . Be yourself." Senator
Edmund S. Muskie, in *Harry S. Truman, Late
a President of the United States*, p. 172.
"I still get around . . . cover me up." Letter
of Oct. 15, 1963, to Edward D. McKim, PPF,
Name File, box 55, "McKim, Edward D."
Off the Record, p. 408.
248 "He doesn't look . . . nice picture."
Wabash (Ind.) *Plain Dealer*, May 8, 1972.
"He's a skull . . . old man." *Loc. cit.*
248–9 "It takes . . . satisfaction by service."
Memorandum, July 1954, PSF, box 334; *Off
the Record*, p. 306.

INDEX